With

THE SAME SIDE

OF THE MOON

Coral Perfitt

Coral Perfitt

30/12/24

Silverslate Fiction

Silverslate Fiction,
The Bungalow, Milcombe, OX15 4RS

First published as a Kindle eBook in January 2024
This paperback edition published by
Silverslate Fiction in May 2024

A CIP catalogue record for this book is available from
The British Library.

IBSN: 978-1-0686591-0-2

Book Cover by Jacqueline Abromeit.

Printed on Carbon Captured paper
Holywell Press
14039900282

Printed by Holywell Press Ltd
16-17 Kings Meadow, Ferry Hinksey Road,
Oxford OX2 0DP, on carbon captured
paper from the Woodland Trust.

Prologue

My two women captors gave a cruel shove, making me cascade down a flight of wooden stairs into the dark. There was the grating of a bolt being slid across above me. Lying bruised and shaken at the bottom, I latched onto to the slim hope that when Will came to rescue me, he wouldn't need a key—he would only have to release the bolt.

….Moving stiffly back to the top step, away from the cellar's filth, I found a draft under the door diluted the pungent smell slightly. With my mouth still aching from the magistrate's blow, I leaned wearily against the brickwork, my ear to the wood of the door frame, to listen for my husband's voice.

PART ONE

1. Eleven Years Previously

1844

Frances

I lay in my narrow bed, listening to the snores of the other house maid for the last time. Neither she, nor the others had spoken to me for nearly a year, except to be unkind. It no longer mattered quite so much, as I would be gone next morning. My small bag was already packed. Above me in the flickering candlelight, fine cracks in the ceiling whitewash made patterns like a map, but nothing that made sense of what had happened. Didn't everyone deserve to be accepted for who they were? To be respected, treasured, even loved?

It all began a month after my arrival at Kirkdunham House, when the women realised I could read. I had my mother's older brother to thank for that. Uncle Robert made all the Ferguson's lives more interesting. Against all the odds he'd become a schoolmaster. He lived with our grand-da just four cottages down the lane from us, back home in Long Newton, County Durham.

When it began, we were crammed around our table in the gloomy downstairs room, devouring our supper after a long day. The butler produced a letter. For me. As the buff envelope passed along the table, each servant squinted at my mother's neat writing. Looking down to avoid their gazes I mumbled that I would deal with it later. Letters could bear either very good or very bad news, but this I hoped would just be gossip from home.

Once the last person had finished eating—a stable boy who was extremely slow at everything—I could finally excuse myself. All eyes followed me as I left the table clasping my letter. No-one spoke. It was a deafening silence I would soon be well acquainted with.

Stepping outside, the soft notes of a woodpigeon filled my ears. It was a fine midsummer's evening, and the low sunlight on my face felt immediately cheering. Leaning against the wall by the servant's entrance, I hungrily scanned through our ma's words. In the next few days they would be read again and again. There was no other reading material. With the smell of warm earth, the gentle bird calls and a reminder of village life, it was possible to forget where I was for the moment. In my mind I was strolling across a field at home. A gentle breeze was moving through the ripe wheat; gold glimmering in the low evening light. High in the elm trees, a group of swallows were enjoying the last warmth of the sun. Raised voices from inside Kirkdunham House gradually intruded into my daydream. Finally all peace was shattered when the other maid stormed outside, to remind me exactly where I was.

'Lazy devil. Get inside to wash the dishes.' Her face was sour.

Tucking the papers inside my apron, I followed her to the scullery with a sigh, rolling my sleeves as I went. There was a glint in her eye. Without doubt, the pile of crockery was higher that evening but there seemed little point asking her to help me.

'Who does she think she is?' she said, supposing I was out of earshot. 'She'll expect to be treated better than us.'

The women would have been far nicer if I was stupid.

The master of Kirkdunham House was an engineer for the North Eastern Railway Company, a small man, slightly less than middle-age, with an air of quiet importance about him. His face was pocked, but it didn't ruin his looks, rather it gave him a rugged, handsome appearance. When he was at home, his young wife dressed brightly and they would take walks along the lane, she holding lightly on to his arm. When he was away on business—which was more often than not—she wore somber gowns with a long face, behaving like a railway widow.

One damp day in August, things got worse for me. I finished lighting the fire in the small library, but it was too tempting to leave without first examining the books my employer collected on his tall polished shelves. With the sky dark from the threat of rain, I had to lean forward and squint slightly, to read the titles: *The Theory of the Earth*; *Principles of Geology*… I wasn't sure what that last word meant but it was obviously a favourite subject of his. I was unaware of any books about railways but perhaps he would write one himself? As well as the large tomes, there were a few novels, boys' ones mainly: *Ivanhoe; The Pickwick Papers*… I was reading aloud to get my tongue around the new words when the door was flung open, and the mistress swept into the room, bosom first, dark blue gown swishing. She screamed when she saw me, a piercing sound which made me jump as much as she did. I must have looked a strange sight in the half-light gripping the silver coal bucket.

'What *are* you doing, girl?' Her voice was still high-pitched like her shriek.

'Sorry ma'am. I've just bin lighting the fire.'

'Get out now. Do not ever let me catch you looking at the books again, do you understand? What's your name?'

'It's Frances, ma'am.' I made a swift exit, clutching the bucket so hard my knuckles were as white as her face. Later that day she complained about me to the housekeeper who told the other women servants. They largely ignored me after that, unless to order me about.

Being used to family life with all its noise and banter, it was a shock to be shunned. I asked myself if such a brief peep at the master's books was worth it. Maybe not, I decided. It *might* be though, if I had a further opportunity. I kept watch for a chance to enter his study again, but perhaps on the instructions of his wife, another servant was tasked with lighting a fire in the library grate each day, from October right through to the end of March. It wasn't until April when it turned cold again, with sleet in the air, that my moment came. My employer was away but the warmth of a fire would prevent the damp damaging his book collection. There was nothing to lose so I offered my services. The housekeeper may have forgotten the previous library incident by then, or it might have suited her for me to light the fire for some reason.

It was already feeling dank in there. I lit the wood in the grate efficiently, blew on it gently to keep the flames coming, and stood to scan the shelves for the book I was most interested to read: *The English Boy at the Cape: an Anglo-African Story.* I eased the book down, spreading the others out a little so there was no gap. It went easily into my apron pocket feeling solid and significant against my stomach. Then I crept upstairs to the attic to tuck the story safely under my mattress. It was strange the master had a child's volume on his shelves, but maybe the subject was a matter than concerned him.

Finding moments to read was a challenge, but I did it, a sentence or two at a time when no one was nearby. I grew more confident, starting to keep the book in my apron. Making a bed upstairs, I would spend the first minutes reading about the English boy's troubles to forget my own. Sent to the cellar for coal, I used the candle to finish a chapter. Suddenly the world was opening up, making me almost sorry for the other servants who couldn't read, so much that I nearly offered to teach them. I was immediately enthralled by the descriptions of the Cape, 'The deep green of tropical vegetation, the deep blue of a tropical sky,' and fascinated by the flora too, at the same time familiar and unknown, such as the tree whose leaves and acorns resembled the oak, but instead of the gnarled and twisted shape we knew, stretched stiffly into the sky.

Most of all, I was gripped by the story of the English boy who was in such danger in Africa. Near the end, the tale was so absorbing, with young Charles delirious, dying from thirst, that eventually I became careless one evening, reading for just a moment too long. The other housemaid came into our attic room after taking her bath, as I should have known she would. I was still in Africa.

'What the heck.' she shrieked, dropping her soap and towel in shock.

I emerged from the story, slightly confused at first because I was so engrossed. Then realising my mistake clutched the book to my chest.

'Give that ere, thief.' It was the first time she'd spoken to me for some time. She seized the book roughly, holding it high as she departed through the still open door, clad in her nightgown looking like a jubilant ghost. I stared after her, sinking on to my mattress to wait for more trouble. But no-one came in that night, save the maid again, with nothing more to say, a smirk all over her face. The housekeeper had to wait until morning to inform her mistress, since the lady had already turned in by that late hour. I felt the mistress' wrath directed at my back as I cleared away the dishes in the breakfast room, but I had to wait for the evening to learn my fate. The moment her husband returned home from his business, when his hat and coat were barely hung on the stand in the hallway, she instructed him to sack me.

'My hands are tied,' he said, sounding genuinely sorry when I was standing before him quaking, in that same library with its dark paneled walls and forbidden shelves, to be handed my punishment. He said he would give me the book if he could, waving his hand over it as it lay, unloved, in front of him. 'But I have to think of my wife.' He looked up at me then with doleful eyes from his seat at the ivory-topped desk. 'The best I can do is just let you go and say no more about it, eh?'

Although I was shaking as he told me, next morning as I looked up at the ivy clad house it felt like a release from prison. I had no way of knowing what the future might hold; that I would later experience imprisonment for real.

2. The Sound of Bird Song

Frances

I was lucky at the time. The trouble was there were so few options for a country girl. You could usually only become a house servant or perhaps a cook if you had the skills, or get married if someone wanted you. Being literate wasn't much help unless you were clever enough to be a governess. In a quirk of fate, it had been precisely because I could read that the clergyman took me on at his rectory far away, despite not having a good letter to recommend me.

The Reverend Theodore Beard wasted no time setting me on the right path. His first sermon left me in little doubt the master of Kirkdunham House had warned him about the 'stolen' book. In which case, I supposed it went in the clergyman's favour that he accepted me into his household. As the Reverend reached the eighth commandment from his pulpit, the sunlight shone through a stained glass window onto his thick red beard, making him look even fiercer.

'THOU SHALT NOT STEAL.'

To give Reverend Theodore Beard his due, that first Sunday was the only time he addressed my moral wellbeing from the pulpit, in my presence at least. Of course I could be mistaken, so that the subject of the Ten Commandments had nothing to do with me at all. Whichever the case, as I sat on the hard servant's pew, I didn't mind. If I needed advice to keep the job, so be it.

As it happened, it wouldn't be the last time I would question his choice of sermon, although that would be in much more ominous circumstances. By that point in time, even his wife would have concerns.

Mrs Theodore Beard was as different to her husband in looks as chalk and cheese. In contrast to his large frame and hairy face, the reverend's wife was tiny and fragile, and being beardless you could see her chin, which I could tell was determined. If the Reverend Beard could read my thoughts he might have another sermon in mind: I'd wondered how they embraced, because if they did, her nose would be on a level with her husband's portly belly. Also, he would have to bend double to kiss her, if he ever did that.

Mrs Beard preferred to be called just that. She liked to lose the Theodore part as it was too cumbersome. While they contrasted in looks, in another way they were similar. Like the Reverend Theodore Beard, his wife wasted no time getting down to business. I supposed it made sense for the pair to make haste, with only one week to decide my true colours.

Once lunch was cleared away that first Sabbath day, Mrs Beard came downstairs to collect me. Seeing her standing small and diminutive against the cook's solid frame, I took an unexpected liking to her.

'Shall I call you Fanny?' she asked as we ascended the rear staircase from the kitchen.

'Yes ma'am.' I wasn't about to tell her otherwise, being grateful for her addressing me, at all.

'Have you read from the Holy Book before?' she said, as we entered the Bible room. She opened the large tome reverently where a strip of material marked the place she sought.

'No ma'am, but my uncle has a story book about Palestine.'

'And you've read it?'

She smiled. 'Good. You can start from here.' She pointed to the open page, before leaving me alone.

Hardly believing what was happening, I pulled out a chair tucked under the Bible's table and read, letting the words sink in, with no idea it was a test.

The merest feeling of guilt about being away from my chores, prevented me from fully enjoying the moment, but there was no need to feel that way. The rectory was as different from Kirkdunham House as you could imagine. It was a modest home which didn't require many servants, as the reverend's wife wasn't above doing chores herself.

When Mrs Beard reappeared, she asked if I liked the story.

Taking her cue I recounted what Queen Esther did to save her people. Esther was young and brave. I didn't go on to say it reminded me of the *'English Boy at the Cape'*, even though I hadn't read the ending. In that story, the people you'd expect to behave well did not and instead it was the poor coloured people that were kind and brave. It made me think.

'That will do very well,' my new employer told me, not reading my thoughts, indicating that I could go back to work. 'Oh, and Fanny, you'll be helping me with our new mission.'

The Sunday school mission was a vision of Mrs Beard's, although the Rev Theodore Beard went along with it. Mrs Beard may have preferred a more remarkable beginning. In the event, the youngsters gathered in the front room of the rectory at three o'clock on the following Sunday. I wasn't as tiny as Mrs Beard but neither was I large, so having changed out of my maid's clothes it was easy to slip unnoticed beside the older children. I couldn't stay hidden for long—my job was to read the story. Crammed between two of the girls in that rectory sitting room, I tried to make the chapters live. To start with, knowing I was on probation, my voice trembled from nerves. I'd had little chance to talk out loud in front of people for the last year at Kirkdunham House. Nevertheless, once I had the group's attention, my storytelling became more confident, even ending with a flourish. Mrs Beard cleared her throat before extracting the lessons she wanted her audience to remember. The next Sunday was easier, with the reverend's wife and me soon settling into our routine.

Intent on learning the children's faces and names which changed each time, I didn't immediately notice the problem. Once I'd seen it, I couldn't stop making the observation one afternoon, whilst we planned the coming Sunday's lesson: at no time during the weeks the Sunday school had been running, had we seen children from two of the town's largest, poorest families who lived near to the mill.

'Ma'am,' I said carefully, 'I wonder if they're too shy to come along without shoes and in their shabby clothes, or even too hungry to make the effort?'

It didn't take her long to see.

'Then they need enticing.' She decided on buns, considering the idea her own from then onwards. But Mrs Beard first had to broach the matter with her husband.

Raised voices were coming from Reverend Beard's study. After a quick look behind me, I pressed my ear to the door.

'My dear, we're already doing our Christian duty by keeping your maid on at the rectory.' For the first time since arriving at that house, my heart sank. Was that all they thought of me? Did I have so little value, apart from the easing of their consciences?

Mrs Beard obviously wasn't giving up that easily on her mission. 'But surely there are no limits to our Christian duty to provide charity, Theodore.' My spirits rose a little.

I visualised the scene. He would be tall and imposing behind the cluttered desk, upright in his chair; she, leaning forward in hers to claim his attention. I'd been in his study on just one occasion, on my arrival from Kirkdunham House. His book shelves were populated with religious books, while the whole room was plainer than the library which had cost me my previous job. A faded rug took up the main part of the large study, pale colours contrasting with the dark polished boards at its edges.

Light steps sounded on the boards, so his wife was approaching the door. I needed to move, and fast. Reaching the turn of the hallway before the study door opened, I raced down the stairs, flopping down at the big kitchen table to take it all in. I'd learned a lot: firstly, although Mrs Beard was tiny, she was willing to stand up to her husband; secondly, despite his wife's resolution, Reverend Theodore Beard had exercised his rights as head of his household to overrule her plan; finally, I was being kept on at the rectory, not because of any value, but as a charity case, certainly in the Reverend Beard's opinion, but probably his wife's also.

Mrs Beard must have somehow persuaded her husband that evening. The next day, I found our cook, Mrs Cherry, elbow-deep in flour while a delicious aroma of fruit buns arose from her oven. That afternoon I was sent into Northallerton to spread the word. Half of me was pleased about the outcome to my idea, half of me miserable about my lack of worth in the Beards' eyes.

The promise of buns worked well. So many children crowded into the rectory's front room, we moved the Sunday school across the road into the church itself. Mrs Beard was so pleased with herself that on the spur of the moment she invited me to help with the Old Testament story.

'Would you care to draw out some lessons, my dear?'

'Thank you ma'am.' I shut my eyes quickly to help me think.

'I reckon it means some folk are too fond of their own opinions, while these children can have a lot to teach them.' I indicated along the pews in front of us, which caused a few stifled giggles. Mrs Beard tutted. She wasn't sure she would put it quite like that. But certainly pride wasn't a good thing.

I resumed without seeking further encouragement. '….and small folk, can easily be scorned or looked down on, yet can be so kind, and have an important part to play.' By then my mind had slipped away to Africa again. I was thinking less about the little maid in the Bible story, who was sent to give instructions to a great man; more about the brave little Bushman girl who helped the English boy at the Cape, in the story of that name. Mrs Beard perhaps saw yet another application—herself, immediately seeming to grow taller in her seat. 'Thank you Fanny.' She had that look which meant she would need to reconsider my points later, to decide it they were valid.

It was a good while before she risked me taking Sunday school without her, but in the end that was out of her control. She fell ill with a heavy summer cold, taking to her bed with no time to make other arrangements. When I carried in her breakfast tray, she told me weakly that I would have to take the school alone that afternoon.

I was doubtful. 'Are you sure ma'am?'

'We can't let them down, Fanny.'

'No ma'am. Aye I will then.'

After I'd pushed away my reservations, a thrill of excitement went through me. Finally, I could hardly wait. That afternoon, I rushed through the story, brought out the lesson as quickly as possible then led the children through the rear door of the church. We trooped into the garden where it was a sparkling summer's afternoon, light glinting through the foliage. With sunshine warming our spirits, I began to point out each flower lovingly tended by the old gardener. I remembered my ma doing the same, showing me each plant in our borders. Caught up in the moment, I taught the children different ways to remember the blossoms, even making up a story for the foxglove, of a fox that needed gloves. 'Do you see these lupins?' I said. 'If we look after them, any seeds that fall to the ground will grow into a new lupin flower next year. If children are kind to people, they grow into lovely flowers.'

'Is that what happened to you, miss?'

It brought me to my senses. The girl who spoke, reminded me of myself back in Long Newton, before my spirit was crushed by the women at Kirkdunham House. It also reminded me that I was employed simply to be a maid at the rectory, not a teacher, so had probably overstepped my position. By evening I was worried there would be trouble. The reverend's wife would stop talking to me. That was my biggest fear.

Nothing immediately came of my fears, but the following week, when Mrs Beard still wasn't fully recovered, I was determined just to teach the Bible lesson as well as I could and do nothing else. By the end of the story, we could hear rain beating against the stained glass of the church, which meant any idea of venturing out, had to be abandoned anyway. Yet, seeing the dirty but hopeful faces of the mill-side children dashed, realising we wouldn't go into the garden, made me sad. I asked if anyone could recall any bird songs they'd heard. A couple of boys could.

'Could you whistle them?' I asked. They reckoned they could. Then it wasn't long before everyone was joining in, with the church full of bird song. When we'd exhausted that line of entertainment, one of the little girls wanted me to teach them a children's song. As it happened, I could think of several.

'Surely you could have taught them a hymn,' Mrs Beard croaked, emerging from her coughing fit. She'd reluctantly had to leave her bed to receive a visitor downstairs, the mother of one of the children, who had come to complain. The reverend's wife didn't tell her husband about my sins, or stop talking to me. Those punishments would have been worse, but she no longer invited me to contribute of a Sunday afternoon, other than to read the chapters from the Holy Book. It was not unexpected. Mrs Beard would be worried about her husband's feelings, while if he ever heard there had been whistling and bird song in his church, Reverend Theodore Beard would be concerned for his reputation.

I didn't regret inspiring some of those Sunday school children. It felt right to fire their imagination, especially knowing the hard lives the bare footed children must have. But neither did it sound a bad thing to have a husband to be concerned about as Mrs Beard did, so long as the Reverend Theodore Beard also worried about his wife's feelings. At least the master at Kirkdunham House had been kind to *his* wife. I said as much to Martha Cherry. With a tear in her eye, the rosy faced cook told me that her own hubby, before he was lost in the war, had been decent to her too. She patted my hand. 'With a sweet character like yours,' she began, reading my mind, 'I'm certain a nice lad will turn up very soon.'

Mrs Cherry may have had a psychic moment, because the following morning while I was sweeping leaves in front of the rectory, a pony and cart ambled past. The occupant didn't appear in a hurry, or have a particular place to go, especially as the waggon slowed almost to a stop. It was almost as if he was looking for me. When he turned back to call 'good morning' or something similar, I saw he was little more than a boy, scrawny, still to develop fully. As the cart picked up speed again, I focused on the back of his head. The man-boy had dark shaggy curls.

3. The Chance Encounter

Will

He blended into the group of children and youths gathered outside the smithy, where the first light of day was only beginning to reveal their expectant faces. A hum of childish conversation hung in the frosty air. Later, the children's chatter might have been dwarfed by the heavy *thwack* of the looms, but at that early hour most villagers were still at home stoking their fires and drinking tea, before starting their labours.

There'd been no opportunity for Will to pause for breakfast. His day would be a long one, with every moment of daylight needed. The bread and cheese his sister had prepared was wrapped in its cloth, in a bag strung across his lean chest. He thought about the food then, making his stomach rumble.

Several carts and ponies were being loaded in the square, with some of the youngest children already taking hold of the animals' halter ropes, staking their claim to lead the ponies, laden with linen, out of the village. Will sighed. The little ones were excited at the prospect of seeing the world outside Appleton Wiske. He'd been the same, once, but he'd made this journey too many times. He rubbed his hands together to warm them, before going over to help the men heave the heaviest packs onto the carts. Then the procession was off.

It was a long ten miles, but after unloading the linen and then loading the flax ready for the homeward journey, the mill workers let them warm their backs at the fire. The journey home was more tedious. Will's legs ached as he walked alongside one of the carts, waiting his turn to ride in the back with the flax. Guessing the boy's boredom and misery, the driver let him come up beside him to take the reigns and was rewarded with a broad grin.

Will chatted about what he'd witnessed that the morning on his way to the smithy; the group of men walking past him, heads held high, striding out of the village with their picks or shovels resting on strong shoulders. Starved of much excitement, he'd watched their jaunty steps with envy. He'd shouted after the last of them before they disappeared into the gloom.

'Where you going, mister?'

'We're off to dig the railway. Want to come?' the fellow called back cheekily.

The cart driver wasn't surprised by what the boy had seen. 'Plenty of villagers are swapping their looms for a shovel,' he said with a grimace. 'No doubt the railway will run past Appleton soon, then if they make us load our linen onto railway trucks instead of carts, I'll be out of a job.'

Will knocked his boots together to warm his toes. He could no longer feel them. He absorbed the new information: a railway to carry the linen. It would be better than their current journey. In fact, the railway sounded grand to him, but he said nothing, to avoid hurting the cart driver's feelings. Perhaps a seed was sown in his young brain though, as he watched those men in the early morning chill.

Will pushed open the creaky door without enthusiasm. He was still tired from his march through the lanes the previous day, especially as he'd lain awake for at least an hour turning things over in his mind. Like most weaving families, his father's handloom sat in its large wooden frame in a shed behind the house, but the old weaver was absent. He had business elsewhere that morning. It was 'huckaback' business. They made so many huckabacks in the Vale of York, Will's father told them they were to blame for the smarting faces of children all over the country, dried with those coarse towels, after their mothers scrubbed them clean.

The raw cold hit him as he entered the loom shed. It had been the same brutal blast of air years before, in the next door wood shed, the day their lives changed. That was one thing he remembered. Will didn't bother to light the fire before settling at the loom. He always avoided fetching logs from that wood shed with its awful memories. Anyway, even without the added burden of numb fingers, he was too easily distracted to be an able weaver. Their employers demanded a high quality weave, whereas the boy usually found his mind wandering at the loom. That morning was worse. With all the thoughts of railways in his head, proper attention to the warp and weft was nigh impossible.

'You've not secured the warp properly,' said the old man, shaking his head, when he returned at midday. He softened his voice then. 'Leave it to me. Go into the house to see if your sisters need owt.'

He sat glumly on the window seat watching his two sisters at their wheels. Normally at that time of day there would be a thin beam of light settling on them from the spinning window. It was dull outside though so they'd already lit the smoky tallow candles. They all hated the acrid smell, loathed the smoke making their eyes sore. Even so, Elizabeth and Sarah were ready to commiserate.

'Poor Will. It's a hard life here for folks as don't take to weaving.'

'You want owt doing?' he asked them, suddenly remembering why his father had sent him.

Later that evening, when they'd eaten their bread and cheese, the old weaver cleared his throat. Will caught his youngest sister Elizabeth's eye. Their father obviously had something to talk over, but it was a rare thing for him to be included. Once the old weaver was sure he had their attention of his three children, he began to describe the meeting he'd had with the other weavers that morning. Many other villagers like them in the Vale of York, who made a living from weaving, were losing out to linen production by the new factories. It was a worry.

'Will we be safe, Pa?' asked Will.

'For now, we're reet lucky in Appleton,' his father said happily, seemingly glad the boy was taking an interest for once. Will wasn't sure he agreed they were lucky, but he knew not to argue. Their own employers were shrewd, the weaver explained, because a new railway line would run past the mills where Will had delivered the linen yesterday. Soon the huckabacks they made in Appleton Wiske would be distributed to the large cities by rail.

There it was again, more talk of the railways. Will began to wonder if it was an omen.

The weavers' meeting seemed to spur his father forward. The old man was like a dog with a bone, with Will bearing the brunt. His father sat close behind him at the loom every day from morn til dark, determined to teach the boy.

'Watch that weft. Steady with that warp.'

He did his best to learn, but by the end of the four weeks they'd both had enough.

'What do you call this?' The old weaver held up the poorly woven huckaback, then threw it on the floor. Hobbling towards the door of the loom shed, he called out over his shoulder, 'ah, be off with you boy, you're good for nowt.' Will already knew it, but it still hurt.

That summer, the linen cart driver went away to dig the new railway line before it was forced upon him. Fewer weavers in the villages meant his job was no longer secure. Everyone agreed that since Will was unsuitable for everything else, he should drive the cart instead. Therefore, once a week, he found himself going back and forth to the mill at Northallerton.

He wasn't sure why he'd never noticed the house opposite the church on the outskirts of town. He must have driven past at least a dozen times. A young woman was in the garden. Will guessed she'd been sweeping leaves from the path, because a birch broom was propped against the wall beside her. As he passed by in the cart, she was bending down examining something in the border—perhaps a struggling bumble bee on its last legs. It was hard to know what interested a young woman such as her. Feeling bold driving the cart, despite his rear-end hurting from the jolting, he slowed the pony to a walk, and called to her, 'a grand morning to you, miss.'

'And yourself,' the young woman replied. He felt his cheeks colouring, but fortunately the cart had rattled past by then so the lass wouldn't have noticed.

Once he'd unloaded their huckabacks at the mill and was on the way home again with the flax, he slowed the cart right down near the garden, but there was no sign of the girl. She must have gone inside. Will might have forgotten the incident but for some reason he was ensnared. Although it was such a brief encounter, she played on his mind for the rest of that day, and part of the night. The next day too, when he least expected it her face flashed into his consciousness.

When it was clear his vision of the girl wasn't fading even after several days, Will knew there was only one thing to do; he would have to see her again. But although he was determined to see her, he needed an opportunity. With winter coming fast he would be making fewer trips to the mill, especially as with a heavy crop of hawthorn berries that autumn, local farmers were predicting a hard one. It was also unfortunate that on his final trip before bad weather set in, several village children were with him. They'd come along for the ride, which meant stopping to look for her would be difficult. It didn't prevent him slowing down near the church, but in any case, the garden opposite was empty. He would just have to put the young woman out of his mind.

December and January were harsh as expected, but in February the snow began to clear, revealing patches of vivid green grass. The sun, as it rose above the moors, felt deliciously warm on Will's face. Snowdrops were appearing on the margins of the track leading to the fields, their tiny white bell-like heads hanging coyly, and before long some of the youngest village children had stooped to pick some. It gave him an idea. On the morning of his first trip to the mill that year, Will picked a few of the best blooms when no one was watching, carefully wrapping some twine around the stems. Then he tucked them safely behind the seat of the cart, where the unusually large load of linen wouldn't flatten them. He'd already thought of a plan. That was one advantage of being snowed in over winter. At about midday, once he'd made the delivery, Will drove the pony and cart away from the mill, past the ominous House Of Correction which always made his skin creep. He would never want to enter such a prison, with the blood curdling yells heard through its walls. Then with his usual sign of relief he was out of the town, rolling downhill towards St Thomas' church. By then, both beast and boy knew the location well, although without foliage on the trees of the churchyard, the square towered building looked different, even imposing. Halting the pony at a short distance, he watched a tall figure in the black garb of a clergyman leave through the front doors of the church. The man made his way along the long path, across the road, straight into the garden where Will had spotted the young woman. Perhaps she lived at the rectory then?

Will jumped down. 'Wait here,' he told the pony, rubbing her nose with his thumb. 'I've an errand to do.' He bent to take the posy from its hiding place, hurrying off before he could lose his nerve. To the rear of the rectory, there was a small door which must be the delivery entrance, and used by servants. Beside it, a rope hung from a half rusty bell, which he had to pull on several times before it finally rang out a reluctant clanging sound. It seemed an age before a voice sounded from within.

'Come inside and leave your fowls on the table.'

He let himself into a tidy kitchen area, the flowers grasped behind his back. 'I'm not the butcher's boy,' he called. 'I'm looking for somebody. Can you help?'

The woman who appeared, wore a cook's hat and apron, and was large like her voice. Her face was flushed, evidently from some exertion. Suddenly Will felt less confident. 'I'm sorry. I thought there were some lass working here?'

'A lass, you say?

'With a pretty face and shy smile.'

'Oh, you must mean Frances.'

'Please can you give her these?' Blushing, he thrust the snowdrops forward, ready to disappear quickly, but she winked at him then.

'No, no, you must do that yourself. What's your name?'

'Err. It's William—Will Bell.'

4. Impossibly Far Away

Will

Frances had stood quite still, surprised and reticent, mouth open slightly as he held out the bouquet; her face as familiar to him as those of his sisters. Shyly she admitted forgetting his own face, or perhaps she never really observed it, due to the cart having already gone past when he wished her a good morning. She didn't know him immediately, as he stood before her with the snowdrops, but once he'd explained, she let out a small cry.

'Ooh, flipping heck.'

She might not have a clear recollection of his features, but hadn't forgotten his greeting or dark curls. She remembered that morning, she told him, because it was a marvel, coming so quickly after a prediction by her friend, Martha Cherry, the cook. She turned then, to the large woman stirring a pan at the stove and they exchanged knowing looks.

It had been a similar scene the second Thursday, although without snowdrops that time. They were in the rectory kitchen, with tea and cake in front of them, sitting timidly side by side at the table. She smelled of fresh air, the sort of freshness you find high up on the moors. He breathed her aroma deep inside.

He discovered she was one of eleven children, but unlike his own family, most were still alive. Almost of full age, it made her four or five years his senior. He was never exactly sure of his age. He blushed when she told him. Perhaps she would think him too young?

Frances was the name she preferred, although her employers called her Fanny. She had a free afternoon on Mondays, and on Sunday mornings the whole household went with the clergyman and his wife to St Thomas' church across the lane. On Sunday afternoons she helped the clergyman's wife with her Sunday school mission. She wouldn't say if she was happy in her job as house servant.

'The walls have ears,' she whispered when the cook had left the kitchen for a moment, her lips dangerously close to his own ear. He felt her warm breath on his cheek and knew he didn't want her to pull away again.

Mrs Cherry gave a little cough.

'You'd best change your free afternoon to Thursdays, Frances,' she said with a wry smile.

He couldn't always visit on a Thursday. It depended on the mill, and sometimes he had work as a labourer on a local farm. Even so, several times that spring, Frances and he had been walking out together.

'Aren't you going to kiss me?' Frances teased when the pair first walked beside Brompton beck. He hadn't needed further encouragement. The world had stopped for those few minutes as he pressed his body against hers. It was his first time, but it came naturally. Maybe kissing a girl would be something he could be good at?

But things changed between them in the thunderstorm. For the first time, on the afternoon of the storm their parting had been difficult. They'd hardly said goodbye.

With the early summer afternoon stretching out before them, they'd taken a path into the countryside. He recalled how they rested at a gate. Her waist felt soft when he pulled her close to him, her head against his chest, looking across at the moors. Until without warning, the sky had darkened ominously. The first rumble of thunder rolled, rain falling on their shoulders like a million tiny spikes.

'We'll need to take cover,' he'd said, taking her hand again urgently. Heads down against the onslaught, they'd run for the woods.

It was a little cooler since the rain. Will was out in the fields, unable to sleep since the sun sneaked over the horizon. The golden rays were casting out the predawn chill, but weren't yet as stifling as they'd been in the first month of summer. All morning he'd been reliving the storm of the previous day. In fact he was about to go over it all in his mind yet again as he walked about aimlessly, when he heard his name being called.

'Will. Where have you been? We've been looking everywhere. You're to come to the house.' Elizabeth wouldn't say why, just turned and ran back so he was left to follow his sister, curious and increasingly breathless trying to keep pace with her in the returning heat.

Back at their cottage Elizabeth pulled him into the spinning room to tell him the news. Their father had suffered a 'bad turn' during the night, probably due to the heat the previous day, so was too weak to work the loom. Sarah had been filling in for their father that morning as best as she could.

Will collapsed onto the window seat to consider what he'd been told. He felt dizzy from lack of sleep and from thinking round in circles all morning. He made himself focus on this new matter, which sounded ominous. 'Sarah's our best weaver,' he mumbled after a while. 'Father knows I'm hopeless at the loom.'

'That's true enough,' Elizabeth said, sitting next to him. 'But you *know* our Sarah's about to be wed.'

Of course he knew. Their eldest sister was having her banns read out that weekend, ready for her wedding day, miles away in Middlesbrough. Heavily pregnant, with the father from a church-going family, their little son or daughter mustn't be born on the wrong side of the blanket. In one way Will had been pleased for Sarah when she'd informed the three of them happily one suppertime, but since then, he'd tried to push away the fact his sister was in such a hurry to leave them—like his mother. Sarah was always the one to soothe them if they were hurt, even before they lost their ma. Several years older than Elizabeth and Will, Sarah would hold their tiny fists when the linen carts rumbled dangerously past. When they were older she would find apples to eat when their stomachs were grumbling. Still, although it was hard to think of Sarah going, Will needed to be pragmatic. He ran his fingers through his hair to help him think. 'Then perhaps *you* can work the loom, Lizzy?'

'Perhaps I will do. We must see what Father wants first. He may be wobbly on his legs but his mind's sharp as a pin.'

It was unclear where all this left them, but no doubt they would find out soon. Their father was resting that morning but wanted to see Will before the end of the day. At least it took his mind off the worry that he'd upset Frances the previous afternoon.

It was shocking to see how gaunt and pale his father looked, but the old weaver's voice was strong enough and he wasted no time saying what he wanted. There was a plot of twelve acres vacant on the north side of the village. The man who had farmed it for years was riddled with gout and bent over from working in all weathers.

'Hasn't he any sons to work his land?' Will asked this as if this were just an interesting conversation. But no, apparently, the gouty farmer was son-less, although an old labourer lived in a cottage with his wife. Will had a good idea where this was going, so tried to steer the conversation away from it. 'How are you feeling after your rest, Da? Will you be back at the loom soon?'

John Bell fixed him with a stare. 'And if I'm not able to weave again, would you prefer to sit at the loom or work on the land?' As Elizabeth had said, their father was still in full control of his senses.

Will shook his head. The land *was* marginally better than the loom.

'So hear me out, William. I want you to look at that land, see if you can farm it.'

Feeling sorry then, the boy promised to go the next day and if the plot was possible to manage, they could talk to the landowner.

He found the land with difficulty. The twelve acres, which abutted Staindale Beck, were at the farthest point of the village. Although flat, it was still almost an hour's walk on a path which was overgrown in places. The small farm was mostly under tillage with some wheat in reasonable condition, ready to harvest soon. There were beans too, which was a crop Will knew something about from his farm work on the days he wasn't needed to drive the linen cart. He decided it might be possible to manage those few acres with the farmhand's help. The problem was the latter was a cantankerous individual, none too keen to show the boy round. Despite his age, he rushed from field to field muttering and repeating himself, with Will hard on his heels.

'You won't like this soil. You won't like it. Tis hard work, being clay and all.'

'Well I would need your knowledge, mister,' Will called after him, having no idea if his words penetrated through the farmhand's bad temper.

On the long walk home, the flies were more annoying than usual, so Will picked up a stick to wave it round, as cows did with their tails when bothered by flying insects. He took his feelings out on the nettles, then occasionally on the prettier flowers too, which made him think of Frances, making him even more miserable.

'D' you think you can do it?' Elizabeth asked later. 'Can we farm that land?'

'I think we have to,' he said glumly. The place was impossibly far from the rectory, far from Frances. He would have to give up driving the linen cart too. Well, he thought with a groan, maybe it *was* for the best, after what had happened just two days before.

5. The Thunderstorm

Frances

It had felt safe with Will in the rectory kitchen, sharing those first glimpses of each other's lives, the table strong and sturdy in front of us. Martha Cherry did her best to put off her mixing or kneading for the few minutes we had, before I returned to my chores and Will drove the flax waggon back to his village. She was never far away though. The first time we walked outside was quite different. The sudden freedom threw the boy into uncertainty. Once we were through the door he wasn't sure how to be with me. Seeing his anxiety, I led the way across the lane into the large church yard, where an old wooden seat was set amongst the jumble of tomb stones. It was my favourite place to escape to, with the sweet, woody smell of yew trees always having a calming effect.

'It's a grand place,' he admitted, stretching out his long legs. 'It reminds me of my ma.'

I let him continue.

'That was the last time I was in a church, but it was so long ago, I can hardly remember.' His voice dropped. 'I wasn't good enough for her.'

'I disappoint my father too,' he said after a while. 'He thinks I'm hopeless.'

I didn't believe a word of it but he clearly did himself. There was nothing else for it: I reached out, taking his hand in mine. Neither of us spoke for a while. Behind us in the trees, the woodpeckers drumming for insects filled the silence.

I could feel his eyes on me, so he would have seen a tear gently roll down my cheek. As well as being sad for him, I think I grieved for all the misery in the world; for the isolation I'd felt at Kirkdunham House too. He gripped my hand until the loneliness began to lift.

After a bit, he grinned. 'That's enough of being miserable. Shall we walk on?' He stood to pull me up and we set off hand in hand, arms swinging a little.

That spring when Will and I were together, we liked to walk beside Brompton Beck imagining what might be lurking in its deeper pools. One warm afternoon we collapsed, giggling, onto a grassy bank which the rabbits kept trimmed and neat for us. Will propped himself onto his hands and knees, leaning over to kiss me. Slipping my hands under his shirt to pull him closer, I could feel his ribs. Then he collapsed and we lay there for a while sensing each other's heartbeats. I sighed. It never felt enough. In a moment I would have to return to help Martha Cherry with the Beards' supper, while Will had to drive his cart back to Appleton Wiske.

For our last minutes together that afternoon, we turned onto our backs, side by side, holding hands, gazing up at a clear blue sky, wishing we could stay longer. Swifts were flying overhead and then dipping down out of sight behind the trees to the next curve of the stream, searching for insects. It was one of those perfect afternoons when the moon was visible in daylight, clear as anything. A crescent; hanging high above the moors; waiting for dark.

He frowned for a moment when I pointed it out.

'Every time I see that moon from now on, Frances Ferguson, I promise I'll think of you,' he said squeezing my hand. It made me giggle, but as I lay in my bed later that night I wondered if he somehow saw the future, that we would soon gaze up at the silver crescent quite alone.

Then on the last Thursday before I lost him, our mood was different, not only because of the thunder. We ran into the woods that afternoon, to find shelter. Will chose a dry patch where the canopy was thickest, and we sank down thankfully between the roots. He shook his long curls like a dog then ran his fingers through them, which was a habit of his. I shivered as I wrung out my skirt.

We sat with our own thoughts for a while, which was unlike us, but Will could never be silent for long. 'It's like your church in here. It's so quiet. Maybe we should get wed,' he said.

'Are you asking?'

'Perhaps I am,' he said, suddenly serious. He took out his knife to cut back some of the woody creeper clinging to the nearest tree trunk, turning away then so I wouldn't see. As he worked on the task in hand, I busied myself thinking about my Uncle Robert. He would have been glad to see the tree's life saved from being choked by the creeper. My tree-rescuer then got to his feet and pulled me up to face him, producing a twisted ivy ring.

'Frances, do you take me to be your wedded husband?'

I kept my face straight. 'I do,' I said solemnly.

'Then let this ring be a sign.'

I leant forward and kissed him gently on the mouth to seal the ceremony.

The sound of rain and peals of thunder were muffled by a dense canopy, but the storm above was unrelenting. There was no choice other than to stay there under the trees, unless we wanted to look even more like drowned rats. Will took my hand and pulled me down beside him on the dry leaves. He turned to kiss me. 'We're wed now Frances.'

'Aye, so we are.'

We must have fallen asleep, probably for quite a while, as my clothes felt almost dry. I extracted myself from his arms and shook him awake softly. He looked so young sleeping there.

'Will, wake up. It's late, I need to get back.'

As he opened his eyes the memory of what had happened gradually dawned on him. He frowned. 'Are you alright, Frances?'

Perhaps I nodded, but in the rush to get away, it went unsaid. It was hard to keep up with him in my long clothes, as he wove his way purposefully through trees and brambles, in the direction we'd come. Outside the woodland, the ground was sodden. Avoiding the worst puddles, I followed him as best I could, my skirt gripped in tense fingers to hold it up. We covered the ground quickly. Back outside the rectory Will went straight to his patiently waiting pony, hitched her up to the cart, jumped up and flicked the reins.

'I have to go,' he said under his breath. For the first time, it seemed we would part with barely a glance. Then on second thoughts, Will turned and called, 'I'll come again soon.' I watched them grow smaller and smaller, he and the pony, until finally the cart disappeared from view. When I could wait no longer I turned to go inside.

Martha Cherry stopped making her dough to eye me carefully. Did she see something new about me? Other than the state of my skirt, which was black at the hem and crumpled from sleeping on the earth?

'All right bonny lass?'

'I am thank you. That supper smells right grand.' I did my best to give the impression of normality but in fact there was nothing normal about the way I felt that evening. As I went to my room to change, I had a stab of conscience in my stomach thinking of Will driving back to his village, concerned and late. I should have reassured him better.

'Your lad's not been this last month,' Martha Cherry accused one Thursday evening, hands on her hips. She had a soft spot for Will since that first morning he arrived bold as brass in her kitchen, boyish and lanky, his cheeks flushed partly from the cold east wind, partly from awkwardness.

'He's busy with the harvest probably,' I said, hoping Will was alright, just labouring on one of the village farms, which he'd told me he did.

'He wouldn't let that stop him. He'd find a way to come. The two o' you had a row?' The tears came to my eyes then, but I scrunched them away. I was concerned about Will myself.

'Can't you write a letter?' Martha Cherry asked.

I'd considered this too but Will couldn't read. I'd offered to teach him, but at the time he'd quickly changed the subject. I suspected he was worried he would fail me. Even if I did write him a letter, and someone was on hand to read it to him, I had a feeling he would be embarrassed. On top of all that, I was feeling unwell, with the reason slowly dawning on me. Martha took a little longer to work it out but she realised soon enough.

'No. Frances!' She shook her head from side to side in disbelief. 'You'll get us all sent away if they find we've been hiding it.'

I knew the clergyman would show me the door once he discovered the truth, and I had no desire to stand in front of another employer pleading my case just yet. This time it would be worse than my exit from Kirkdunham House, especially as I hated to disappoint his wife. Mrs Beard had been good to me.

'You can't leave it much longer,' the cook urged, afraid for her own skin. But in the end I managed to conceal my condition for nearly four months, before I did as she wanted.

The clergyman's wife sat absently beside her husband's desk, intent on her embroidery. She was usually out visiting on a Saturday, but I'd asked to see them both.

'Now what is it you wished to say to us,' Reverend Theodore Beard began. 'I hope there is no illness in your family?'

There was nothing to gain from delaying. I hung my head at an appropriate angle. 'I'm sorry to tell you both I'm expecting a bairn, sir, ma'am.'

I stole a glance at their faces. A tiny blush had developed above the Reverend's thick red beard, while Mrs Beard was motionless now, her embroidery paused.

'I'm right sorry to disappoint you.' I felt her eyes hover over my belly. I knew my bulge was just visible. His eyes followed. 'You didn't think to inform us sooner?' His voice was so soft it was impossible to tell his emotion.

'I'm sorry,' I said again. 'I like it here; will I have to leave immediately?'

'I must say, you should have thought of that. This shows you are not at all concerned about other people. What will my parishioners say when they learn a woman under my roof, found herself in this position?' His voice was steady, his eyes shut as he tried to imagine how this could possibly have happened.

I hung my head low. 'It's not quite as you think, sir.'

'And how does she know what I think?' He turned to his wife briefly before facing me again, a flash of anger on his face now. 'You'll marry him I presume?'

A tear rolled slowly down my cheek. 'I hope so sir, when I find him. He'll need permission from his father though.'

The clergyman sighed and rubbed his beard. 'I can't believe I'm hearing this. I'm surprised that a woman of full age like you could do this.'

'I'm sorry I'm so wicked, sir,' I sniffed.

'It is certainly unfortunate,' he agreed.

His wife spoke up then to soften the atmosphere as I had hoped she would. 'As my husband says, we are disappointed but we wish you well, Fanny.' She didn't go on to thank me for my contributions to the Sunday mission, so I suspected she still saw me as a charity case.

'Yes,' her husband granted somewhat reluctantly. 'I think it's best if you make arrangements to leave the rectory tomorrow. I imagine you still have a family who will take you in?' He didn't wait for an answer, instead returning to the papers on his desk. I wondered if it was his sermon for the next day and if so, whether he would need to change it now. I saw myself through his eyes—a foolish country girl, shapely enough to attract the opposite sex, with no other remarkable features other than the slight glow of pregnancy in her complexion. Similarly, I had no other basis to form my opinion of the Reverend Theodore Beard, other than he first took me in, but then let me go. I had no other interest in his morals—or perhaps lack of them, at that point in time.

As I turned to leave the room, it occurred to me there was something that needed saying to Mrs Beard. 'Sorry ma'am, but I'm known as Frances now—my given name.' It was sharper than I was proud of, a parting shot, born of disappointment, plus as I saw it then, a lack of appreciation.

The Beards arranged for the gardener to drive me home to Long Newton in a waggon, so there was no opportunity to look for Will on the journey. I held tightly onto the side of the cart with one hand; with the other I held onto to my belly. It was a long bumpy ride.

My parents had run out of handed-down names by the time I was born, so I had become the first Frances in our family, christened after the Marchioness Frances Anne Vane Tempest who owned the estate land we'd laboured on all our lives. My brothers said it was perfect timing, my coming home. They'd just taken over the tenancy of a plot of Tempest land.

'We're husbandmen ourselves now,' they told me proudly, puffing out their chests, 'so we'll be glad of your help.'

My daughter Ann was born five months later, vigorous, a real force of nature. I named her after my ma and grandma, which was an easy decision to make.

When Ma put the newborn infant in my arms, she pointed out Ann's few dark curls. I thought about the day Will had called 'a grand morning' to me from his cart, his curly locks memorable as I watched his receding figure. I remembered the way he came to find me again, single-minded, determined. Something had gone wrong this time,—this time when my heart skipped a beat whenever I saw him in Ann. He hadn't come looking for me, despite his promise as we parted at the rectory after the thunderstorm, before I watched him drive away again.

6. An Unlikely Trio

Will

As he opened the door to the farmstead, the pair of them were almost knocked back by the filth.

'This hasn't been cleaned for years,' Elizabeth cried.

Will only just stopped himself gagging. Grabbing his sister by the arm, he pulled her out into the fresh air, coughing and spluttering. He wanted to get as far away from the building as possible. Still reeling, they drifted past the farmhand's cottage and out into the fields, where the wheat was golden in the mellow evening sunshine. Brother and sister stood and surveyed their kingdom, although for Will, it wasn't a heartwarming sight. The crop needed harvesting very soon, yet he had no idea how they would achieve it.

'We need a plan,' Elizabeth decided, 'we'll come back tomorrow.'

Things did seem slightly less daunting after a night's sleep. Back at the farmstead, they rushed through the cottage with handkerchiefs over their mouths, thrusting open every window they could find. They spent the next minutes taking stock. It was easier to breath with the fresh air, but with the windows open the stench was attracting house flies. The insects did at least help them identify the main culprits: dirty bandages; an unemptied night pot; rancid food.

Will swore out loud.

'I'll deal with it all. You go outside now,' Elizabeth urged. He didn't need telling twice. A rickety barn and a small tool shed stood near the cottage. The barn was dry, although not swept. The tool shed was the first piece of good luck they'd had. Evidently, the gouty old farmer loved the shed more than his cottage. Neatly hung on the wall was an array of scythes, hoes, shovels and rakes. While not particularly shining, the tools were rust free, largely mud free, and reasonably sharp.

The small farm was too far from the centre of the village to keep trudging there each day, if they actually wanted to get anything done, but there was no way Will would sleep in the filthy cottage. Elizabeth had an idea. The next day she collected blankets, a clean cooking pan, cups and plates from their father's house, so they could camp in the barn. At least his blanket felt soft there, stretched out on the remnants of hay they'd raked together. The smell of animals and crops stored over the years was almost pleasant. In the half light of dusk he could see the shape of his sister nearby. He spoke softly, not sure if she was awake. 'Its three days since I put my mark on that paper for the landowner, yet what have I achieved?' He'd asked the landlord for the shortest tenancy he was prepared to grant. They'd settled on two years but even that period seemed daunting when he thought how inadequate he was, and remembered the stink of the farmstead cottage.

'What will you do next, brother?'

'Start our harvest if I can get that miserable Mr Crank to oblige.' They'd found out the farmhand's name. It suited him.

Will had used a scythe before, to clear nettles while labouring on local farms. But when he'd helped with last summer's harvest, the tenant farmer quite wisely had cut the wheat himself. How should he swing the thing? It looked easy, but he knew things that looked easy, seldom were. No doubt his father would think him just as hopeless at harvesting as he was at weaving. He picked out the scythe that looked sharpest, along with all the rakes and laid them in the cart.

They started the harvest on the Thursday, one week after the thunderstorm, when Will should have been sitting with Frances in the rectory kitchen, or walking hand in hand along the cool side of the burn. It was backbreaking work out in the shade-less fields, even when he began to find some sort of rhythm, which meant before long the sweat was pouring off him. The wheat seemed to stretch out endlessly. Only Crank the crabby old farmhand really knew the proper system, but he was slow to give advice, so it was more by luck than judgement that the four of them made any progress that first day. Will's shoulders ached as he pushed the cart back to unload it in the barn.

Elizabeth took charge the next morning. She had Will cutting the crop, herself gathering, Crank's missus tying the swathes, and Crank stacking them on the cart. Later they would go over the same field, raking and collecting the loose stalks.

'Keep those apart,' Crank growled. 'There'll be stones from 'raking. There'll be *stones* in them!' He obviously didn't want to break any more teeth on the bread his wife baked.

On the third afternoon there was more of a breeze. Will stood up to straighten his back. At last with Elizabeth's plan they were making some progress. Also, as far as he could see, he got the cut about right. It was low enough to reduce the stubble but not enough to blunt the scythe on the soil. He wondered if his father would agree; probably not. But even thinking about his father's opinion, or lack of it, or of the fields still unharvested, and despite a large blister on the palm of his hand, Will felt a little happier. Also, the following day was Sunday, when he could sleep.

But there was no chance of rest because half the village arrived. Those that owned scythes brought them, along with extra carts, a pony and even some jars of cider. Their father came too, riding on one of the carts. Getting away from his cottage into the fresh air put the old weaver in a cheerful mood. In fact, he kept them going with his toothless smile and harvest tales they'd all heard before. 'You're all doing a grand job,' he said so often it made everyone laugh each time he repeated it. At one point, Will even started to believe him.

They were spreading the first bean crop out to dry in the barn when Elizabeth discovered a young terrier bitch hiding with her puppies at the back. 'Will. Come and look who's here.'

As he approached, the creature cowered further into the shadows but he could see she was brown and tan, with dark, silky, floppy ears. The two pups looked the same. 'Good girl,' he called gently. Then after several attempts, her tail came out from between her legs to give an exploratory wag.

'She likes you,' said Elizabeth. 'I wonder what she's been eating.'

'Probably mice—or cats,' he said, to see her reaction.

They took care not to disturb the dogs too much, but noticed Crank's wife bringing a saucer of milk from her cow. Elizabeth wondered if she knew the dog from before, when the gouty old farmer lived on the farm.

After the urgent business of harvest was done, the next concern was how to settle the rent with the landowner, and pay the old couple for their work. Will needn't have worried because Elizabeth had it in hand.

'Father says I'm organised, just like mother was,' she reminded him proudly with her face radiant seeing how impressed he was. She should have added '*on a good day.*' Will had no idea who he took after himself. He'd probably inherited the worst traits of each of his parents. Appearance was easier. It was well known that he took after his ma in looks.

Elizabeth sold some of their beans and grain in the village. The rest they divided between them. She also scrubbed and tidied the farmstead until the farmer's stench was only noticeable when the weather was very warm. They had a few of those days that autumn, although that would be the least of their problems.

With the rest of their crops under cover, Will decided to walk the fields and choose where to sow next year's wheat. He set off just after sunrise when the ground was still soaked with dew, and hadn't gone far when there was a soft noise behind him and something wet brushed past his legs. It was Bonny, the young terrier. Will had suggested that name because she was such a handsome girl. It must be the first time she thought it safe to leave her pups. Bonny kept him company all through that morning despite him having no titbits for her. Sometimes she would rush into the long grass at the edge of the fields, searching for a vole or another tasty meal. At other moments she would be content to wander beside him sniffing the air. Later on when Will sat for a while on a fallen trunk, weary from thinking, the dog lay down next to him panting quietly. They felt the breeze and watched a flock of birds pass overhead. Frances would have known exactly what sort the birds were and where they were going. Will had desperately wanted to explain everything to her, but the rectory was too far to reach easily on foot, with the demands of harvest unforgiving, even assuming she still worked there. She might be with someone else by then—a pretty girl like her—he told the dog lying beside him. The terrier stood up on her hind legs to lick his face, whimpering softly. He thought of Frances' warm body, her soft lips. His shoulders relaxed as a decision drifted into his consciousness. He would visit his father in the village the next day, find out what day the linen cart would be going to the mill, ask for a ride, go to find Frances.

John Bell was ashen grey as he stood swaying in the threshold.

'Da, what's wrong?' it wasn't part of Will's plan for his father to be unwell again. He was just expecting to ask the old man if he needed anything before heading off to find the cart driver. Instead, he followed the unsteady man inside, feeling slightly dizzy himself. His father held out a crumpled letter. Will looked anxiously at the paper, but didn't take it. Neither of them could read. Eventually he got the story from his father, who'd been to the blacksmiths to learn the letter's contents. It was from Sarah's husband in Middlesbrough. Will's favourite sister had given birth to a bairn, but neither she nor the little one had survived. He slumped to the floor and leant against the door frame, while his father watched him candidly for a few minutes.

'You'll have to fetch Elizabeth.'

Will nodded, pulling himself up again with difficulty. He wiped his eyes on his sleeve and set off on the long walk back to the farmstead to break the news. Any chance of visiting Frances had departed along with his eldest sister.

Will and Elizabeth took the news very badly. The realisation they would never again see or touch Sarah brought back memories of their mother leaving them. By contrast, on the surface at least, their father seemed quite stoic. He'd had plenty of experience losing children. Nevertheless, his grief and shock must have run deep, because the old weaver was found collapsed over his loom a few days later. Sarah had been the only one of them to take to the weaving, which he loved himself, so this gave them a special bond. He must have gone back to his loom, to remember. A neighbour discovered him blue and cold, and carried him to his bed. He was light as a feather.

'There's no need to fuss,' he moaned, pushing Will and Elizabeth away when they tried to feed him with wheat porridge, or plump his pillow. He rallied slightly when they got him warmed up; coming to his senses a little, pointing to each of them in turn, with instructions which were barely audible, while they strained to look attentive and hide their tears from him.

The old weaver closed his eyes for the final time in the silent hours before dawn. They buried him a week later. After the funeral, Will went back to their farmstead to prepare for winter.

With the smallholding taking all Will's attention he hardly noticed Elizabeth was unwell. They both had coughs every winter but hers went on well into spring, while she said nothing about the blood. Even so, he should have seen her struggling. He was appalled at himself. When he found her, she was collapsed in the barn, after trying to fill the grain sacks to sell in the village. He carried her into their farmstead, desperately searching for signs of life. There were none, but he couldn't believe it. 'Wake up Lizzy, you're safe now,' he told her over and over. When there was no response, he lay next to her sobbing, until he fell out of consciousness. Crank's wife found them there the next day after Will had failed to collect the milk she gave him from her dairy cow. The farmstead door was still wide open.

'She's gone, Master William. There's nowt you can do now,' the woman said firmly, leading him away.

After that it was just the three of them: Crank the miserable farm hand, his wife and Will—an unlikely trio. Will sank about as low as it was possible to be, while still pretending to be a husbandman.

7. The Same Side of the Moon

Frances

When I wasn't working the land with my brothers or helping Ma indoors, I was gently bouncing my daughter on a knee, getting to know every new achievement and sound. As she grew, I started taking her into the fields, placing her basket in the shade; scarcely lifting my eyes from her while I worked, scanning her features and reactions for any I recognised.

'Just as soon as you're old enough we'll look for your daddy,' I promised. It was frustrating I couldn't at least write Will a letter. It made me sad some folk never learned to read or write, although it gave me an idea, so I wasted no time asking my Uncle Robert's opinion. Leaving Ann safely with my ma that evening, I marched to my grandfather's cottage, hoping my uncle would be at home rather that at the boarding school for boys, where he still taught sometimes. Uncle Robert had never married, or maybe he was married to his vocation instead. A dedicated teacher, he loved nothing more than sharing his knowledge of biology, philosophy, or anything really. How he achieved such knowledge, coming from a labouring family was the subject of wonder for some in Long Newton, but only of pride, for the Ferguson clan.

Uncle Robert spread out his few books on the table: a map of the world; the book on Palestine; one of poetry; *Elements of Botany*. Compared to the collection at Kirkdunham it was paltry, but these books had certainly been lovingly read.

'Take any of them to read,' he offered generously, 'although I believe you already know enough to teach young Ann when she'd old enough.'

I explained my plan to teach some of the other village children. It was the first time I'd voiced it out loud. 'Shouldn't all children learn to read and write?' I asked him.

'They should, my dear.' He scratched his balding head for a moment. He could probably bring me a few old slates from his school, along with some picture books. Perhaps I could use those to stimulate the youngsters' interest?

I rushed over to embrace him.

'Well that's enough of that, girl,' he said reddening, immediately heading back to the kitchen to finish his supper. 'I'm happy to help.'

I opened the map book, trying to commit the African continent to memory, especially the Cape. We would start with that.

Lessons began in my brothers' farm kitchen just a few days after I had the idea. First it was just Ann's cousins, but on the second day other village children began to join. I kept them inside for no longer than an hour each morning, because most had chores to do. As I'd promised myself, we began with the shape of the African continent. Using the markings on my uncle's map, we imagined what the landscape was like in Africa; what wild animals might be there. From memory I described the fauna the eight year old English boy saw in the storybook from Kirkdunham House. There was the rose-coloured flamingo, slender and long-legged, sailing through the air; the honey-bird, which enticed the boy away causing him to get completely lost; the antelope which was calmly drinking from the river bed but had to take flight when a lion and lioness arrived. We had the picture books from Uncle Robert to help.

'How long would it take to reach the Cape?' asked an inquisitive boy, 'I want to go there.' I couldn't say, but I thought many days or even months on the sailing ship.

'But Frances, how *many* days and months exactly?'

There was such a lot I didn't know, and in particular, numbers were not my strength. I confessed as much to Uncle Robert one night later that first week.

'Then have the children do some work themselves,' he suggested.

Outside, the October hunter's moon was rising, tinged with red, and large. It must be almost at its zenith because the old man in the moon was clear as anything. I leaned on the gate to gaze up, wondering if Will was watching at the same moment, thinking of me as he'd promised. It suddenly came to me. I could ask the children to count the days and nights until the next full moon. As well as helping with our arithmetic it would give me another reason to think of Will every day. Not that I needed one, he was never far from my mind.

The idea was received with enthusiasm by the children, which meant I knew it was exactly eighteen days after hunter's moon, when a silver sliver was waxing again, that the first parent came apologetically into the classroom. Her daughter was needed to mind her younger sisters, so could no longer attend for lessons. At twenty days, when we'd almost reached a three quarter crescent, an irate farmer stood before us, arms akimbo, come to pluck his two sons away. He'd only just found out his boys were 'skiving', because his wife had kept it from him until that morning. His boys should be working on the farm, not dreaming about a country on the other side of the world. When the rest of us had counted twenty-four nights, an older boy arrived to fetch his brother, who was supposed to be counting sheep, not lunar nights, so his father told him to say.

I braced myself for more.

'Will we have to stop learning, Auntie Frances?' worried one of my nieces the morning after the second full moon. The five children still there in addition to the Ferguson family, had kept one eye on the door that lesson, waiting for their turn to be dragged away.

'Not if I can help it,' I told them while shepherding them out.

I had to check some things with Uncle Robert. Such as, would you see exactly the same moon at the South African Cape as we did? I thought so, but wanted to be certain. He demonstrated, with the aid of a couple of turnips, how the same orb travelled around the earth with always the same side showing. He chuckled to himself. But the moon would look upside down in Africa! Then he ran his clean teacher's finger long-ways down the map from Greenwich, in London, to the bottom of the page. If my brothers or Will had done the same, there would be a dirty line left on the map. My uncle's invisible line was known as a meridian, he told me. His finger passed through the ocean to the left of the Cape, but not too far away.

'That means although time won't be exactly the same in Cape Town, night and day will still be similar,' he told me. 'Now,' he pointed across to map to the New World. 'Here, its likely night will fall during our day, because it's so far away from the Greenwich meridian. Do you see?'

I didn't, completely. It worried me that I would never know enough to teach the children properly. Even if I did learn enough, some of the parents may not like it, if they were anything like those women at Kirkdunham House who'd taken a *skunner* to me.

'We can never please everyone,' said my uncle with a shrug. 'Some folk just don't like change, or else they worry they'll be left behind. So they punish those of us that want to make a difference, or rise from our station in life to start to understand our world.' I'd never told him about the housemaid who made my life a misery, so was amazed to hear his description, which fit her so well. I suspected my uncle knew of such punishment first hand; a teacher arising from a farm labouring family; although he seemed to deal with his disappointments better than me.

One thing did please me greatly. Even if the man in the moon was upside down in Africa, the English boy at the Cape would have seen the same side of our full moon. *'Our moon.'* I desperately hoped Will and I would gaze up at it together again, one day soon.

Meanwhile, counting lunar nights gave us endless material for learning as well as entertainment. Some boys and girls kept counting after the November moon, including one boy whose father had pulled him away by his ear. After the December full moon, he escaped from his father's tenant farm just outside Long Newton, to pay us a visit. He hovered for a few minutes on the threshold to explain, his breath visible in the frosty air, one eye on the lane in case his father had followed him. The boy had carried on counting. He'd wanted to find out if it was the same number between each full moon, or different. He pulled out his slate from under his smock.

'Here's my numbers miss,' he announced, before speeding off again.

He wasn't the only keen individual. One of the boys from the poorest family in Long Newton still came, wearing shoes that flapped about, his thin coat threadbare with the sleeves only reaching his elbows.

'Ma says to learn as much as I can,' the ragged little boy informed at the door the very first morning he arrived, 'then I can get us out of poverty.'

After each lesson, I slipped him some bread and cheese for his dinner, an apple, or whatever we could spare. He was bright, would be brighter than me I felt sure.

Uncle Robert made discreet enquiries into a bursary for him at the boys' school where he taught, but to no avail.

'This is wrong,' he said frowning. We were both disappointed.

The boy's family knew nothing of our frustration at the way things were. His mother sought me out at St. Mary's church on a February Sunday when her son had been coming each morning for four moons.

'You've made such a difference to us, knowing there's some hope,' she said with her eyes full of tears. My own eyes filled up after that. I needed people's appreciation. I needed thanks. There was even more reason to be grateful that February Sunday in 1848, the day my daughter Ann turned one year old. She was healthy and strong, although that was about to change.

8. The Guest Speaker

Will

It was Crank's missus who had gradually dragged Will out of his depression.

'You need to take the grain and beans to the market,' nagged the farmhand's wife. This was when the sun was high in the heavens yet Will was still under the covers. 'We can't live on bread alone,' she persisted annoyingly. 'Says so in the good book.'

He grunted, well aware of their precarious situation, but with absolutely no enthusiasm to do something about it. It was better just lying in bed, letting other people do the worrying. It had always been Elizabeth's responsibility to sell the produce. He knew they would also need to purchase salt for salting down the vegetables from the garden, bacon for their stew—they had no livestock except two hens and the Crank's dairy cow—and soap for washing, but it was all too much effort.

'And what about paying the rent this month?' Mrs Crank insisted.

Will wondered vaguely what she knew about that, or what she was even doing in his sleeping area.

'I know,' she said firmly, reading his mind. 'I weren't born yesterday.' She'd brought him wheat porridge sweetened with honey, and tea, to coax him out of bed. The previous evening, because she felt he'd had a productive day, she'd rewarded him with a jug of sweet elderberry wine, apparently kept stashed away in her own cottage. He'd drunk it when the sun had sunk low in the west, when he could feel the gnats dancing around his head, but not see them. It had been a fine evening, with a flame-red sky turning dusky pink, but he'd gazed without seeing into the distance, his brain numbed for a while by the alcohol. After that, he slept long and dreamlessly.

Eventually, he prised himself from under the covers to do what Crank's missus told him. The first week after he buried Elizabeth, the old woman had called the two dogs to jump on him, biting, playful, and slightly wet from the dew. Later, he speculated whether she'd used these tactics on the cantankerous old Crank when they were younger, or if they'd ever had children themselves.

The weeks and months passed, but everything was harder without his sister. Harvest, particularly. Last year, Elizabeth had taken him in hand. It had been hard, but they'd had each other. This second year was far worse. The old couple and he had to struggle on their own, since the villagers didn't turn out to help again. Will couldn't understand why they didn't come, until he realised they were embarrassed, not knowing how to behave around the grieving boy. It took until the autumn for him to emerge from his dark mood, five months after he buried Elizabeth, and when he surfaced, he vowed never to let himself descend there again. He was also determined not to die just yet. His father used to call him a survivor and he wanted to prove him right.

Crank's missus turned out to be a good cook. When the wheat was safely in the barn, she came over to Will's farmstead cottage with a rabbit stew. It contained a herb or two; one he recognized as rosemary, the other he couldn't quite identify. The stew had settled nicely in his stomach, making him feel full for the first time since Elizabeth. It was gestures like that which pulled him through. In fact, not only was he rubbing along nicely with the old farmhand's wife, a strange thing had happened with her cantankerous husband, since Will lost Elizabeth. Crank was less cranky. When Will bemoaned the fact they were getting so little wheat sown, instead of making some unhelpful remark, the farmhand told him, 'Nowt wrong with that. Fields like to rest.' But that wasn't all, because he added, 'we could sow some turnips after harvest next summer. It's better than leaving the ground fallow.' Will hadn't told Crank yet that he would be quitting when his tenancy ended next July. Later when Crank's wife brought Will's eggs, she congratulated him. 'You've managed to drag out the better side of my husband. Not many folks can do that.'

It was so cut off on the farm; he couldn't remember the last time he'd spoken to another person if he excluded the old couple. When he roused himself enough to venture into the village one afternoon at the end of winter, he heard conversations outside the smithy about a new farmer's club. There was to be a special meeting on its opening night to kick the club off, with an important guest speaker. It would be held at half past six on March 19th, in the large barn at Tomlinson's farm. Will made a mental note of the details; it was time he made the effort.

He arrived early on the Tuesday evening, but found the large barn already packed out with men and boys; a white sea of smocks. He'd never seen so many people gathered in one place. He launched himself into the throng, eventually emerging at the far side of the barn, reasonably near the front.

'This'll do me,' he thought. The noise was deafening. Young men like him were laughing and chatting excitedly, whilst old men were shouting to each other over the din. A few wooden crates had been pushed together at the front with two chairs perched precariously on top, the farmer on one of them. The second chair was mysteriously empty. Will was surprised to see a few gentlemen landowners in their smart coats and cravats seated on benches at the front, visible in the gas light. Then before long, a slight figure entered through a side door, pushed his way through and sat down next to the farmer. There was a surge in the crowd's chatter for a moment as they noticed the newcomer, with the noise gradually dropping away to an expectant hush. The room was so full of humanity, Will could feel the warmth of those closest, sensing a slight tremor of anticipation coming from them too. At last, the farmer got to his feet and cleared his throat nervously.

'I'd like to welcome all you fellow farmers to this new club.' He let his words sink in. 'And I'm sure you'll give a warm welcome to our guest speaker.' There was a hum of approval from the packed floor followed by a few shouts of encouragement from a group of youths behind Will. 'He's come all the way from Newcastle. Thank you for coming to talk to us sir.'

It was difficult to tell the guest's age in the poor light, but he was young enough to bounce to his feet on the rickety stage.

'Friends, the world's changing and we can't be left behind! 'Bout three years ago I saw something in Newcastle I'll not forget and I want every farmer to be ready for it.'

'He's a smooth talker,' someone standing behind Will said.

'I expect some of you've heard about the Royal Agriculture Society, haven't you?' The speaker paused for a moment then, to gauge his audience's reaction. 'Aye,' he went on, 'and you know every year they're on the road for a show. Well, it was our turn in Newcastle in forty-six, and I can tell you all that's what changed my life.' He cast his eyes along the rows of the crowd to make sure they were with him. They were. 'My friends, you plough, you sow, you reap and thresh, then it all starts over again and you get knackered. Well let me tell you gentlemen, this'll change very soon. The future of your farms is going to be totally different. And you know why? I'll tell you. It's the age of the engine. Because what I saw at that show, was me first farm engine.' He paused for effect, which gave one of the gentlemen in the first row the opportunity to speak up.

'Sir, using a threshing machine powered by steam in one's barn is not unusual nowadays with large landowners, although I admit I've not yet seen the machine myself.'

'Aye it's true.' The guest speaker agreed, bouncing a little more so that the boxes creaked, while the farmer next to him looked nervous. 'However gentlemen, what *I* saw at that show was even more amazing. I saw a traction engine for working the fields.' There was a hum as the farmers took this in and whispered to their neighbours. Then the speaker had to raise his voice slightly to regain the audience's attention so they could learn about the self-moving steam engine, which had so captured his imagination. This machine could even pull a plough. It had enthralled the speaker so much that the company demonstrating the engine gave him a job. Now he travelled all over the east of England, mainly by train, telling farmers about it.

'Where can we go to watch this engine in use?' one of the landowners asked.

'Give us another year or two and they'll be everywhere,' the guest speaker promised, bringing his hands together for emphasis, at last sinking into his chair.

The hours had flown by. Will had hardly noticed his legs aching from all that time on the hard floor. After the farmer had warmly thanked the speaker, followed by a great rumble of applause, a door behind them creaked open so the audience could slowly leave. Will was pleased to be at the other side of the barn. He wondered how it would feel to be shoved like cattle or sheep through such a narrow exit, which used to happen at the livestock market in Northallerton, near where he delivered the linen.

He was one of the last to pass through the exit. The sun had long since set, the air felt cold after the warm barn. Looking around him, he saw most of the men had gone home to their farms but a few had stayed to talk in the moonlight, including one tight group with long faces and low voices. He wondered what their problem was. Will could definitely see a future for farm engines even though it wasn't what he wanted to do. He was no good at farming. His father would have confirmed that. But engines to travel up and down the country like the guest speaker? Now *that* was a different matter. He liked the idea that engines could take him to new places, rather than taking root on his farm. He guessed the little group of farmers didn't relish the idea of change. As he moved closer to hear the men's hushed conversation one of them pointed upwards. The others followed his finger. Two old farmers rubbed their beards in astonishment, another hid his face. The moon was turning deep red in front of their eyes, making their smocks pink.

'Tis an omen,' another said shaking his head. 'Nowt good can come of this engine talk.' They dispersed then, as if bathed in blood, leaving Will to do the same.

The long walk back to his farmstead gave him plenty of opportunity to think. What did a blood red moon mean? It couldn't be good. He'd promised to always think of Frances when he saw the moon in the heavens, but this time made him uneasy. Was something bad happening to her? How had he left it so long?

9. Crimson Moon

Frances

As the cold spring wind whipped across the farm we both caught colds, with Ann's fever so high we were forced to close the school. I was worried about my daughter, but also unhappy at letting the other children down. The previous evening, Uncle Robert had made a surprise appearance at the farm. The enthusiastic man had chosen the armchair by the stove, rocking back and forth a few times before telling us his news. When he was being enthusiastic he grew two pink circles on his cheeks. He'd heard the news at school in the master's drawing room. One of his colleagues had an acquaintance at Durham Observatory he explained. A total lunar eclipse was expected around full moon, just two days away. Sun, earth and moon would line up that evening, with the earth getting in the way. The orb's colour would change to gold or perhaps orange or red.

He thought the children should witness it, assuming it wasn't a cloudy evening. Hopefully it wouldn't matter for them to lose a bit of sleep.

Although I didn't completely understand about the lunar eclipse, it sounded grand. I struggled to sleep, thinking how I could explain to the children. But there was none of that once I felt the heat coming from Ann's forehead at sunrise. When the first child arrived for lessons, we stationed her at the door of the classroom, to send the others home. Then once all the school children had been turned away I went back to Ann.

Even during those ten minutes she seemed worse. Since daybreak she'd been crying fretfully but she was swiftly becoming listless. Ma and I exchanged worried glances. We hurriedly stripped off her clothes, sponging her down gently with cool water, but both her chest and back continued to burn.

'We'll just have to hope this fever breaks soon,' my mother said wringing out the cloth grimly. I sank into a chair. I wasn't well myself, my throat was like a washing board while my head thumped with fever and anxiety.

'Rest awhile, Frances. Maybe the little one will be better when you wake.'

She wasn't. The heat was still coming off her in the afternoon. I took hold of the cloth frantically, trying to cool her small clammy body. Then I rocked her in my arms desperately.

Throughout the night and all the next day we took turns sponging her, or lifting her up to spoon a little water between her lips. By the second evening I lost all hope. The worst thing was that Will would never have the chance to meet his daughter. He would never gaze at her in wonder as I did each day. He would never lift her high above him in his strong arms, as my brothers did sometimes, watching the smile broaden across her little face.

Sitting at the window I stared out hopelessly into the night. The moon was flushed crimson, like our daughter's feverish body. Time passed as I watched blood red turn back to silver.

'Frances, come and see.' My mother's voice cut into my misery.

While I'd been at the window Ann's fever had broken, she was coughing a little and beginning to cry.

When lessons resumed, there was such a clamour in the farmhouse kitchen I had to quieten them down to think properly. Girls were crying, boys shouting.

'Talk one at a time, if you please.'

A little girl spoke first. They'd thought I was dead. When the clouds parted, the moon had been crimson. Her brother told her it was blood, which meant I must have died.

'Well, as you can see I'm very much alive.' I smiled as broadly as I could, while remaining serious so as not to make the child feel stupid, an experience I knew only too well.

'My Gran says you should never look up at a red moon, it makes you go mad,' said another. Still another child recounted how their farm dogs had lifted up their heads and howled. I explained about the eclipse as best I could. After that I knew it was time to stop.

'Thank you children for all those observations, and now we are going to leave the moon to do what it does.'

Young Ann watched proceedings intently. Everyone loved her. Her hair was growing long, dark and curly, and she had the most beautiful smile. It was Will's smile. A motley group of children continued to join us in the farm kitchen most mornings, even in the growing season which was a busy period for their families.

It was hectic for me too. After our lesson, I worked in the garden, tending the vegetables until the sun had sunk behind the hills. My sister-in-law was away visiting her folks, so there was weeding and harvesting to do without her help. But when my brother announced he was taking the waggon over the river next day to collect his wife, my heart gave a leap. The radishes could be thinned later. His wife's family came from a village just past Appleton Wiske, where I hoped Will might still be.

Our journey started badly. Sitting at the front alongside my brother with Ann propped between us, I had an excellent view of the racing cart coming towards us. Two youths were whipping their donkey, which was weaving back and forth across the bridle path towards us. There was nowhere for the nearside wheel of our waggon to go, except the ditch.

'Fools,' I shouted, before we tipped over. My brother grabbed Ann's clothes to stop her sliding after me to the ground. A layer of sludge in the bottom of the ditch cushioned my fall. The waggon carried on without me in lopsided fashion, until it found a sort of level again a few feet further along, where the lower ground widened. I pulled myself up with a groan and together we assessed the damage. My shoulder and hip felt bruised where I'd landed; my dress was black with silt and I was trembling. But it was the waggon that had come off worst. The wheel was broken. The better news was our pony was grazing on the long grass beside the ditch, apparently unfazed by what had happened.

We thought we might limp along slowly to the wheelwright, but we'd need the waggon back on the path first. It was easier said than done. I tried to persuade the pony onto higher ground while my brother pushed the waggon from behind, but it was too steep. Next we tried unhitching the animal and pushing the waggon up without her. That didn't work either. We could either walk home for help or wait until someone passed by. We decided to wait.

Having already spent more time on the ground than I preferred that morning, rather than sitting down with the others, I wandered further along, round the corner. Someone was approaching on foot. He was tall and dark, so my immediate thought was of Will, but then everyone I saw made me think of him. Instead, it was a neighbour walking home after a night in town, slightly the worse for drink. Together, the three of us manhandled the waggon back onto the path. Our neighbour then lurched off home, while we set out carefully for Yarm.

It took several pleas to persuade the wheelwright to do the job that morning. His face told us what he thought about the mess our waggon was in, so I wasn't at all confident we'd get to our destination. But when he came to find us he was smiling.

'Easier than I first thought,' he admitted.

Despite my fears, we picked up my brother's wife from her village and rolled into Appleton Wiske on our way home. My bruises were sore, I was battered by the rutted lanes and flushed from the sun and wind, but we'd managed it. It was worth all the bruises to learn about Will from an old man outside the smithy.

'Aye, I can tell you about William Bell,' he said, laying a slightly rusty scythe down on the ground first. It looked as if we were in for a long story. The old man cleared his throat theatrically then told us what he knew. Will had lost all three members of his family, but was working the land his father insisted he take as a tenant farmer. His farmstead was isolated, difficult to find if you didn't know it and had poor soil, by all accounts. The most worrying news was that the tenancy was up that summer when Will would likely be leaving the area. He couldn't say where the lad would go.

I thanked him for his information. It was too late that evening to search for the farm but I knew I'd be back.

10. A Mystery

Will

Crank caught Will arriving back wearily from the smithy, with the good-as-new scythe resting across his shoulder. 'Some lass were seeking you a day or so ago,' he said. Apparently this occurred when Crank had taken the scythe into the village to be fixed ready for harvest. Will turned round carefully to face his farmhand. The handle of the scythe was resting safely against his body but the other end was sharp. "'Some lass", did you say? Did she give her name?' He wondered why the old man had left it three days to tell him. It occurred to him that Crank was getting forgetful but seeing the gleaming scythe had jogged his memory.

'Nay, she didn't. She had a youngster with her, if that helps?' Crank told Will the woman and child arrived by pony and cart accompanied by two others. A man was driving and another woman who looked vaguely familiar sat in the rear. Crank thought the second woman might be from a local village.

'And this lass with a child asked for me by name?'

'Aye she did. I told her a bit about you. Pretty woman she was.' Crank was being mischievous. 'Bonny child too,' he continued,   clearly enjoying the young man's perplexed look and even making the terrier prick up her ears when she heard her name. 'Over a year old I'd say, with lovely brown locks o' hair.'

It was definitely a mystery. Will couldn't for the life of him recall any woman with a child, who would come asking after him. He ran his free hand through his own curls.

'They said they couldn't hang around. They'd had a difficult day and needed to get home,' Crank finished.

Will had had a tough day himself with a headache coming on. He hung the scythe in the tool shed ready for the new tenant, following the dog's example to take a long deep drink. It was unseasonably hot for May so he felt prickly in his winter clothes, but once he'd stripped off and put his head under the pump for a few minutes he felt a lot better. That evening after supper, they sat outside, the three of them—Crank, his wife, and Will—enjoying the cooling air and listening to the field crickets singing. A tiny breeze had picked up from the direction of the sea bringing with it the sweet smell of rain from far away.

'Mebbe we'll get lucky and have a nice shower,' the farmhand hoped.

'But not a downpour to spoil the wheat, please God,' countered his wife. In the end, the rain came to nothing, so neither of them was happy. It was farmer's talk which reminded Will how uncertain their occupation was, and how good it would be to leave it behind.

It took longer than he thought to leave his farm. Will was determined to tidy everything up so the new tenants wouldn't curse him, as he and Elizabeth had cursed the gouty old man who preceded their own tenure. He cleaned the farmstead cottage from top to bottom, even sweeping the chimney. He oiled the tools in the shed, after checking all the mud was cleaned off. He swept the yard. It was almost as if he was putting off his departure. In the end it was early evening before he got away. If he spent another night at the farmstead he would have to say the goodbyes again, so it was best to go, despite the hour. Strangely, he would miss Crank and his missus. Since Elizabeth's passing they'd been kind to him. He wondered if the old farm hand would get on with the new tenant farmer, or if he would revert to his cantankerous side.

He'd decided to leave Bonny with the Cranks, where she was happy and knew where to find shrews and mice, but she was having none of it. The terrier followed him into the village. He was taking a last drink at the pump in front of the church gates, pausing to take one final look at the place where he'd spent most of his life, when he heard her panting behind him. Her ears were back, tail wagging sheepishly as she waited to hear if she'd done the right thing. Tears sprung to his eyes when he saw the dog. He ruffled her head and then they set off together past the weaver's cottages with their spinning windows and sheds, quiet now at that time of the evening, until they'd left the hot smell of baked mud pavements behind them. The coolness of the countryside felt welcome. He took a deep breath. 'It's just the two of us now, girl,' he told the dog. 'We'll have to make some new friends.' It reminded him how hard it was to keep hold of the people he cared about.

It was the route he used to walk as a child with the ponies, then when he was older, with the linen cart; a steady rise out of the village that you noticed more when you were walking. It was the way he'd driven the day he first saw Frances in the garden, the route he'd taken the day of the thunderstorm. It seemed an age away. Two years away in fact, during which time he'd lost everyone he loved. He'd lost his father, two sisters and he'd lost Frances too, or perhaps just mislaid her? That was why he was heading out to St. Thomas' church, to find out for certain if he'd lost her too. It didn't bear thinking about, but at least then he could decide where to head for railway work. Earlier that day Will had discarded the smock Elizabeth had embroidered prettily in blue. He hoped someone else could make use of it. Without it, he was aware he looked like a vagrant: shirt and breeches, bag over one shoulder, blanket over the other, dog by his side. None of his clothes had benefitted from the care of a woman lately. He would be sleeping in a barn, so would be even more vagrant-like the next day. He must take care not to be arrested. It felt good to be free, but with the sun setting and the chill creeping in, there was a flutter of anxiety in his breast.

A glow from the occasional cottage told him at least some folk were still awake, people with family, with love in their lives. Although it was dark, he knew the lane well. He also had an idea which barn he would choose. He crept along the lane to the farm he had in mind. No-one seemed to be about. He would be away first thing in the morning before anyone saw him. He chose the third of their three outhouses which was unlikely to be a grain store so far from the house. The wheat should be in the large middle barn. When his eyes accustomed to the gloom, he realised the building he'd chosen was a kind of workshop, with a lathe and bench. Spreading his blanket out on the floor he flopped down on it. Bonny did the same. They shared his hard boiled eggs and two bread buns before settling into an uneasy sleep. Bonny always slept with one ear open, but Will did too for the first half of that night, on tenterhooks in case the farmer discovered him, with all the explaining that would require. Eventually he fell asleep more deeply so was wide awake, refreshed, before the first tentative notes from two wood pigeons in the rafters above them. Once the first bird made its call, he moved quickly. Prodding Bonny fully awake, he rolled his blanket, checked he'd left no body shape on the floor, and peered outside. No sign of movement—'good.'

They were creeping back past the buildings when a cat came into sight, green eyes glowing, back arching seeing the dog. All hell broke out. Bonny went mad, tipping her head back, letting rip with her voice box. The two animals faced each other off in the half light, neither prepared to give way. 'Shush you stupid girl,' Will told the dog, no longer bothering to whisper. 'Leave it.' but it was too late to escape unnoticed. First, an upstairs window of the house creaked open, then a face peered out. Will squashed himself against the barn until the person looked away. After a moment or two when he thought it was safe, he squeezed through a gap between the buildings, leaped over the stone wall behind the farmyard, escaping breathlessly into the field. Bonny followed eventually, hearing his whistle. Once on the lane they ran and ran. He was still looking behind him for at least an hour, half expecting an irate farmer to catch up with them.

Late that morning as they neared St Thomas', shock from the cat incident began to merge into panic. What would he say at the rectory? What if Frances was there but no longer wanted to see him? He'd let her down, should have returned to see her two years ago. Finally, when man and dog turned the corner to face the church's squared stones and parapets, Will broke into a sweat. They got only as far as the gate to the rectory garden.

'I just can't do it,' he told the dog.

Everything was a blur after that. He knew he slept under a hedge that night, because he woke at dawn with thorns in his hair and ants in his breeches.

But where was Bonny? He couldn't see her anywhere. A terrible sadness washed over him. She must have returned to the farmstead, to the Cranks. Who could blame her?

He heard her eventually. She was rustling in the undergrowth looking for breakfast. His eyes moistened to find she'd been so faithful.

'I'll make it up to you,' he told her, unsure whether he meant his terrier, or Frances.

Something drew him to the old seat in the graveyard; the usual tap, tap of a woodpecker beating time in the horse-chestnuts or yews. It was the seat he used to sit on with Frances. Sitting there in the dappled light, he began to make some peace with it all. It was that sort of place. Until by mid morning he knew he could find the courage to ring that bell and face the consequences.

It was no surprise when the woman tried to shut the kitchen door in his face. He could imagine how he looked after two nights: the first sleeping in that barn; the last one in a hedge. He wasn't giving up easily though. He pulled the reluctant bell again. To give the new cook her due she did open the door a second time, although not wide, it was true.

'Look. I can tell you for sure there's no Frances or Fanny working here, and hasn't been for almost two years, since I've been here. Now clear off before I call the reverend.' There seemed little point asking where Frances might have gone, but the woman did reluctantly reveal what she knew of the old cook, Mrs Cherry, who she said had moved with the former rector and his wife to a new town.

He returned to the seat to find Bonny waiting patiently as he'd told her to. Hunching forward, he reviewed what he'd learnt. Frances had left the rectory, so he needed to find her. He would start with her village, which he recalled was miles away over the river in County Durham. Long Newton, he believed. He would confess to her what a bad person he was, then be on his way. Even if she was married, he could still apologise, admit he was useless at everything, and ask for her pardon. He'd thought about sleeping in St Thomas' church that night and leaving in the morning, but the door was firmly locked. It must be a sign.

He spoke to his terrier, stood up, and brushed himself down. They would set out immediately, heading northwards towards this Long Newton, to find Frances.

11. The Ecclesiastical Grapevine

Frances

I was crouching in the soil, just as I had been the first time he said the words. But on this occasion, I was amongst the cabbages at Town farm, rather than in the pretty rectory garden. I intended it to be the final morning tending and harvesting before I left Long Newton for a few days to go in search of Will. I'd saved enough shillings for us to stay at an inn on the journey, to make the long road up and down to Appleton Wiske manageable even with an infant. I planned to set off the next day, with Ann.

After all the times I'd imagined seeing Will in a passer-by, or in the figure of a man at the market, or maybe in the handsome features of a boy driving a cart; when I did see him after over two years, I didn't recognise him. The features were unfamiliar as he walked towards me with his dog. This figure was gaunt and shabby, like a vagrant; older, certainly. The tall frame was bent slightly, the hair wild and matted.

'A grand morning to you, miss.' The voice was gravely with anxiety but there was no doubt it was Will's. His voice was the one thing I did recognise immediately. The dog sat down next to him, panting quietly, wagging its tail. Time stood still for a moment. I extracted myself carefully from the cabbage patch, stepped towards him, took him in my arms and buried my face in his chest. When I was as sure as I could be he wouldn't run away, I lifted my head to whisper, 'you came.'

'At last,' he said; his voice still croaky. 'Sorry it's taken this long.'

Eventually I asked him, 'do you know you have a daughter?' The surprise jolted through his body, close to mine.

He stood back to look at me quizzically, his mind full of questions.

'Her name is Ann and she favours you in looks.'

'Then…?'

I didn't let him finish. 'Aye,' I cried out. It wasn't certain what he would have said. Perhaps he was about to mention my visit to Appleton, if the funny little old man I met outside the smithy had told him about us. My guess was that he meant the afternoon of the thunderstorm. I pulled away again slightly to grin at him.

'Now don't you want to meet our daughter?'

I half expected my surroundings to have changed when I looked around. The summer colours seemed brighter certainly, but there was still the farm house with its roof due for a repair, the red door needing a touch of paint. There were the same cabbages, the usual white butterflies which tested my patience and the identical rows of late potatoes ready for digging. The purple headed hills were still visible in the distance. But something *was* different I realised. It was Ann. Will's dog had been standing over her where she was playing in the soil, licking the child's face. As we watched, our daughter pulled herself up holding onto the dog's neck then started to follow the animal. It was the first time I'd seen her try to walk. The creature didn't complain; it seemed to know to treat her gently. Ann chuckled happily as she flopped down again, so I could tell she had also fallen in love. I lifted her up in my arms and handed her to Will.

'Here's your daddy,' I told her. 'I said you'd meet him soon, didn't I?'

*

Late that afternoon, after Will had stood under the pump and I'd fed him with farm fare, I put Ann in her cot in my mother's cottage and led Will by the hand into the fields. We spread out a blanket where the stubble was softest and sat close together watching distant heather clad moors sparkle in the low sunlight.

'I could see the moors from my farmstead too,' he told me, squeezing my hand. 'So we might have lost each other but we were still connected.'

Tears of joy sprang to my eyes, hearing his words, and I leaned against him, sleepily. But when he slipped his arm round me I felt the old spark light up inside. We could wait another day to share each other's news.

While we waited for banns to be read in Appleton Wiske as well as in Long Newton, Will knuckled down to help my brothers on the farm. He was a capable husbandman they told me, and even made some fine suggestions about improving their cropping. It would be no good complementing him though. He was convinced he was as poor at working the land as at everything else. I wondered if he associated being bad at something, with work he didn't enjoy? He left me in no doubt that farming wasn't popular with him.

'It's too uncertain,' he said straightening his back and brushing the soil off his hands. We liked to walk back to the farmstead together, at the end of a day in the fields.

It was a time of suspense, waiting for our wedding. For Will particularly, because he'd added about two years to his age. He was worried the vicar in Appleton would realise, especially as there was no-one left in his family to give permission. It was a concern, as who knew what would happen in that case?

'What you thinking about?' I whispered when we were sitting on the hard pews of our Long Newton church. The vicar was casting his eyes over our own congregation, to see if any folk in my village objected to our marriage. I was waiting with dread in case there was a problem, although there was no reason to be. Will's mind was far away in Appleton Wiske.

'I'm wondering how your vicar will know if everything's fine in Appleton?'

I thought back to my time at the rectory and tried to think how Reverend Beard knew what was going on in local parishes. I had the answer.

'They've an ecclesiastical grapevine for that,' I whispered.

'A what?'

'Seriously Will, I reckon no news means good news.'

He nodded, but there was something more on his mind.

'And I'm trying to remember my ma's face. But I can't.'

I whispered it would likely come to him when he wasn't expecting it. He agreed that did happen sometimes. The vicar eventually looked our way with a frown. It brought us both back to the present; to the hard pews of St. Mary's. We didn't want to upset him.

Fortunately, no-one objected to our union, or noted Will was only nineteen, so we were wed properly this time, with bells, rather than in a damp wood with an ivy ring. They all came this time too: my brothers, their wives and their children, Ma clutching hold of our Ann, Uncle Robert of course, but most of the village too, dragged along by my school children. Will had nobody. Not even his dog, as she wasn't allowed in the church. He'd have wanted his sister to come. When he said those words, he couldn't face me. Instead he bent to fondle Bonny's ears as he explained. He'd told me how he'd found Elizabeth in that barn, collapsed, lifeless. Never having met his sister it was impossible to grieve for her properly, but I cried for Will's loss nonetheless.

'I wish I could have met her,' I said, 'especially if she was just like you.'

'I'm not like her at all,' he said sadly. 'Elizabeth was good at everything, *and* she was beautiful.'

'Then she was *exactly* like you,' I told him, taking his hand firmly.

After our wedding, we could have stayed on longer helping my brothers but Will had too many dreams. Uncle Robert knew this too. That autumn he took Will, as he had taken each of us when we were children, but now ambling slowly due to his creaky knees, to the ancient woodland behind the village. I knew he would be showing my husband the bats roosting in the crevices of a rotten oak tree. Once, Will might have been polite but uninterested at being forcibly immersed in nature, but he'd changed in those years on his farm.

'Watching the birds and bees made me think o' you,' he told me, when I pointed this out.

'Sweet man,' I said, standing slightly on tiptoe to kiss him.

Uncle Robert took me aside after their expedition. 'Things are changing in the world,' he said to me as we sat together on the village green. 'You young people need to embrace it all. Some folk will stay the same but it's not right for everyone.'

When I told Will, he grinned. 'That's more or less exactly what the guest speaker told us at the farm meeting,' he said. 'We have to embrace the future.' He'd cheered up considerably since he arrived at Long Newton, sheepishly, with Bonny beside him. But it wasn't until after we were wed, and when I'd told him about my conversation with Uncle Robert, that he became really bold again; the Will I remembered; the same person who had called from his cart outside the rectory, then turned up again at end of that winter, trying his luck with the snowdrops. All of a sudden now, he had the bit between his teeth. It was time to embrace the railway engine, he said.

He'd even asked Uncle Robert to search the newspapers in his school library. The York Herald, Newcastle Courant and Northern Star turned out to have a great many advertisements as expected, but nothing to say which railway jobs were available. My husband was disappointed, but didn't give up. The breakthrough came one day when he was in Yarm, on business for my brothers. Will was about to untether our pony from the stake where he'd tied her, when he spotted a line of men outside the national school room. There was something about them that attracted him, he told me afterwards. They looked proud in their working clothes. They weren't wearing smocks, so definitely not farmers, and probably weren't weavers either. When he crossed the road to ask, the men pointed to a sign pasted on the door, but then, luckily for Will—he admitted this would have been a useful moment to be able to read—they explained it was the annual meeting of the institute of mechanics.

'So you're engineers then,' Will suggested. It was obvious they felt flattered because they crowded round to shake his hand and became chatty as anything. Taking his chance, he asked if they knew of any railway jobs. They were full of ideas. Some thought Stockton was the place to try first, others thought Darlington. 'I'd start with Hartlepool, beside the ocean,' one said. 'They need railway workers there. My brother lives near the station so I know that for a fact.'

'Hartlepool?'

I could imagine Will repeating the word with a degree of wonder in his voice.

'Aye,' said the man, 'That's where I'd go.'

'Have *you* heard of Hartlepool?' Will asked me with a broad grin across his face as he described his conversation with the engineers.

'Aye, I reckon so,' I told him, despite having no idea what the place was like, nor how far away it was, or how you reached it; just that it was probably too far to walk easily.

'Look, we'll only go if you want to, but wouldn't it be nice for you and Ann to see the ocean?' my husband continued with a glint in his eye.

I could think of fifty reasons not to go to Hartlepool. As it had a railway line then it would probably be noisy and dirty. I didn't have any friends there; I would miss teaching the children, while Ann would be healthier in the country.

I looked across the fields to the beautiful Yorkshire hills, then up at Will's radiant face.

'Hartlepool it is then,' I said with an enthusiasm I didn't feel.

It would take just days for my sense of gloom to be realised.

PART TWO

12. Hartlepool

Frances

My husband offered to go on ahead, except there was no way I was agreeing to that. I might lose him for a second time. 'I'm coming with you and that's final,' I told him, standing tall to my full five feet.

It was already a dreary day with a steady rain falling when we arrived at Hartlepool railway station amidst a grey fog of steam and smuts. Will needed to secure railway work, so we waited at the station for the foreman to show up. It felt risky to me, trusting the word of an unknown youth back in Yarm that work would be available. At least we'd left young Ann safely at the farm which was one less worry. By mid-afternoon though, even my husband was growing edgy, listening to the relentless patter of raindrops on the tin roof, watching the mud beside the track grow moister. He paced the deserted platform, unheeding of the damp soaking into his shoulders, leaving me to my own thoughts. Then all at once when he'd passed me twenty times or more, through the haze an engine pulling a truck-load of men came to a noisy halt, with a burst of steam and a hoot of its horn. An older man in a railway cap jumped down first to let his men out. Will almost accosted him. Then it seemed an age while the foreman finished with his men, filled in his book and explained where to turn up for work the next morning. By that time it was late afternoon so we were both tired and hungry.

Outside the station walls was another world. The rain had ceased, although in its wake it left rivulets of brown water to step over. We found the hostel easily, but it was full. Holding back the tears, I picked up my skirts and followed after Will as we scoured the streets one by one. Finally when we'd almost given up I grasped his arm. Not recognising the words, he'd passed by the roughly penned sign which hung inside a grubby window: '*ROOMS,*' it said simply. My heart leapt as we waited for the door to be answered.

The advertised rooms were nowhere near the main town, instead we had to trudge along a dirt track clutching our few belongings, passing grey shed after grey shed, eventually emerging in a completely new area.

We came to a stop at an old brick terrace with some of its walls missing. Those that remained were blackened with soot.

I clutched Will's arm in panic. 'Can this really be it?' Only part of the building had been pulled down, but the rest should have been, too. There were holes in the roof, windows were gaping. A black cat eyed us from the shadows.

Next morning, despite a poor night's sleep, Will had a spring in his step as he set out towards the station. I could tell he was thinking of his day ahead. Standing in the half light at our grimy entrance, I gave him my best encouraging smile. It had rained again overnight, which meant waste water was flowing freely along the street, even beginning to trickle down our stairs. I watched my husband disappear from view then went down to fetch my cloak, keeping to the driest patches. With Will away at work, those four walls would feel even more like a prison, although outside offered little improvement. The stench made me retch. The night's rain had turned to a drizzle, and mixed with the dense haze of Hartlepool's industry, it painted a depressing scene.

It was hard to get any bearings, but I took a guess at which way was south; homeward, the route we'd taken into town in our uncomfortable Third Class railway carriage. I just needed to find some green, but the whole area was like a building site. Even at the town's edges there were sheds or smoking chimneys, which my husband had pointed out with some excitement from the train. Standing there alone that grey morning without Will beside me, I never wanted to call Hartlepool home.

It was the same story walking west, but desperate for fresh air or trees, I just kept walking. At last reaching something akin to countryside, I pulled myself onto a gate to drink it in, that wonderful fresh smell of fields. Greens and browns were dulled under an overcast sky, trees were losing their leaves, but it was beautiful. I took one last look, before turning back to face the grey of Hartlepool.

It was dusk by the time I retraced my steps to our lodgings, heavy, tired, and muddy, although at least looking forward to seeing Will. Yet I'd given no thought to buying food for our supper. What would become of us if I couldn't do something so simple? He was already in our basement room, trying to find his way round in the dark. With only one small grated window high up, there would be scarcely any light even during daytime. I was supposed to buy candles that day, but Will didn't complain. Nor did he grumble when for the second time we ate only bread. I couldn't see his face, so had no idea if he was concerned that the dried up loaf would be gone next morning, once he'd taken the last chunk for his lunch. A hard working man needed more. Without the supply of fresh eggs, milk, and the stock of preserves I was used to at the farm, it would be hard, but I promised myself the next day would be better.

Once we'd eaten that evening, there was little else to do except go to bed; I was too downhearted to ask him how his day had been. We curled up together under the thin cover, sinking into an exhausted sleep.

On the second morning I set out towards the north, although I didn't get far, instead reaching a dead end which made me gasp out loud. Beyond me was the vast, blue-green German Sea reaching to the very edge of our world, as exciting and mysterious as the storybooks pictured it. I immediately thought of my school children; few of those would have seen the ocean as *I* certainly hadn't. The sea breeze blew away some of the town's stench, replacing it with a new smell—a saltiness, mixed with the smell of vegetation. Perhaps that came from the weeds lying at the edge of the water? I stood, breathing in as much fresh air as I could. To my left was a great stretch of sand; ahead and to the right were fierce looking rocks. Turning south then with the rocks on my left, I continued round a sort of headland passing a strange whitewashed building that must be a lighthouse. Another corner brought me to a small harbour frantic with ships and people. I stood watching, amazed. The sudden activity was strangely comforting; it meant I needn't do anything for that moment in time, since they were doing it instead—people with lives uncertain like ours. There were long-trousered sailors probably separated for months from their wives or children, there were families travelling to foreign lands to seek their fortunes. A sailing vessel waited patiently, rocking lightly in the breeze, its sails furled and almost docile. Ladies held on to their hats as they boarded, to avoid a little gust catching them out, while men and boys struggled with their awkward boxes. Youngsters grasped the hand of those accompanying them, although some were alone. I needed to know to which land those children were going.

I grasped the sleeve of a young sailor. He nodded towards the ship docked nearest to us. 'We're bound for Trinidad,' he told me. 'That one's from New York,' he said, waving seaward at a vessel approaching. He was kind to take the time, so I took my chance. 'Do ships go from here to the Cape of Africa, mister?'

He lifted his sack to his shoulder. 'Not from here, miss. You'd mebbe have to go from Southampton.'

Before stepping out past the docks back to our miserable basement, I stopped at a market on the headland, for bacon, candles and coal, as well as another loaf. It was a start. Once we had a wage packet at the end of the week I would buy more essentials.

While Will chewed on his bacon that evening, I told him what I'd seen at the harbour, but he didn't share my enthusiasm for imagining the lives of folk roaming the high seas.

'I shouldn't care to be a sailor,' he muttered, his mouth full. Later on after supper, he told me, 'On a ship you're at the mercy of the weather, just like farming.' He had the faraway look in his eye which I was becoming familiar with.

I longed for the evenings, listening out for Will's tired steps on the stairs, but more especially for Sundays, when we had a whole day together. A full month after we arrived in Hartlepool I dragged him along to the harbour. While the usual hustle and bustle was missing, the docked ships seemed poised for it to begin again next morning.

'I wonder how if feels setting foot on foreign soil. Do you think the smells are different as well as the flowers? I mused, thinking about what I'd read of Africa, as we sauntered arm in arm. Will couldn't say.

It was always the railway engine which had my husband animated. 'Now with a train engine, you know you'll get to where you're going,' he informed me later that evening. We had different dreams, but it wasn't worth disagreeing.

I poked him playfully in the ribs. 'Aye, especially when William Bell looks after the railway tracks so nicely, shooing the cows off the line.' We fell onto the bed laughing after that.

It was good to see Will happy at his work, but his hours were long and I worried for his safety. It sounded so dangerous having to leap between trucks to couple or uncouple them, and being tall, his back suffered from unloading goods. Yet our time together was precious, so it was better to forget our worries that evening, which included the damp walls and the soiled mattress I'd covered with Will's blanket. But we couldn't carry on this way. 'When do you think we can go somewhere better?' I asked carefully, re-buttoning my dress. I didn't like to put pressure on him but things were getting desperate. Ann was safe and content on the farm but she should be with us. It was already far too long.

'I reckon soon enough.' He bent to kiss me again, but I pulled away from him so he would answer my question.

'Will?'

'Don't worry we'll fetch our little one to be with us soon.'

They were the usual empty words. He never gave me the straight answer I needed.

13. The Important Railway Official

Frances

Will always had a good story to keep us amused of an evening in our damp basement room, before we lay down together on an even damper mattress. The last week's tales included the cows on the line at Seaton. He was the only railway worker who dared to move them away. It was no bother, he admitted, because he was used to dealing with his old farmhand's cow. But often the stories were gorier. I felt sick when a boy's hand was trapped between two trucks, whereas my heart skipped a beat when he described how a young woman leapt out in front of a locomotive. I was concerned for Will. It would have been close to home for him.

Soon after coming to find me in Long Newton, Will had told me properly about his mother. Some of the memories were his, some handed down: before she went to live in Appleton Wiske, Jane Bell was a

Richmond lass. One summer, three young weavers from Appleton borrowed a donkey cart, driving to Richmond to fish in the River Swale. Jane was perched on a rock, bare feet dangling in the fast flowing water. All the young men were captivated by her dark curly hair and bright smile, but it was John Bell who won the prize. It was a whirlwind romance. Soon their first bairn was born and others would arrive every year or two. However, only three of her babes survived past six months, and this made Jane Bell very sad. When she was well, she was as sweet a mother as you could want, and managed the household like clockwork. Unfortunately, her mood was up and down like the moors and the dales. There were long weeks or months when she was as low and flat as the vale of York. Then all of a sudden, once Will was born, the flow of babies dried up, which meant the run of mortality did too. It was not for a lack of love or intimacy because the weaver was apparently as much in love with his wife as he'd always been. Her body was simply too exhausted to make more offspring. But when Will was eight or nine years old, his mother gave birth again, one final time. It was another boy, but born too early and fragile to survive long. The bereaved woman went into her deepest depression yet, until one grey morning Will and

Elizabeth discovered her in the small outhouse where the wood was stored. She was hanging from a beam. She'd climbed up on a ladder then kicked it away beneath her. The children couldn't bring themselves to look up at her face, just watched in horror as her feet swung a little one way then the other in the icy draught.

As well as dealing with the shock and grief, it was a defining moment for Will. He feared he'd been a bad child. He believed he was to blame because his mother didn't want to be near him any more. No-one thought to put him right. Instead, his father's strict parenting, however well meant, made things worse. I desperately hoped one day my husband would be free of all that.

Fortunately for whatever reason, the body of the young woman on the tracks failed to trigger my husband's worst memory, perhaps because the circumstances seemed quite different. But I was always on edge that something would remind him of the family he once had, disturbing any fragile peace we had.

One evening as we settled down to make the best of our time together in our basement, Will was especially keen to tell me something.

'You'll never guess what happened today?' He told me, with his words coming out in a jumble of excitement, how an important official from the North

Eastern Railway Company had been to address them. 'He made us gather in a big shed. The man was small and nothing to look at, but you could tell he was important the way our foreman treated him, nodding and saying "*sir, this*" and "*sir, that*".'

His description immediately reminded me of my first employer—the master of Kirkdunham House, who I remembered was an important railway man. I must have been told his name once but I'd had other things to occupy my mind at that place and it escaped me. Still, I could easily recall his looks. 'Did your railway official have a pocked face by any chance?' I asked when I could get a word in edgeways.

'Aye, reckon he did. How did you know?' My husband glanced up astonished, even losing his train of thought for a second.

'I'll tell you in a minute—what did he have to say first?'

'He said The North Eastern Railway Company holds us workers in high esteem when we're loyal and takes a pride in our work.' Will grinned. 'He was apologetic that it was our lunchtime. He hoped we would understand because he had good news to tell us.'

I was even more convinced that I knew this railway official by then, especially when Will imitated the man looking around earnestly at the workers as he demonstrated his regret. In my mind I was standing in that library again, as I had four years before, with the stolen book before us on the desk.

The railway man told his workers they would all be getting safety training and the opportunity to learn basic numeracy and writing skills. Will imitated the man's quiet, well-spoken voice. My husband was quite the actor when he got going. A low murmur of appreciation had rippled through the shed while the important man had nodded in recognition.

When I'd finished chuckling, I agreed with Will and with the important official that this was very good news—if or when it happened. There was no doubt Will would benefit from learning to read and write, especially if he wanted promotion, but I somehow doubted if he would take up the offer. He was still refusing my help.

On the evening of the railway official's visit, when we were finishing supper, I explained to Will about the pock-faced master of Kirkdunham House and his book, 'The English Boy at the Cape'. I told him how in the story, some people acted out of the kindness of their hearts to help the orphaned English child, while others behaved terribly. 'Makes me wonder if we should do more to help children like that,' I finished. I meant what I said, but Will had other concerns.

'We can hardly look after ourselves, for goodness sake.' I could see his point. Our stools were pulled up close to the fireplace to keep us from shivering in the dank room. The few pots and other utensils we'd been able to afford were blackened from coal smoke.

But Will had more to say too. 'I'm more worried your old master will remember you, so I never get promoted.' His shoulders dropped for an instant.

I stood up wearily, rubbing my back. 'I doubt the man would know me now, that was years ago and he probably has to get rid of housemaids all the time for 'is wife,' I said with a sharpness I regretted. It was our first real squabble. I was sorry to be sharp with Will but being on my own most days wasn't helping my mood. I didn't wish the mistress of Kirkdunham house harm either, wondering if she had an infant now, to give her some pleasure while her husband was away on railway business. 'We all deserve some happiness,' I muttered to myself.

I couldn't sleep at all that night. The thoughts kept coming. With no family nearby and with Will out at work, life was lonely. By morning, when I rose wearily to make our tea, I'd already half decided what to do.

The steady rain was adding to our street's muddy puddles as I stood outside to watch my husband leave for the station. The scene was so common I barely noticed, but indoors, something was new. Holding the candle high to see better, I traced the rain water as it trickled through the ceiling beams, down the mouldy chimney breast.

I could stand it no more. That evening I would tell Will that I would return to the farm.

14. A Worthy Candidate

THE important official from the North Eastern Railway Company sat at a spare desk in Hartlepool station. He was enjoying being there for an extra day, especially as the building was aesthetically pleasing. It was a curved building constructed from an ancient Dutch ship, with the manager's office housed in one of the old cabins. He liked being so close to the sea too. He put his pen down and stretched out his short legs. The next day he would be back in his library at Kirkdunham House, so he must make the most of his time here in Hartlepool. He would do that shortly, at the Crown Inn—although those were not the exact words he used to tell the station manager he would take his leave soon.

WILL had spotted the important official in with the station manager, so after finishing his unloading job in one of sheds, he slipped back to the station. '*Good*'—the man was still there. He felt his heart beat a little faster as he hovered in the office doorway observing the official's pocked face. If this was actually the master of Kirkdunham House, he hoped the man wouldn't discover Will was married to Frances, an employee he'd dismissed four years ago. But this would be worth the risk if it made his wife proud of him; if it cheered her up. He knew what was amiss with Frances, but unless he had a wage rise, they simply couldn't afford better accommodation. Perhaps if he were cleverer he might get a promotion. Standing there though, he soon began to wonder if his railway superiors were ignoring him. If he didn't make his move soon, his foreman would come looking for him. He rapped lightly on the open door.

The station manager looked up from his work.

'Yes?'

'Sorry to bother you. I'm here about the help with reading and writing.' Will indicated towards the engineer at the opposite side of the room. 'The mister mentioned it yesterday in the shed?'

THE important official also looked up from his desk, where he was tidying his papers ready to leave, to take a long hard look at the speaker. He wanted to remember the young face. It sounded as if his words to the workers yesterday had taken root, here at least. Anyone prepared to better their education struck him as interesting. Once the wiry lad with the unkempt hair had left, with an assurance from the manager he would look into it, the official turned to his companion.

'Here's a worthy candidate for our train crew, I believe.'

WILL was summoned back to the office by the station manager, but by that time the railway engineer had left the building. Although relieved the older man had disappeared, it meant he had no idea of what part, if any, the engineer had played in the manager's offer, so therefore couldn't answer his wife when she asked him just that, an hour later.

He'd run home breathlessly with the news his station manager had given him.

'I just had to come and tell you,' he puffed.

He never left the railway quite as early as he did that afternoon, so Frances looked startled when she looked up from the washing she was wringing out, red fisted. He took her wet hand to lead her to the table, pulling out a chair for her. He wanted to savour the moment.

'I've got a job with the North Eastern train crew so we can move into a railway house!'

She didn't look convinced.

'How can you be so sure Will?'

That was when he noticed her tear streaked face. It looked as if she'd been crying all day. In fact, ever since she waved goodbye that morning outside in the puddles, before it was fully daylight.

'Tis as certain as I'm standing here before you, Frances; as sure as eggs is eggs; the manager told me. I'm to be a fireman, and it means we can fetch our Ann home.'

Even with dusk falling outside, she insisted they put on their coats and go to this Railway Row to see where they would live. He took her arm as they traipsed past the docks and the harbour, where just a few fishermen remained, preparing for their night's work. Will cheerfully bid the men a good evening. When they reached the station, he told Frances to shut her eyes so he could lead her to Railway Row.

'Ooh flipping heck.' Frances cried, when she saw the place. She turned to kiss Will on the mouth, with neither of them bothered who might be watching. Then, with no desire to return immediately to the basement, they sat close together on the harbour wall listening to the waves crashing on the rocks. The rain clouds had moved away and the man in the moon was clear as anything that evening. It was the first time they'd gazed up at him together.

WILL kept from his wife the fact he was taking lessons. He wanted to surprise her one day, on the sort of occasion the ability to read would be handy, such as that first afternoon in Hartlepool, when his wife noticed the sign advertising *ROOMS*. Although he might have guessed at the meaning of that hastily scrawled word, he wouldn't have been confident enough to knock on the door.

One problem was he would be late home every Tuesday evening. He told Frances the train crew worked for an extra hour on a Tuesday. He didn't like lying but since they were in their new accommodation, and Ann was with them, he was no longer so concerned about her. Their new lodgings were clean and dry. The houses were still narrow and built of the same dark brick, but they now had a shared back yard where Frances could dry their washing, rather than have it gathering mould inside the house. Best of all there were no rats scurrying over their feet when they used the privy. They'd moved to Railway Row on Christmas Eve, spent the whole of Christmas day cleaning and making the place home, then before New Year they'd gone together to Long

Newton to collect Ann. As Will sat in the school room with the other train crew on the first Tuesday of the New Year, he cast his mind back over everything that had happened. At last he could try to build a proper life for his family.

He'd told her the truth in a way. Learning *was* work; harder than railway work really, on his brain at least. He felt exhausted afterward. He'd never been to school, so it was strange sitting in the church schoolroom with the other railwaymen. Once he'd put his name forward, others had too, quite a group of them.

THE important railway engineer was in Durham for a winter court session on a railway matter. A man was accused of stealing a chain from the North Eastern Company, found guilty and sentenced to two week's hard labour. It was hard to contemplate what that punishment might mean for the man's family, but the engineer accepted the verdict. It was better than being sent to the colonies. While the railwayman was in court that morning, a second case caught his attention, so he stayed in the gallery to observe the outcome. A boy of nineteen had pleaded guilty to stealing four books from a shop in Hartlepool. Again, the engineer was pleased with the judge's fair decision. With it being the boy's first offence he was let off with a warning. 'Now that needs following up,' he thought, wondering why the lad stole the books in the first place, and taking note of his address. It reminded him it was on a Tuesday evening that the railway workers had their weekly encounter with books. His horse had been stabled overnight so she was well rested, and as it was still early in the day he would ride over to Hartlepool to observe his workers' education first hand. He smiled to himself. He would stop on the way to water his horse at an inn where they served a good beef stew. Then after observing the lesson, he would stay at his usual place in Hartlepool for the night and avoid going home to Kirkdunham House.

WILL had also had a long day. He'd been on the early train to Sunderland. It wasn't all about shovelling coal either. It was quite a skill to keep the fire glowing steadily, so he had to concentrate hard. He'd been looking forward to sitting in the classroom for an hour, resting his legs and arms. He certainly wasn't expecting the important railway official to be present, sitting at the back with his notebook. It meant the atmosphere was completely changed. The young teacher was more self conscious; the men and boys quieter, until eventually the observer spoke up. 'Please carry on as normal. Imagine I'm not present.'

Things did gradually warm up after that, but Will made sure not to draw attention to himself, keeping his fingers crossed he would answer the teacher correctly when it was his turn. Whereas most of the men had had some knowledge of letters previously, he'd had none— he was acutely aware of it that evening. Even keeping his head down, he could feel the railway engineer's gaze resting on him at times. Since Will was already known to the man from that day before Christmas in the manager's office, he was wary of his intentions. As soon as the lesson ended, Will slipped out. For once he didn't stay behind for the usual friendly slaps on the back or shouts of '*see you in the morning*'. He needed to get away.

Outside, a heavy frost had already descended, which was unusual for the seaside town. For some reason, perhaps to clear his mind, he walked towards the docks. The houses there, behind the docks, were in various stages of disrepair. He wrinkled his nose at the thought of who might be living there. He'd forgotten it might so easily have been them. As if to prove his point, a man stumbled out of a tavern, clearly the worse for drink before setting off in a zigzag line towards one of the more squalid homes.

For some reason that night, he could feel all his senses heightened: the crunch of ice under his feet where water in the cart ruts had begun to freeze; fetid breath steaming in the moonlight from a small pack of feral dogs, on their way to the harbour to find food. It made him thankful he'd left Bonny at the farm, despite Ann's squeals. Hartlepool was certainly no place for his terrier. He'd even heard of folk putting poison out and he'd seen the stiff bodies along the railway line.

He shivered. The docks were devoid of human life. Everyone would be in their homes keeping warm, eating whatever supper they could afford. It was time he did that himself. When he reached Railway Row his ears and nose were stinging from the frosty air, but inside, a decent fire—even by his standards—was burning in the grate. A delicious smell of sausages filled the room. He hung up his cap and coat, went over to kiss his wife and stole a sausage from the dish. He'd never been so happy to be home. He wanted to confess what had happened that evening but that would mean his secret would be out. He wasn't good enough at reading yet, for that to happen.

15. The Brawl

Frances

I was glad our new street was free of putrid waste water. Nearer the headland the breeze kept the worst smells at bay too, yet I still found myself retching of a morning. I also had an aching back, which couldn't entirely be blamed on lugging Ann about when she tired of holding my hand. I didn't breathe a word to Will until it was certain. The other wives noticed before he did. That was another good thing about Railway Row. The neighbours looked after each other—before it all went wrong. We ranged from the wife of the booking clerk to those of drivers, right down to a couple of women whose husbands worked in the railway gangs, as Will used to. Wives of gang workers were lucky to be allocated a railway house in my opinion. But in the women's eyes we were all equal. There was usually one of us about to give birth, or struggling with a new-born, so we rallied round to help whatever time of day or night. When Will and I first moved in we had a succession of visitors. It was as different to the miserable basement as could be. The women shared their wisdom about most things. Such as the best day to visit the market, the cheapest corn salesmen, the tried and tested methods to help the sickness which dogged most of us in the early weeks of pregnancy. We chatted in the backyards which stretched the length of our Row while hanging out the washing. Of all the wives, my husband's clothes were the filthiest, from coal dust and smuts. Despite my best efforts, their charcoal grey was plain to see against the clerk's white, but I was fiercely proud of Will, and his clothes. The job of fireman was skilled work so without him, the trains were going nowhere.

I'd not been sure about the other wives. I worried that once on my own, with Will out at work, they might shun me for some reason. The way the women had treated me at Kirkdunham House was never far from my mind. That didn't happen at first, but I did notice one thing about the railway wives: whilst they looked after each other and us, they weren't so accommodating towards the less fortunate families in Hartlepool. Ann and I had seen plenty of those poor unfortunates near the docks.

It was a sparkling day with a gentle sea breeze shifting the town's haze for a while, when I first encountered the little girl with fair hair.

It was so pleasant sitting on my upturned box observing the comings and goings, in sunshine which signaled the end of winter, that I forgot to keep my daughter close. When I came to my senses, she was nowhere to be seen. I cried out with concern. Ann was growing up fast and becoming inquisitive but she'd never disappeared like this. I couldn't even remember how long I'd been daydreaming. Someone might have taken her. It wasn't unheard of.

A group of people were collecting on the wharf, already embarking on the vessel moored up there. I ran towards them. 'Have you seen a little girl with dark curls?' I turned first to one person then another. Most didn't respond, concerned with their own kin, pulling them together, making sure their offspring were with them. I was growing more and more frantic as people ignored me, until one particular lady seemed to sense my distress. She appeared self assured, as if she was a regular voyager. She believed she had seen a child matching that description boarding with a family. My mind jumped a mile. Ann was being stolen by a family who were taking her across the seas—not to the Cape, like the English boy, but still far away.

'You can't board without a ticket, miss.'

When I explained my child had been taken aboard by mistake, he urged me to stand back; he would send someone to check.

Eventually another sailor approached, older this time. 'There's no youngster aboard matching those details love.' I wasn't sure whether it was good news. Assuming it was true, then where was Ann? I mumbled my thanks. Nobody noticed me rushing to first one side of the harbour, then the other, calling her name. There was no sign of her anywhere. I walked along the edge peering into the murky water. Would I even know if she'd gone under? Then a moment of hope took hold of me. Perhaps she'd wandered home. If she'd gone towards the station then I had less reason to worry because people might recognise her, keep her safe. On the other hand—if she'd gone towards the docks! All sorts of scenarios formed in my mind. She could be knocked over by a cart or even a train engine. How would I break the news to her father that a train engine had collided with our daughter?

I worked my way slowly away from the harbour, peering desperately behind each pile of coal, around each mound of fish heads. I heaved a sigh. She was crouching behind a stack of crates, her dress trailing in the fish waste which littered the whole place. Another child was with her, probably two or three years older than my daughter, also crouching. This child had on a tattered straw hat, such as a country dweller might wear in the summer, she had tangled fair hair, clothes that didn't look at all clean, whilst her boots had large holes at each toe. I don't know why I even noticed the boots when my eyes were concentrated on finding Ann. The footwear was as expected, I supposed, for a child living in poverty. The two girls were facing, not really in conversation but clearly comfortable in each other's company. The ragged girl even appeared to be looking after her new friend. 'I found her, she was lost,' she announced.

Once the distress of losing Ann had begun to ease, I wondered about the girl with fair hair and grubby clothes. I could understand how women let their children go dirty. It wasn't easy to keep a clean home. Cooking on a coal stove was dirty work, and washing clothes was hard. Some women had it worse if their menfolk spent their wages at the Crown. I was lucky having Will, but even so it was hard to cope, especially being pregnant again. I wondered who the child's mother was and what her life was like. Why was she out on the docks alone? Not that I could judge, having lost my own. The girl had run off as soon as Ann padded over to hug my skirt. Thinking about it, she might live in one of the run-down buildings behind the docks. I decided to keep an eye out for her, without realising just how dangerous that would prove.

Ann and I loved the harbour, for watching people and imagining their lives, but it stopped being our absolute favourite the day we discovered the beach. That was the day the first shoots appeared on the tree near the lighthouse. The tree was one of the few living things in our grey town existence. It was a day of firsts. On the first afternoon we ventured down to North Sands I felt the baby kick inside me, so she could also feel the thrill.

'Wait till I tell your daddy,' I told her.

The tide was out when we arrived, exposing hundreds of worm burrows along the damp shore. As Ann occupied herself making marks in the sand with her toes, I stood watching the breakers, the wind in my hair. We followed the water's edge almost to the headland before climbing back onto the coastal path. A few youths were fooling about on the rocks. Surprisingly the girl with fair hair was with them, or actually not with them, because she was slightly apart, playing by herself. 'Out on your own, at such a young age,' I said aloud. She wouldn't have heard, with the sound of the waves washing up on the rocks. We saw her often after that: by the market; on the beach; at the docks again, sometimes with other children, but more often alone.

I placed Will's hand on my belly and watched his face. I didn't want my husband to lose out this time as he had with Ann. Sometimes he had to stay away from home though, if he was needed for the crew of an early train. Those nights were lonely again.

It was after one of those nights when my husband was away that things changed. It was still early summer, but the weather was so warm I'd turned Ann out of my bed because of the extra heat we produced together. My legs were swollen to match my belly so it was harder to get around, yet I wanted to go to market all the same. We would need a good stock of food in the cupboard.

A group of neighbours were gossiping outside. 'Not long now lass,' they called.

'I hope you're right.' I told them, already panting slightly. 'I reckon I'll burst soon in this heat otherwise.'

The sultry weather was making everyone irritable. A cart was being driven at breakneck speed; children were fractious; horses danced restlessly. That day a fishy smell from the docks pervaded everywhere.

Once my basket was full, I slumped on a bench kindly installed by the new municipal borough in the shade of a building. Wiping moist fingers on my dress to get a better grip of Ann's hand, I helped her climb up to sit beside me, and cast my eyes around the square. I didn't like the flies swarming over the meat stalls. A child bent in the gutter to catch a potato as it rolled away. He pocketed it neatly, casting a sneaky look back at the stallholder. The man cried, 'oi!' but from the sweat on his brow he had no energy or inclination to chase after him. Most people were doing their shopping then swiftly leaving to go somewhere cooler. The girl with fair hair was hanging around though, so perhaps she was waiting for someone? Suddenly there was a huge commotion just in front of us. Two women were fighting tooth and nail, snarling and screaming. Dust was flying around as they scuffled together on the ground. People were coming over to watch, with some urging the pair on, backing one or the other. There was no chance to move away without crossing the women's fighting ground, so I clutched Ann close to me covering her eyes and ears as best I could. Gradually the two women moved towards the centre of the square, as one backed off but the other went for her again, leaping on her back, pulling her back to the ground by her hair. It was a relief to be spared such a close view. I couldn't see the faces, but the fair girl knew at least one of the women. Unable to stand it any longer, she ran screaming over to join the struggle pulling at the main aggressor's blouse. 'STOP. Leave my mama alone.' It was heart-breaking to watch.

Most onlookers had their opinions, as people do: it must be the heat that frayed their tempers; it was surprising they had the energy in this heat; there must be bad blood between the women as they'd fought before; no doubt there was a lover at the centre of it; best to keep away from that lot; and so on…

Finally a beefy man intervened. 'Come away Hilda,' he instructed the distraught fair haired girl. He talked to the women sternly. 'Stop now. You've made your points.' Pulling the child away gently he separated the pair with some skill, as if he'd had to do it before. The more aggressive woman stepped away, brushed herself down and walked off, head held high. The other woman also brushed her dress down, looked for the girl, picked up her basket, which miraculously was still intact although empty of food, and they slunk off together.

I took hold of my daughter's hand and we trudged home as fast as I could manage. I had a new feeling of weight on my shoulders. I felt my waters break as we wearily pushed open our door at Railway Row.

'Fetch one of our neighbours please darling,' I told Ann, shakily. Someone must have also sent word to Will. He arrived full of concern as I lay panting in earnest on our bed. Our second daughter arrived that afternoon. We called her Peggy. Maybe it *was* nearly the right time, but with Peggy coming so abruptly I knew it was the women's fight that set things off, on that day I first heard the fair girl's name.

16. The Secret Is Out

Frances

Will took Ann to stay with her grandparents in Long Newton so I could concentrate on looking after Peggy. It would be good for our eldest child to get some country air, too. When we went to collect her and show off our second daughter, it was astounding how much she'd grown up in those few weeks, also how clever she was getting. She brought back with her a picture book which had simple words written on each page. The strange thing was Will seemed very interested in the book, in fact more than once I caught him with Ann on his knee pronouncing the words together. I didn't say anything, but I could see he was learning reading and writing from somewhere.

I made the discovery quite by accident, late one Tuesday afternoon when I went out to collect some sewing. Ann was playing at a neighbour's home at the time. Peggy was strapped to my front. There was no hurry to get home because Will would be working late as he always did on Tuesdays, or so I thought. I paused at the tree near the lighthouse, noticing its leaves just beginning to turn. Sauntering casually back towards the station, I caught sight of my husband's dark curls disappearing into the church school room. Other men wearing railway clothes were about to do the same. I speeded up in time to ask one of them what was going on inside.

He looked embarrassed. 'Why it's the North Eastern Railway Company's attempt to make us read and write. We come every Tuesday.'

I thanked him, laughing to myself. One day soon, I would teach my husband a lesson. The opportunity arose when I received a letter from my ma, giving us her news. I propped it on the mantelpiece behind the penny tin as usual. Will saw the envelope that evening.

'Aren't you going to read it to me then?' he asked cheekily.

'You're welcome to read it yourself if you want,' I said walking away, to leave him wondering.

The colour dropped out of his face.

'You know about the classes?'

'Yes I know about them, you clever old thing. Now prove it and read it aloud to us.' I took the envelope down and handed it to him. Sitting at the table he read my mother's words out, hesitatingly the first time, then more confidently.

'Now Husband, do you have any other secrets?' I asked him later when the girls were in bed. Actually he did. He told me how the important railway official with the pocked face often sat in on the lessons, seeming very interested in the men's progress. He'd felt the man's eyes on the back of his head, as his father had done when checking up on him. Will wanted to show the railway official he was making progress, but worried he wasn't good enough. It was the memory of trying to please his father, all over again.

'Well let me tell you William Bell, you are certainly making progress,' I assured him with a kiss. I *was* very pleased with his progress, but more especially that he finally agreed with me on the importance of being able to read and write.

It gave me pause for thought regarding the master of Kirkdunham House; the important railway official. The way the man had behaved after sacking me, it made perfect sense that he would still be passionate about literacy amongst the working classes. I hadn't gone quietly when he fired me. I pleaded my case in the library with the story book lying before us. 'But sir, I only borrowed the book and would've returned it. It was so interesting and there was nothing else to read.' The master had sat thinking for a while, tapping his fingers on the ivory topped desk, while I stood, quaking slightly. Where would I go? he asked. Did I have any idea what work I wanted? I had no idea how to answer, after all what choices did I have? I said any work would suit me, especially if it involved reading. Perhaps a small smile crept onto his face then. 'Do you know Northallerton?' he'd asked eventually. I didn't. Well it was a fair way away but he'd noticed with interest, an advertisement for a maid who could read and write. It was at a rectory near Northallerton. 'I'm obliged to you sir,' I remembered telling him with a tear in my eye. He agreed I could stay one final night at Kirkdunham House. The following morning he had railway business in Northallerton so would take me there. We would just have to hope the position was still open.

Thinking about it all again now Will's secret was out, I became acutely aware of the part played by the master of Kirkdunham. If he'd not found work for me with the Reverend and Mrs Beard on the outskirts of Northallerton, Will wouldn't have seen me in the rectory garden. I hoped nothing would go wrong now, to jinx the railway official's good will. In any case, as I felt my husband's arms around me that night, it occurred to me we had every reason to be grateful to the railway engineer.

Seeing the benefits now Will could read and write, I was even more determined for Ann to practise her writing and arithmetic at home, but she was a sensible girl and didn't need nagging. She helped me with Peggy too. As Peggy progressed from babe in arms to taking her first faltering steps, the two girls became inseparable. One Saturday when I was off to the corn market, Ann pulled a face. She didn't want to come. Instead, she begged to take Peggy to the harbour. At four and a half, she was too young to be out alone with her sister really, but she was so insistent I found myself relenting. I knew I would be back promptly. Also it wasn't one of those days when passenger ships were docking.

The girls were still out when I returned, which was worrying, but soon enough Ann came stumbling through our door, clutching a crying Peggy in her little arms.

'Whatever happened, dear?' I asked Ann while taking my youngest daughter from her. I was glad they seemed unhurt.

It took a while to pull the story out of her then make sense of it.

'It was Hilda. She had a basket 'n was stealing coal from a heap.'

A man had grabbed hold of fair headed Hilda, holding her tight, while it seemed another went away to fetch the port constable. Hilda's ma turned up too, followed by a lot of shouting after the girl's basket was confiscated.

'I can't believe there was enough coal in the basket to make that much fuss,' I said. Ann wasn't able to say, because she'd pulled Peggy behind a fish crate and couldn't see everything, but she could hear the conversation.

'The man asked if Hilda's ma told her to steal the coal.'

'And did she?' I asked, but Ann would only shrug.

I was furious that the men could hold the girl so roughly, but even more cross if she needed to collect coal to keep them warm.

When Will arrived home, he knew our girls had been at the harbour from the stink of rotting fish coming from them.

'They must have been crouching in the waste behind the crates,' I agreed.

As their father listened to the tale, his face which was already black with soot, darkened even more. He pulled Ann close to him. 'Now listen up.' He stooped with his face close to her. 'What you saw at the harbour was wrong. Stealing's wrong and that's that. If I ever catch you stealing, you'll be for it. D'YOU HEAR?' After he was certain she realised the import of his words he strode outside to the back yard for his wash.

When her father had finished his rant, Ann followed me looking shaken, into the scullery-kitchen. But it wasn't her father's words which bothered her.

'I'm worried 'bout Hilda,' she told me. 'Will she be in bad trouble?' Her voice quivered.

'I hope not love, but maybe she will. It depends on the constable probably.'

'I want to help her,' she said looking up to gauge my response.

'We'll do that then,' I agreed quickly, putting my arm round her. 'I'll try to find her tomorrow. Once I know where she lives I can take some stew 'n some coal.' It was more than likely Hilda's mother was struggling to feed her family and keep warm. I stepped away then and caught my daughter's eye. 'And we'd best not tell your father 'bout it.'

I knew why Will was so hard on our girls, so determined they wouldn't learn to steal. Train robbery was escalating so we were always learning about crimes on the railways. Wives of the train crews waited on edge for their men to arrive home if their train was carrying post that day. I didn't join in, as the other wives worried about train robbers while they hung out the washing or in a little huddle on their front steps. They had an unhealthy distrust of some areas of town, especially behind the docks, where they thought less respectable folk lived. I didn't share their opinion, but Will was not immune to this idea, himself.

'If any of them from behind the docks jump on board while I'm fireman, I'll just wallop them with my shovel,' he whispered loudly with a mock menacing look.

I threw a pillow at him.

'Shhh you'll wake the girls.' We were behind the heavy curtain we'd strung up to separate our mattress from the girls' cots. He reached out to touch me tenderly, which as usual, promptly put an end to our conversation.

Later, as I turned on my side to go to sleep, I considered how we were only safe while on the subject of railways or engines. It was different when I tried to tell Will about my own passions.

Sometimes I doubted if my husband would ever be happy to help unfortunate children like Hilda. However in one way he *was* helping—he just didn't know it. When I took provisions to Jeanette Stott, Hilda's ma, behind those very docks, Will was paying for the extra food. It wasn't without a shred of guilt on my part.

17. A Driver's Job

THE important railway engineer smiled. Tuition in literacy and arithmetic for his workers had achieved what he'd hoped for. Now he would have to find a new reason to be away from Kirkdunham House, and needless to say he had the perfect excuse in mind. Following on from the scheme's success in Hartlepool, the revolutionary engineer had plans for other railway towns. It would kill two birds with one stone. It would take him away from home while at the same time fulfilling his dream to help other workers read and write.

Kirkdunham House had depressed him since childhood, even before he inherited the dismal place. It was during boyhood there, when they thought he would die from the pox that he discovered his love of reading, stuck inside, not allowed out because they thought it would weaken him. Later, his obsession with geology led the North Eastern Railway prospectors to approach him. The company needed to understand the landscape for its tunnels and cuttings. Before long, other railway companies had sought him out, an arrangement which the North Eastern gladly accommodated for the appropriate fee. Becoming a railway engineer was the best employment the heir to Kirkdunham House could have hoped for. Kirkdunham still had a sheep farm, but that was managed by others. Anyway, farming was of little interest to him. Since he married, he felt bad about his wife being incarcerated in the large house, but she appeared to enjoy being its mistress, and with a son to occupy her by that time, he worried about her less. In a way it had been a marriage of convenience. He supposed he loved her. Her older brothers had done well for themselves, making them the apple of their parents' eye, while growing up she was largely ignored. He'd saved her from that. In return, although she said she missed him when he was away, she didn't make too much fuss. She'd had her moments with the staff, but she'd mellowed and was turning out to be a good mother.

His mind went back to his work and he smiled to himself again. He recalled how every railway worker who set foot in Hartlepool station had the opportunity to brush up on their literacy. He recognised it as another obsession. Not everyone had taken the lessons, it was true, but most had done, very impressively in some cases. He thought of the tall lad with dark curls who had obviously started from scratch, knowing nothing, but was now a man, confident, mature, and from what he could tell, as passionate about engines and railways as he was himself.

Will

The footplate was warm enough from the hot coals and the cheerful hustle of two men working as a team, but around him there was a nip in the air. With no roof above them Will was exposed to the elements. A blanket of autumn mist had been slow to lift that morning. As they chugged out of the station, he could just make out a gang of men, raking leaves from the track further down. Even with his short experience on the North Eastern Railway he'd noticed saplings take advantage of the waste land. Foliage was thickening beside the rails, which meant leaves were beginning to cause problems at that time of year. The gang would stand back out of harm's way when the driver beside him sounded the horn. Will couldn't help grinning to himself. He would still have been part of that gang if he hadn't been promoted to fireman.

As the morning mist cleared, a flock of starlings came into focus, feasting on the remaining dark elderberries, unbothered by the noise and steam. Blue-black feathers glimmered in the bright sunlight. He was glad flora and wild creatures were sharing the line with them. Often there were smaller birds in the hedgerows too, pretty and colourful, although he would need Frances to identify those.

Once they'd left the gang of men behind, the engine began to pick up speed, the air ruffling his curls where they stuck out from beneath his cap. He turned back inside to concentrate on his job again. The boiler was full of steam thanks to his efforts, and he watched with envy how the driver released the steam down to the pistons, turning the wheels. Will was still an apprentice, so it would be a while before any promotion to engine driver was likely, but it didn't stop him wishing.

It was a shock next day when the station manager jumped up onto the footplate of Will's train, the 8.05 to North Stockton. 'There's a driver's job coming up soon, if ye're interested. Someone thinks you're ready for it.' He'd caught the fireman with his shovel in the tender, getting up a head of steam ready to depart. The weather that day was as different to the previous one as you could imagine. Both driver and fireman were already drenched from the steady rain, collars turned up, caps pulled down. The station manager looked pleased he could go inside his cosy office once he'd delivered the message.

'Ye'll take it then?' The manager didn't sound convinced himself. He nodded civilly to the engine driver at the controls, and without waiting for the answer leapt off again, in time to watch the locomotive pull away.

All day the rain seeped through Will's jacket into his undershirt but it didn't dampen his excitement. The worst thing was the long wait before he could share his good news with Frances.

'Ooh flipping heck,' she said as she usually did when he surprised her, before reaching up to kiss him. He loved it when that happened because it reminded him of her surprise years back in the rectory kitchen, when he'd first heard her say those words.

'Your clothes won't be half as sooty.' She was still bending over the steaming, grimy water of the washing pot as he told her his news. Frances always seemed to be washing those days with their two children to keep clean, as well as his clothes to deal with. He took her hands in his own to check how rough they were. They weren't much smoother than his.

'Here, let me help you, m' love.' With difficulty he lifted the heavy material out of the water onto the drainer for her. 'One day there'll be a machine for this.'

Frances gave him one of her looks of pity, but it was true, he could see into the future. Anything was possible, in fact probably someone had already patented one. He left the subject then, not wanting a row to spoil the good news. 'Come on, let's tell our girls.'

'Your daddy's going to drive an engine,' he boasted. It was every railway man's dream to be an engine driver, possibly the height of his career too, although there was a hierarchy with driving an engine. Once they'd all calmed down, he admitted this job was at the bottom of the scale. 'Once I've learned 'basics, I'll be driving goods locomotives back and forth between 'yards and engine sheds, up in Sunderland.' He watched his wife's face but she didn't reveal if she was disappointed. 'I can get a ride on a goods train to Sunderland each morning, that way we won't have to move, unless you want to?' It was always a sign Will was getting excited when his broad Yorkshire surfaced.

'I've to write a report tomorrow,' Will announced near the end of his first week driving between the engine yards and industry of Sunderland.

'Flipping heck, what will you write?'

In a way it was perfect timing for Will. One duty of an engine driver was to write a report about each week's goings on, if he noticed any repairs needed, for instance. He could read and write as well as the next man now but all the same….

'Dunno,' he said with a grimace. 'What do *you* think, love?'

'Well, who's the report for?'

'The gaffer, I suppose.'

'The important railway engineer perhaps? Or would your report be beneath him?'

He shrugged.

She considered it with her usual look of concentration. Her brow furrowed.

'Well, what's it like in Sunderland and what did you notice this week?'

There was a lot going on in Sunderland. Some of it he liked but other bits unnerved him—such as the sinister prison-like building on Silver Street, near the docks. It would take several horses to drag him in there. It reminded him of the House of Correction back in

Northallerton; both places gave him the shivers. Rumour had it that children were kept in the Silver street building—a place with no windows.

On a more positive note, a new station was being built, with a crisscross of lines springing up across town. Properties were going up in the new suburb of Bishopwearmouth. 'Perhaps we should move there after all,' he wondered.

'Mebbe. But keep on the subject. You can't tell the gaffer about those things in the report, he'll already know—unless they caused a problem?'

Frances was so clever.

One thing Will noticed as they chugged along the tracks was the poverty in some areas. He saw children barefoot and thin, their clothes hardly enough to keep them covered or warm. Sometimes they tried to climb aboard if he slowed. When he told Frances, he could see the sadness in her brown eyes. That was his wife all over. She was kind as well as smart. 'You'll put that in the report won't you?' she pleaded.

He went to stand close behind her at the sink, putting his arms around her. 'What would I do without you to help me?' he whispered. 'I'll have to thank you properly later on.'

'Oh you will, will you?' she giggled.

If they went on like this, there would be another bairn in her belly before long. It was a good job they had an engine driver's wage coming in.

There was one thing he hadn't mentioned. He did so then, slipping it past Frances as if it were nothing, just a minor thing. Earlier that day they'd had a near miss. Another engine was being driven too fast along a line which intersected with theirs. It scared him, but he didn't tell his wife that much. He'd sounded the horn when he saw the locomotive in the distance, but so had the other driver. Then the other engine speeded up, hoping to cross in time. He had too, thrusting the regulator downwards. There were just inches to spare as his last truck cleared the intersecting rail. Sweat ran from his forehead, mixed with the grime, when he'd realised they were safe.

Perhaps Will's reports pleased his gaffer, or maybe it was just luck, but gradually he was asked to drive the passenger trains. The first time, a driver was sick with fever, which was hardly surprising according to Frances, with the weather conditions they had to cope with. The second time, an experienced driver was needed for a royal visit. Soon, Will was given a regular route between Hartlepool and Stockton. It meant another wage rise. Frances agreed it was perfect, so long as it would be safe, driving trains at forty miles an hour up and down the countryside. Sadly, he wouldn't be able to promise that.

18. December 6th 1854

Will

According to the *Hartlepool Free Press and General Advertiser*, individuals working both near and far that Thursday morning heard the terrifying sound, wondering if it would never end, that scrunch of metal and splintering of wood might go on for ever. When eventually the sounds did peter out, they were followed by an eerie quiet.

'What on earth was that?' someone cried.

'Something's happened up on the main line.'

It was a cold, crisp morning with frost still glistening on the rails when they left Hartlepool station, at just past 8.05. A mixture of passengers had boarded as usual. Most Third Class fares had been on the earlier train, but a few women wrapped in shawls far too thin for winter, lugged their baskets of goods to the far end of the platform, before heaving them up into their open carriage. Second Class was most popular at that time of day, with clerks and secretaries bound for Stockton or beyond, dressed in tall hats and tailed coats. But at the last minute, a man in servant's clothes rushed up to the engine, weighed down with large cases in each hand. He begged the crew to wait, to prevent him losing his job. Seeing his scarlet complexion, the crew obliged. Shortly afterwards, a tall, fur caped woman with a young girl in tow, joined the others on the padded seats of First Class. Unlike her servant, the woman remained perfectly poised, apparently unwilling to rush on behalf of the other passengers who needed to get to their places of work. As a result, the 8.05 was delayed by just a minute or two. It certainly wasn't early leaving the station.

His fireman was doing a good job getting up a head of steam, but while Will might subconsciously have wanted to make up the time, to his knowledge he didn't exceed the speed allowed. There was only so much speed the engine could pick up in any case. When the 8.05 had gone about three miles south of Hartlepool, it passed the *'ALL CLEAR'* signs which told them it was safe to enter the cutting. The moment they reemerged Will caught sight of the other train in front of them. It meant he had time to brace himself for the impact, although he knew immediately that his passengers had not. He heard the shrieks from behind him the moment his engine connected with the rear of the freight train. But that wasn't the end of it. Both trains continued in unison, sliding forward on the slippery rails until they made contact with something else, something very solid. There was yet more crunching of metal and wood, more screaming from behind.

His guard appeared beside the engine white faced, swaying slightly. He must have run the length of the train despite his creaking joints.

'I heard your whistle but there was no time to brake.'

To be fair, Will had barely had time to blow his whistle, so it was hardly the long drawn out note that was expected; more of a *tweep* cut off by the thump. Later, Will mused about the way his mind worked at that moment; certainly his perception of time changed. Instead of thinking about the length of his whistle, or lack of it, he should be acting. But what to do first? The wails and shrieks had ceased behind him but an ominous silence had descended instead.

'I'll see to the passengers shall I?' the guard asked, much more alert, much less in shock than he, already limping back towards the carriages.

Will suddenly noticed the fireman hovering beside him clutching his hand. Thinking about it, he could see what must have had happened. The boy had been facing towards the rear with his shovel in the coal tender, so hadn't known what was coming. It was a miracle he'd stayed on his feet and only suffered that small burn to his fingers.

'Can you make it back to the signal box?' Will asked gently, taking charge at last. 'We need to stop the next train going into our rear. Also, get a message to Hartlepool to say we need transport for the passengers. We're not going anywhere with that mess.' The empty freight trucks in front had come off badly, separated, and left the rails in every direction. He helped his fireman down from the engine and went to look for the guard.

The old man was busy in First Class, reassuring or calming people, helping them back into their seats. The man was a natural; much better at it than Will would ever be. Several passengers facing forward in the carriages had been thrown onto the floor, with some ladies still weeping from the shock. A couple of gentleman travellers had already helped some ladies back to their seats. Boxes and cases had flown from the overhead shelves; carriage doors with faulty catches had flown open. Miraculously no one appeared badly injured, in First class, at least. When Will arrived, the old man hobbled away to check the rest of the train.

It was the fur-coated passenger making the most fuss. *She* would be having something to say to the North Eastern Railway Company she assured Will, when she saw his driver's cap.

'I'm sure you will madam.'

For once, Will began to see the world through Frances' eyes. First Class passengers had been well cushioned from their falls, appropriately clad for winter, but what of the poor women in Third Class? They had little flesh or clothing to protect them from bruises, or from the snow, which was falling rapidly by then. Even as he considered this, the young fireman returned with his message, that the company would only send Broughams for First or Second Class passengers. Poorest passengers, who had likely left home with only a mug of tea in their bellies, would have to trudge back on foot.

The final horse drawn carriage was ready to leave.

'Get that seen too as soon as you can,' he told his fireman, pointing to his burned hand as the boy joined the guard beside the cab driver. Will had insisted his crew ride back to Hartlepool.

He groaned. Now it was time for him to assess the damage. This he was *not* looking forward to. The empty freight train they'd collided with was in a sorry state, sandwiched between his engine and a fully loaded coal train. The freight driver stood long-faced beside his engine. Will extended his hand, but the other took it reluctantly. The driver's hand was cold.

'I'm sorry. What a mess.'

'Ye're lucky no one was hurt,' the freight driver muttered.

Will attempted to explain. 'The signs said "*ALL CLEAR*", so it gave us no time to brake….' He looked around at the fuel scattered at the side of the tracks. 'Was any one hurt in the coal train do you know?' He tried to ignore the other's sullen attitude.

The freight driver shoved his hands in pockets before turning away. 'Not that I know of. My train came off worst for sure.'

The man was right; the coal train in front was hardly affected; Will found all three crew members keeping warm by their fire box. That's what he should do himself while he waited the inspector to arrive. 'There's nowt to be gained from standing miserable in this cold,' he told himself as he trudged back through thickening snow to his train. That freight driver was certainly miserable. He didn't blame him. Heads would roll no doubt, but it would most likely be his own.

Before he retreated to the relative warmth of his own boiler, he searched the passenger carriages, checking for lost property, shutting doors. He found a monogrammed handkerchief in First Class and a perfectly wrapped wedge of pork pie in Second, both of which he pocketed. He was about to shut the door to the final Second Class carriage when he spotted something. There was a red patch on the floor. Was it blood? He cast his mind back to the people they'd evacuated. It must belong to a bald headed man, who'd been particularly dazed and was holding his head. He'd helped that individual up the slope into the carriage, himself. Hopefully that passenger was alright?—it did seem to be a rather a large pool of blood, almost dry by then.

Third Class delivered up one more object of lost property. It was a posy of artificial flowers, fallen between the seats. Doubtless it was from one of the women's baskets due for sale at Stockton market. That find made him the saddest of all. He was less concerned about the other travellers' days cut short by the accident, they would soon forget after their wives or mothers tended to any bruises. At least it wasn't lives that were cut short. He hoped.

Finally he slumped down against his fire compartment. Thankfully, there was some warmth left. There was a roof to this engine, too. He brushed the snow off his jacket and cap. Some of it sizzled in the embers. Remembering the pie, he extracted it from his pocket, unwrapped it carefully and ate hungrily—it was well made, almost as good as Frances' own. Once he'd swallowed the last morsel, there was nothing to do but watch the snow fall silently, thinking thoughts that turned increasingly gloomy. He started to wonder if he'd really seen the *'ALL CLEAR'* signs, or been dreaming. He wondered if he'd been going too fast. The more he thought, the more he decided he must be to blame. It was the words of his father coming back. 'You're good for nowt.' Will kept one eye out for the inspector's arrival with a degree of dread, but the only movement was of a lone fox, which popped its head through the sparse hedge at the top of the slight incline, before carefully making its way down the slope and across the track. Other than that, it was deathly still outside, the deepening snow muffling any sounds.

19. The News

Will

He didn't recognise the inspector, who arrived with a thick covering of white on his shoulders and hat. The man produced a flask of brandy which he passed round to the shivering men. Following the others' example, Will took an enthusiastic gulp, feeling the spirit descend into his gut and perk him up. It loosened the men's tongues, so when the inspector inquired what had happened, they subjected the poor man to a chorus of different stories and points of view. He shook his head and tutted a lot to himself but made no comment, which added to Will's fears that somehow he was to blame.

Once the inspector had done his inspecting, noted the engine numbers, and made some measurements, he told the drivers they could leave. Will and the freight driver, who were employed by the North Eastern, were to report to their gaffers the next morning. The crew of the coal train would report to their mine management. All, except the coal train driver, were bound for Hartlepool, including the inspector himself who had travelled down from Newcastle and would stay at an inn until the weather improved. Silent and heads down against the weather, they set off together to traipse the three miles through fresh snow.

They looked a gloomy group, each no doubt thinking about their families, and what they would tell them. It was almost dark when the men reached the shelter of Hartlepool station mess room where they could get a hot drink, and by then Will felt exhausted and numb. He didn't immediately head for Railway Row. He needed time to thaw out, get some feeling back in his fingers and toes, then settle himself before his girls clambered over him or Frances asked about his day. Whatever time he pushed open his front door, hung up his sooty jacket, and wiped his snowy boots on the mat, his wife would know immediately something serious had happened. But the longer he sat looking into the station fire-place thinking about the day's events, the longer he delayed going home. Frances would have seen the weather, so if he failed to arrive home, she would assume he'd been delayed at Stockton, where he would spend the night. Sitting there, feeling sorry for himself, he was convinced of one thing: she wouldn't want to see him in his current melancholy state; therefore he stretched out on the wooden bench, rested his head on his still damp jacket, and shut his eyes.

In the morning, the station master was clearly startled to observe Will making himself tea on the stove, unshaven, his hair uncombed and most likely with dark shadows under his eyes. It would be obvious he'd not been home, but the manager didn't comment. Everyone was soon busy, clearing the tracks where the wind had blown the snow into deep drifts. Will was glad of the activity. It numbed the familiar low mood creeping up on him, while also delaying the task of writing his report.

When they paused at midday, the station manager brought Friday's edition of the *Free Press and General Advertiser* into the mess room. Will couldn't bring himself to read the witness accounts, which he anticipated would be biased or just plain wrong, but the other workers had no such problem, proceeding to read them all out loud. It was the first time he regretted the literacy classes, with his colleagues just too keen to show off their skills that day. It soon occurred to him that folk in Railway Row would have seen the newspaper.

For certain then, Frances would have heard about the accident, and therefore be rightly worried. But the paper had clearly reported only minor injuries and no fatalities, so he hoped that would ease his wife's concern. He didn't want her giving birth early and losing another unborn child. He felt an extra touch of sadness remembering that's what had happened last year when Peggy had still been tiny. This time though, Frances was already past the early days of sickness, looking more pregnant by the day.

With his thoughts still in a whirl, Will worked solidly alongside the gang until the afternoon light began to fade, clearing the track all the way down to his abandoned train. It was back-breaking work, but he could hardly complain. The men stood together in the half-light; to marvel at the mess of trains they'd reached, before turning to march the three miles home.

Back at the station, the manager looked at Will sternly. 'As soon as ye've written your report you should get home to your wife, Bell,' he told him, wagging his finger. 'She'll be worried sick.'

'I'm sorry to let you down, my love,' he said in response to Frances' concerned look. She helped him off with his jacket then held the lamp close to cast her eyes over him, as if checking the newspaper report had been correct, that there were no serious injuries.

'I knew nothing good could come of travelling so fast,' she said, hands on hips. 'What's the point, when it means you don't get there safely?'

Will was in no mood to argue, but he could think of many reasons travelling faster could be better, when things went well. Without explaining quite all the details, which would make her worry more, he told her about the women on board bound for the market with their goods. Normally, he explained, it was good for them to travel to Stockton to make a living. He pulled out the posy, which he'd kept safe at the station. Every time he saw flowers like that it reminded him of the snowdrops at his first proper meeting with Frances in the rectory kitchen.

'Do you know of any local women that make these?' he asked, holding them out. 'I found it between the seats in Third Class, after they'd all left.' His ruse to distract Frances worked. From her questioning look, she was surprised. She took the posy from him carefully examining it with interest. 'It's pretty,' she said. 'Some women are so clever with their hands.' She readily agreed to make enquiries to see the flowers were returned to their owner. It had the effect of calming things down between them.

'Thanks love, I'd be happy for that to happen. It would mean a lot if something good came from all the mess.'

Next day, on the Saturday, an icy wind continued to pierce through their clothing, but with no more snow falling over night, they could start the recovery. Will drove the empty passenger train to the first turning point then back to Hartlepool for a full inspection. He was slightly happier having done that, realising he could still drive the thing.

It always happened to him, that just when he began to feel more positive, things would deteriorate rapidly. It was mid morning on the Monday that he was called into the station manager's office. Two unknown men stood there, serious looks on their faces. When they asked Will to clarify his name and address, a feeling of alarm washed over him.

'William Bell. 7 Railway Row,' he told them with a dry mouth.

'I'm afraid we have distressing news for you, Mr Bell. Would you like to sit?'

When he'd done so, they did too.

'It concerns a passenger in Second Class, who hit his head when you had your incident last Thursday.' Will wasn't expecting that. He thought it would be a complaint from the woman in the fur coat. One of the men went on, 'the passenger developed a severe headache on the Thursday evening, had visual disturbance on the Friday and became sleepy. His sister, whom he lived with, suggested he go to bed and sleep it off, which he did. When she went in to him on the Saturday lunchtime she was unable to rouse him and called the doctor. I'm afraid to tell you the man didn't wake up, but unfortunately died at approximately three o'clock yesterday afternoon. The doctor confirmed the cause of death to be swelling of the brain following a head injury.'

All Will could think of to say was, 'but the signs said "*ALL CLEAR*", I wrote it in my report.' The men nodded. They asked if he wished to add anything to the report in the light of the new development. His fireman and guard would have to make reports now, so it would look better if everything agreed. Will told him shakily there was nothing to add, except how sorry he was to hear about the poor man.

'Then thank you for your co-operation, Mr Bell. You'll have to stay at home now until a verdict has been reached. Oh, and it would be best if you didn't leave the country,' the officious man finished with a smirk.

He tore off his railway cap and hurled it across the room where it narrowly missed Peggy.

'Will. What's happened?'

'The signs said "*ALL CLEAR*,"' was all he would keep saying.

Eventually he told Frances the latest development. She took hold of his hand.

'If you know in your heart you did nowt wrong, you have to hold on to that thought.'

But he spiraled downwards next day, barely wanting to eat, just going through the motions with the children, helping his wife with the heavy lifting, before retreating back to the chair by the fireside.

'Come on Will, you need to eat.' It was Frances' voice but he kept thinking back to those weeks after he lost Elizabeth, when instead of his wife, it was Mrs Crank the farmhand's missus coaxing him with porridge. He could see Frances was worried sick when by the end of the week his mood was still at rock bottom, but he couldn't help it. His world had crashed around him, just like the trains had done.

∗

THE important engineer, being employed by the North Eastern Railway company, was of course well aware of the facts of the collision, including William Bell's part in it. He was also fully aware of the terrible development following the demise of the clerk travelling in Second Class. He had been telling his employers for some years that they should deploy the absolute block system. He absolutely could not believe the driver of the passenger train was in any way at fault, and was prepared watch the investigation play out, to prove it. He didn't think sticking his oar in at that point would help the situation. Plus, it wouldn't look good for himself, if, by any slight chance things went the other way, especially if it were on record that he had recommended Bell for the job in the first place. On the other hand, if the verdict turned out to put the railway company at fault, then he would be in an excellent position, because his recommendation to use the absolute block was certainly on record in several places. He did feel slightly guilty about Bell, he couldn't imagine what the man was going through, but the engineer had to think of his wife again now. They were expecting their second child, with his wife becoming more demanding of his time.

Anyway, that *was* the engineer's position as regards the three train collision and William Bell, the driver of the passenger train, *before* he received the strange letter. Things had completely changed then.

20. The Letter

Frances

'Where we going, Ma?' asked Ann when I met her from school with Peggy, but we started walking in the opposite direction to Railway Row.

'To see the station manager.' I needed to know when their father would be allowed to drive his engine again. I couldn't take much more of watching my husband wilt away in his chair.

The manager was pleasant enough, although completely unhelpful. He admitted the inspectors still hadn't submitted a report; anyway, it would have to be scrutinized by the magistrate in view of the serious situation with the poor clerk. He just couldn't give me an answer, he was afraid.

'Well that's no help to us, is it?' I replied sharply, immediately regretting it. The manager wasn't to blame. 'My husband is languishing at home, barely a shadow of his old self, yet we all know it wasn't his fault that the trains collided.'

He didn't give an opinion, but just said he was sorry, we would have to be patient.

'And when the railway cuts my husband's wages by half next month? Must we be patient about that too?' Ann squeezed my hand but it should have been Will doing that, as he used to.

'Are we going to be alright?'

I couldn't give her an answer. If I reassured her but it proved wrong, then that would be worse.

'Let's watch the ships,' I said instead, leading the children to somewhere we could perch out of the wind, but face the ocean. We found a box without too many rough edges, in the lee of a wall. It was good to sit. My legs were swollen, as they normally were in the last stages of pregnancy.

'Don't go too near the edge,' but Peggy skipped off, oblivious to our circumstances, unquestioning as to why her father was at home each day miserable as sin. Ann stayed close holding onto my arm. With my shawl wrapped around us we watched a passenger ship toss about on the choppy water. To take our minds off things, I told her about the English orphan boy from the story book, who would have sailed from England on such a ship, then was lost in Africa, missing his mother. I explained that some people, who should have known better, were unkind to that little boy, but the poorest people were kindest.

'We should always be kind to others,' said Ann. 'That's what they say at the church school.'

'That's quite right, love.'

Even Will seemed to be turning over a new leaf in that respect, concerned for once about the women from Third Class on his train. It was good to see him showing his better side. I had the little posy in my basket that day, and it was time to find its owner. Anything was better than going back home immediately to tread on eggshells around my husband. It might even cheer him up if we found the rightful home of the flowers.

'Now we've had a rest, are we ready to do a kind deed, girls?

They agreed they were ready, so off we set towards the docks, passing the crates where I'd found Ann the day I lost her, when she was barely toddling. She didn't seem to remember hiding behind the crates in the fish waste with Hilda Stott. Ann did remember the day Hilda got into trouble for stealing coal. We were so thankful that nothing came of it. She wasn't charged or sent away. If she stole again, no doubt it would be a different story.

Thinking of the fair haired little girl, I reckoned the street where she lived was my best chance of locating the posy maker. I was right. A group of women gathered on their steps recognized me easily, from the times I'd arrived with provisions for Hilda's ma.

'A grand afternoon, ladies. Do you happen to know who makes these pretty posies?' They directed me towards the newest area of town; Hartlepool West it was called. But I needn't go as far as the posh new streets. They expected me to find the posy maker near the dilapidated slums Will and I had once lived in. Thankfully, the terrace where we'd stayed had been knocked down. There was a big space of mud and bricks with weeds growing, despite the desolation. Anything vaguely green was a sign of hope in my mind, so I felt my spirits lift. But the street we ended up at was little better than ours had been. Clearly many families lived in just a few buildings, probably inhabiting a room or two each. I wouldn't want to be back in such a place, but I could see it happening, if we were turned out of Railway Row.

The woman who made the posy was very happy to be reunited with it. She told us more about the morning of the crash. Will had been kind, she said. He was also furious that the North Eastern Railway expected them to walk back to Hartlepool in the snow, while providing transport for Second and First Class. This was news to me as he'd not told me that part.

'Tell your hubby we'll remember his kindness,' the woman said when I took my girls' hands to leave. 'And I hope you reach home, before you drop,' she pointed at my enormous bulge. 'Me too,' I told her with a wry grin.

In fact, I *was* extra concerned about the coming birth, not only because the state my husband was in, was far from ideal, but also because since the accident, the railway wives had been less than friendly. In a rare moment when Will said anything sensible those days, post accident, he mentioned one of our neighbours had a cousin. It was the miserable driver of the freight train he'd crashed into.

'But why would the wives take it out on us?' I asked, '…on me?' He would only shrug, and I could only hope they would reconsider once I went into labour. But it got worse. In a small town like Hartlepool, gossip got around quickly so the wives learned I'd been in contact with women by the docks. Since the great train robbery the previous summer, they suspected those folks even more of being less than honorable. It was disappointing to find Will was just as bad, stuck in his own prejudice. When I told him I'd found the owner of the posy, he was happy for a moment, until he realised where she lived.

'Oh, that part of town?'

'Well where did you expect?' I cut back at him.

I overheard railway wives gossiping, much as I'd heard the women servants at Kirkdunham House, all those years back.

'She thinks she's better than us.'

It brought all the misery and loneliness, flooding back.

On the day my waters broke, I explained to Ann she would need to take Peggy outside and cover their ears. Then I told Will he must be attentive, not sitting staring into space. It was lucky this was my third, and relatively quick. It was also fortunate I had the required experience. Will pulled himself together, so we got through it, the two of us. The railway wives must have seen Ann and Peggy outside, they must have heard my cries, but no one came. That was worse than the labour pains.

I insisted Will talk to the station manager each week when he collected his wages, in case there was any progress. It had the advantage of keeping him out of the house for longer. He always returned with the same dejected face. One day I would probably regret sending him, because we would find out worse news, such as we had to move out of our house in Railway Row, or they would stop his wages altogether. It was already hard, buying everything we needed on half wages, which was all the company was willing to pay the last few weeks with Will still laid off. If the situation went on much longer, I would have to return to the posy maker and beg her to teach me. It was lucky we'd put a little money away for a rainy day. This was certainly one of those.

'Would you take Peggy to the beach,' I asked her father one warm afternoon when buds were developing again on the tree beside the lighthouse. 'Take this picnic…and here's a blanket because the sand will be moist.' He looked dubious, so I had to almost shove him out of the door.

'Won't you come with us, Frances? I'm not sure I'll be any good at it.'

'The babe's too young for the sea breeze…'

I didn't really believe that. If I wrapped her carefully she'd be fine.

'…so we'll wait in for Ann to come home from school.' But I had something else in mind. I had a letter to write and needed my husband out of the way.

I knew where to send it and to whom I was writing. Well, granted I didn't actually remember his name. But how to phrase it? That was the part giving me sleepless nights.

7 Railway Row Hartlepool, March 4

Dear Sir, I apologise for troubling you, especially since our slightly difficult history, but I didn't know where else to turn. I believe you are acquainted with my husband, William Bell. I expect you are also aware of the circumstances of the collision, while he was driving the passenger train. We were so sad to hear a man lost his life. Nevertheless, I believe my husband to be innocent of any wrong doing, as there were 'ALL CLEAR' signs when he entered the cutting. Yet he has had to stay at home these past three months, on half wages the last fortnight. He is a shadow of his former self and worried sick, as am I. We have three young children. The station manager urges patience, but we have little left. I even believe my husband to be at risk of his health if the verdict takes longer. Please, I beg you, is there something you can do to help us? I much appreciate you taking the time to read this.
Yours faithfully
Frances Bell.

I read the final version through one last time. It was the third attempt, with the first and second already gone up in flames on the stove. This *had* to be the one because I had no more paper. I desperately hoped it was the right thing to do and wouldn't make matters worse.

When Ann arrived home from school, I left the baby with her for a while. She was more than capable, and could find me at the harbour if necessary. First I went to post the letter, before any second thoughts popped into my brain, then sat on the harbour wall to wait for my husband to appear round the headland, with Peggy skipping beside him. I stared at the blue green expanse, the smell of salt and seaweed in my nostrils and the thought of what I'd just done in my head. This was surely a moment to believe in providence rather than in fate.

Even so, that night was another restless one. I was downstairs as the sun started to rise. Looked up at the lightening sky, the moon was just visible too; a thin sliver, almost new. Somehow that felt like a sign. Maybe we would soon be able to restart our lives? What form that new start might take, was yet unknown. I'd put all my hope in the railway engineer. He'd saved the day for me once before, but could he, or indeed would he, do so again?

21. A Meeting on the Sands

THE railway engineer read through the letter again carefully, whilst at the same time rubbing a thumb and fore-finger thoughtfully over his end-of-afternoon stubble. Beneath the roughness he could feel his fingers sink into the dips and dents of his scars. They no longer bothered him as they had when he was younger, although they'd never held him back from attracting the opposite sex. In fact there had been several young women before he met his wife. He turned his attention back to the words on the page. He agreed with Bell's wife that the collision report was taking too long. Over three months for goodness sake. Surely that was pure incompetence. He had an added concern as well, that more fatalities were likely with current practices in place, which he would rather not have on his conscience. But those weren't the main reasons for his interest at that moment in time.

He tucked the note paper back into its envelope, hiding it at the back of the top drawer of his ivory topped desk. The letter held many surprises. Firstly, he was impressed to find the wife of an engine driver like William Bell, could write so well. The letter was fluent and excellently crafted. After all, he was pretty sure Bell himself had been illiterate, before the Company provided the lessons which he had introduced. The engineer allowed himself a moment of pride, remembering his part in the excellent programme. Of course, the woman could have employed someone to write the note for her, but somehow he doubted it. It was certainly a woman's hand.

The next matter for consideration was how the engine driver's wife had known his home address? Where he lived was not common knowledge, whilst any railway correspondence would normally be sent to his office in Stockton, especially being addressed to *The Railway Engineer, North Eastern Railway Company*. Finally, there was that very first sentence. If he could remember what the woman referred to at the outset, then it would probably answer his previous question—how she knew his home address. It was the reason he'd pushed the envelope to the rear of his desk drawer. Something had happened between himself and this Mrs Bell historically, but he couldn't for the life of him think what it could have been. He couldn't remember an assignation with a girl called Frances since he'd inherited Kirkdunham House. The name didn't ring a bell from his university days either, but it was just possible he'd mentioned his father's house to someone. What about 'Fanny'? Wasn't that the shortened version of Frances? But that name didn't ring any bells either. Perhaps it was a childhood friend? Well, one thing was clear. This wasn't a letter he wanted his wife to read in her present delicate state. All in all there was a lot to consider.

It was that time of day when the railway engineer needed to keep company with his son. Actually, now the boy was going to school he had become more interesting. His name was Charles, following the family tradition to name each firstborn son after his father. Not many folk knew the engineer's name was the same. Mostly he was simply known as 'sir' or 'the master,' or even perhaps 'that b—railway engineer.' He smiled to himself. Nor did most people remember the nickname his friends at university had called him.

With the work of fatherhood accomplished for that day, before he changed for supper, the master of Kirkdunham House stood on his balcony looking out over the garden, to think what he might do. It was the only place in the house where he felt any peace. The sun was setting and he also noticed the nearly new moon, visible close to the horizon. He stood there for as long as he dared without being called inside by his wife. Anyway, it was getting chilly with the sun gone, so he went to his dressing room to get ready. All through their main course, right up to the end of dessert, which was a delicious apple tart, he was debating his best plan of action. By the time he'd kissed his wife goodnight, and slid between the sheets of his own bed, he knew what he would do.

The next day the engineer slipped a discreet note into the hand of a driver he trusted, with instructions to have it delivered to none other than Frances Bell, who lived minutes from Hartlepool station. He had business in West Hartlepool at the end of the week, where the railway company was considering a second station, better positioned to serve the docks. The new station idea was only in its infancy but he would take a look and make arrangements for the necessary soil survey. The few days available to him until Friday could be usefully spent dealing with the matters raised in the letter.

He'd requested to see her alone at three o'clock on the Friday afternoon, at Carr House Sands, which was far enough away from West Hartlepool and the headland, to make the chance of being seen together and recognised, sufficiently remote. It was also on the best side of the town for him to access easily from his work. He didn't stop to consider that it was quite a walk from Railway Row—until later.

The engineer had a useful day in West Hartlepool on that Friday, and finished making his notes in good time to arrive at the sands by the allotted hour. He spent a pleasant few minutes watching the tide wash up on the beach, before checking his pocket watch again. It was just past three o'clock. He looked northwards towards the headland, unsure of her route. He had a clear view in all directions, but there was no sign of a single woman approaching. Then it occurred to him that she might not own a watch or a clock. Because she wrote so well and was clearly eloquent, he might have been making wrong assumptions about Frances Bell. He probably needed to think of her being from the engine driver's class. He would be patient. He listened to the small waves lapping at the shore; it looked as if the tide had turned while he'd been stood there. He checked his watch once more, and realised he was disappointed. He would have to leave soon if he was to catch his train. He took a last look around him before preparing to walk away. But, perhaps that *was* a figure in the far distance?

He stood where he was, feeling his heart beat a little faster. What was the matter with him?

'I'm sorry to keep you, sir.' She was breathless; rushing. 'My husband was out, and I had no-one to leave the bairn with.'

She was small, although not tiny. Her shape betrayed the fact she'd given birth recently. One or two grey hairs were showing amidst the strands of windblown mousy brown, which had escaped from their braid. She looked about thirty years old.

As she approached along the shore, it gradually dawned on him where they'd met before. She would have been no more than nineteen then. She'd matured, but not past recognition. It was the same intelligent eyes gazing back at him. Then, back in his library she'd been trembling slightly but at the same time been willing to fight her corner, quite rightly, he'd thought at the time. It was the reason he'd helped her. On that day about ten years ago, he estimated, when he'd had to fire her, and also the next morning as they'd travelled to Northallerton to the rectory, she had been reliant on him. He was her superior. This afternoon, on the shore, was different. The woman was anxious certainly, but alongside that, he had the feeling the two of them were equals in some way. They were on equal ground at least.

'I'm glad you came, Mrs Bell. I have something of interest to show you,' he said. 'When you've quite recovered your breath, that is.' He pulled out a manuscript from his bag and gave it to her to read. She took it, appearing to absorb the contents. At the end, she glowed a little.

'That seems to be grand news, sir. May we believe it?'

The engineer assured her that the statement was indeed penned by the magistrate within the last few days, and as far as he could tell, gave every intimation that the untimely death of the clerk would be classed as accidental, with no blame attached, when the court sat the following week.

'Then we must have faith, sir.'

'Exactly,' he agreed. 'Now, about the way the company has excluded your husband from work….' He cleared his throat. 'I have no jurisdiction in that matter but I have suggested to those that do, to reinstate him, at least to some kind of work, pending the full report. It may not mean he can drive the same engine, you understand. With others lodging complaints about that fateful day, the matter could be prolonged. Nevertheless, on Monday, he should report to the station master. We must trust it will turn out well.' He could see the flash of hope in her face.

'Then I'm obliged to you once more, sir.' She looked at her feet as if a little embarrassed.

'Sir, I'm sorry if I'm speaking out of turn.' The engineer looked up, wondering what was coming next. 'But with the '*ALL CLEAR*' signs being so wrong, sir, shouldn't the company take some responsibility for the accident?' When her question was met with silence, she panicked. 'Oh, I *have* spoken out of turn,' she cried. 'When will I learn to keep my mouth shut?'

The engineer looked out at the incoming tide, before turning to glance at the railway line behind them, then back to face his companion.

'On the contrary Mrs Bell,' he said evenly, with his typical look of hangdog regret. 'On the contrary, I believe you are quite correct. What you ask is a fair question, and your reasoning is astute.'

Again, she looked relieved. 'You're too kind sir. Then would you allow me to make one more observation?'

The man gestured that she should go ahead. He was fascinated. Throughout the conversation he'd been studying the woman. He was relieved she was not his type romantically. He'd always been attracted to women with less intelligence, but he could certainly learn a great deal from her.

She explained how the women from Third Class in the unfortunate passenger train, had to walk three miles home in the snow, with probably no breakfast in their stomachs, and barely enough footwear or clothes to prevent frostbite, yet those well-fed women *and* men from First and Second Class, with strong boots and thick topcoats or capes, had carriages provided by the company. Surely it couldn't be right to discriminate again those human beings that already had the odds stacked against them?

'But I've said enough, sir. Now you must get on, I dare say,' she was embarrassed again, but that didn't stop her talking. 'I'm much obliged to you for listening, and sir, may I also thank you for what you did all those years back. If you hadn't found me that position at the rectory then I wouldn't have met me husband, and that don't bear thinking about.' She sniffed to hold back the tears.

At this point, the engineer knew he was beaten. He was hopeless at dealing with women's emotions. He nodded to her civilly. 'Thank you Mrs Bell. I'm afraid I really must catch my train now.' Without waiting for her to speak again, he strode off briskly. It would be touch and go if he reached the station in time, after spending too long, first waiting for the woman, then captivated by her. When he stole a look back before turning the corner, he could see her, still on the sands. She was bending to examine something above the tide line. He wondered if it was one of the wild plants that grew there, or if it was a piece of driftwood, shaped by the waves.

He couldn't help looking out of the First Class carriage window as his passenger train left Hartlepool, hugging the shoreline. He could see the place they'd stood together. She was gone by then. He intended to attend the court hearings himself, keeping a much closer interest in the outcome, now he'd met Frances Bell for the second time. He hoped his assurance about the magistrate and the promise of a return to work for her husband would prove accurate. Whatever happened, he had a strong suspicion their paths would cross again before long.

22. The Full Report

Frances

W e huddled together under our blanket in the pre-dawn chill, unwilling to face the morning.

'Come, I'll make tea. How does a bacon sandwich sound?' I whispered it because the girls were still sleeping on the other side of the canvas sheet.

We were on tenterhooks about what the station manager would say if Will went in to enquire, as the engineer suggested. It was only three days ago, on the Friday, when he'd asked for any news, so it seemed quite persistent to do so again.

To give him his due, my husband left the house in good time to catch the station manager, shortly before Ann departed for school.

He was back before the sun was far above the rooftops, his face serious.

'Well?' I asked raising my eyebrows, my heart in my mouth.

He admitted he'd lost his nerve. Instead of marching into the office, he'd wandered back along the platform to mingle among passengers bound for Stockton. 'I blended in nicely,' he said—'without me sooty clothes.'

'And then?'

'When the 8.05 arrived they all boarded her and left me alone.'

He looked down, not returning my gaze. The 8.05 was the passenger service he'd driven on that fateful day. My heart sank a little.

'Then the manager spotted me on the platform and called me into his office.'

I held my breath, willing him to tell me good news.

'He said I could have me old job again, driving goods locomotives up in Sunderland, back and forth to the docks, until the report's published. That's if I want to.'

'And, do you want to?' I asked, barely daring to hope.

He grinned. 'It's the best news I've heard for ages.'

I gave him a shove. 'You daft blighter, you had me worried.'

The full report arrived on the station manager's desk a month later. When we heard the news, we trooped to the station together. The baby was in my arms, Will held on to Peggy's hand, whilst Ann tagged along behind.

'Ye can stop fretting now, Bell,' the manager said, when we were gathered in his office. 'It seems the inspector was exasperated with our employers. He criticised the North Eastern for refusing to use the absolute block system between signals. Here….' He thrust the report towards us. Will read it, then passed it to me. I cast my eyes over the spidery handwriting. '…*and if the railway is to continue to bring about positive change for the people of our country it has to improve safety.*'

The manager carried on, excited. 'The matter was even brought up in the House of Commons, so we're famous.'

Will stood up taller. 'So it definitely wasn't my fault—I thought it, but there were always doubts in my mind.'

'Time to forget it all and get on with your life,' the manager suggested.

I knew Will would be thinking the same as me; that this wasn't going to be as easy as the man imagined. Too much had changed. We thanked him, and the four of us walked back along the platform, past the ticket office towards the station entrance. The girls could sense the celebration, they were giggling with Will; he was ruffling their hair. I noticed the ticket clerk look our way and nod. It was dark at the back of the ticket office, but behind the clerk's largish frame and clean shirt, it was just possible to make out another smaller individual, seated at the desk to the rear of the room. He was also looking our way.

'Maybe soon you'll be back 'n forth to London, seeing the land of England pass before your eyes,' I suggested to Will, now he was cleared of any wrongdoing.

He shook his head sadly. 'I'll just stick to freight trains in Sunderland from now on. Anything else will be for our grandchildren to do, and mebbe their children too.'

Seeing his serious expression, a lump formed in my throat. The man standing before me was my *Engine Boy*. What about all his dreams? The whole reason for upping sticks to come to Hartlepool, with all the anguish it brought us? Still, thinking about it, if sticking to driving freight trains in Sunderland meant Will would stay safe, then we would get to keep him longer which could only be a good thing. We made our decision that same evening. We would move to Sunderland as a family and make it our home.

Two things of note happened before we left Hartlepool, both within days of our departure. The first matter was worrying. Ann passed on some alarming news about Hilda Stott. The fair-haired girl from behind the docks sometimes attended the same church school as our daughter, but not always, on days she was needed at home. This time Hilda had been absent from the schoolroom for some weeks. Earlier that day, Ann had overheard some of the older children talking in a knot in the playground. The girl's name was mentioned.

I wrung my hands together. 'Why didn't you say before?' I would've been in touch with Jeanette Stott weeks ago.

'I didn't think Dad would like it.'

I grimaced. Ann was probably quite right. I would have to go to the Stott's rooms behind the docks before my husband arrived home. In fact, I didn't waste any time dithering, but immediately instructed Ann and Peggy to mind the baby, pulled on my bonnet and shawl, then set off at pace. As it happened I bumped into the woman on the way there. She was hurrying in my direction as best she could, heavily pregnant. There was a steady drizzle and she looked bedraggled and cold.

'Jeanette, you'll catch your death.'

'I heard you were off to Sunderland. We'll be right sorry to lose you, but you can do us another turn if you've have a mind to?' She looked up, a pleading look in her eye.

She told me Hilda had been arrested and taken to a reformatory in Sunderland—'a right terrible place by all accounts,' she sobbed, her tears mingling with the rain dripping from her hat. The building was in Silver Street. I wanted to know more, but standing there on the dock-side in the rain wasn't the time or place to ask questions. I gently suggested that she should get back home, whilst I would make every effort to visit the Sunderland reformatory as soon as possible.

The second thing of note happened the following day. I answered a soft rapping on our back door with my hands covered in flour. I was baking pies for our journey. One of the railway wives stood there sheepishly. It was the wife of the ticket clerk, who only pegged white shirts on the washing line. Wiping my hands on my apron I quickly ushered her inside. She sat motionless in the seat I offered her, although her eyes carried on moving about from anxiety. She'd come to apologise for their behaviour. The wives had no business taking sides as they'd done, she admitted. She was so pleased Will was cleared of blame, but even if he hadn't been, they should have been there when I gave birth. I let her unburden herself without commenting then brought her some tea. Once we were comfortably seated on opposite sides of our table, I dropped my bombshell.

'You will have heard I go down to the folk behind the docks?'

She shifted slightly on the seat.

'I want you to do me a favour.' I paused to see her reaction, but she indicated I should continue. 'There's a woman called Jeanette Stott. I'll need to write to her from Sunderland. Will you take the letter to her, read it to her?'

'The others won't like it,' the ticket clerk's wife said with a frown. 'But I'll do it.'

Later when she'd gone, Ann asked, 'will you forgive her?'

'Where did you hear that word?' I thought of all the unnecessary hurt those wives had caused me, adding to the worry over Will's state of mind. I remembered the pain of childbirth without them. I thought of the loneliness. Then I thought how brave the ticket clerk's wife was to agree to my request. I looked at my daughter. 'Yes dear, I will forgive her, but she'll have to forgive herself too.' Ann nodded thoughtfully, pretending to understand.

*

We borrowed a railway cart to take belongings and children to our new home in Bishopwearmouth, the brand-new suburb of Sunderland. Even as the crow flies it would be a long twenty miles, so we packed the cart the previous afternoon to give us an early start. The sky was clear before we turned in, so in case of heavy dew, we took down the canvas curtain from our bedroom to cover our belongings as they sat outside in the yard. We'd already packed most of our bedding, so we all slept together on our mattress that final night. The girls were excited, but eventually they settled into a fitful sleep. We watched them drift off one by one: Ann, the image of her father, dark curls flopping over her face, long legs stretched out; Peggy, more like me, was mousy haired and compact. Mary still had her chubby baby features, so it was hard to know who she would favour.

In the morning Will went to bring the pony round, while I loaded the girls. It was a tight squeeze with the baby's cot included in the pile of stuff. Will took my hand as we looked for the last time at the place where our two youngest were born. Then we set off towards the north.

It was early May, and once the sun had fully risen, it was pleasantly warm. Skylarks, with their rising and falling song, fluttered over fields scattered with red poppies, while red and white campion graced the borders of the path. A gentle breeze drifted from the sea. I wanted to stay forever in that place between our worlds.

Will decided to keep to the coastal path wherever possible. The railway also hugged the coast so he knew it must be the most direct route. He made his point several times. 'You see now why railways are so fast?' He pointed at the straight line the rail took through the landscape. 'I can get from Hartlepool to Sunderland in less than an hour with an engine, whereas this is only walking speed.'

Walking speed was just fine by me, but he was right, as we were mostly following footpaths rather than bridle paths, the going was slow. Several times the way became too narrow so we had to turn back and head inland for a while. The coastal path was beautiful. It wound between the hills, up and down. On one occasion we lifted the girls down so the four of us could push, to help the pony negotiate a sudden rise. Our faces were colouring nicely from the wind and sun, and as I could breathe properly for the first time in years, I was in no hurry to arrive back in the smoke of a town. I needn't have worried about my enjoyment being cut short. We didn't reach the half way point until late afternoon, and then it was evening before we could see the smoke of the seaside town of Seaham, below us in the distance. Will pointed out the harbour with its fishing vessels, as we rested high above on the slope. He shook his curls and a boyish grin crept into his face. It never failed to soften my heart.

'We'll set up camp here then, shall we?' He unhitched the pony then got to work with the enthusiasm he reserved for fire and train engines. Between us we coaxed a campfire into life. It was hard to find dry kindling, but once the smoke had died down, we sat in front of it on a blanket, eating the pies I'd brought with us. Will told us stories about his farm, making us giggle with the antics of his cantankerous old farmhand called Crank. When the girls were suitably tired and sleepy, we made a nest for them in the cart.

Will and I stretched out on our blanket under a dense canopy of stars, almost as thick as the leafy trees which sheltered us that first time on the afternoon of the thunderstorm.

'I'm sorry I don't always see the world as you do,' Will said softly. 'I wish I cared about folk like you do. Poor children I mean.'

I had no idea what had brought this on.

'Shhh.' I put my finger to his lips.

It didn't matter at that moment. I loved him for who he was. I suddenly had a vision. 'Anyway, reckon you'll be doing that soon.'

'What d'you mean. 'Don't tell me you can tell the future now?'

'Aye, reckon I can.'

I gazed up at the moon, large and significant above. It lit the ocean below with its silver gleam. Wherever we went in the world we would be led by the same brightness. If Will and I could always see the same side of the moon, it should only be a matter of time before we agreed on everything else.

I curled up close to him slipping my hand inside his shirt.

Our agreement was never in question when we were together like this.

'We'll be alright. Won't we?' he asked under his breath.

We slept deeply until the first bird call. All worry about our new life in Sunderland was on hold. Even the nagging at the back of my mind about visiting Hilda in the girls' reformatory, was forgotten for those few hours. In fact I was blissfully unaware of the trouble that would lead to.

23. Silver Street

Frances

A whole fortnight passed before I could set foot in the Silver Street Girls' Reformatory. Firstly, I had to arrange our belongings into something resembling a home. Secondly, a new church school had to be found for Ann, and thirdly, we all needed to settle into our new neighbourhood. There were numerous other challenges too. Not least, it was a struggle to get the stove to work properly. Even with the chimney swept and those other things settled I needed someone to mind my youngest children. I had misgivings about taking them into a reformatory.

After our two day march from Hartlepool, we'd arrived at the west side of Sunderland almost by stealth. Countryside became a village; fields became pretty gardens; hedgerows became garden walls. Then we crossed a railway line, which Will became excited about, where thatched cottages transformed into rows of brick houses. It was Bishopwearmouth, the place we were to live. We found our new accommodation easily. Although smaller that the railway house in Hartlepool, it was clean and still free of damp. Once we'd unloaded the cart, Will was keen to show me something nearby. He brought us to the edge of an old limestone quarry, where nature was thriving. He glanced at my smiling face.

'They're building a park so folk can get some fresh air. I *knew* you'd like that.'

Most people knew where Silver Street was. It could be found on the far side of the quarry, through the streets of Sunderland, near the docks at the mouth of the River Wear. When a neighbour agreed to watch the girls for a couple of hours, I went to see the reformatory building, to assess what I was up against—what Hilda was up against.

Setting out to investigate that first time, my jaws were clenched. The further east I ventured, the further from Bishopwearmouth I walked, the more obvious the squalor. Roads became congested, filthy waste water drained through some parts, as it had done past our first rooms in Hartlepool, with the same unsavoury smell hanging in the smoky air. All the least inspiring places seemed to be near docks.

It was certainly an imposing façade, with steps leading up to a severe looking door. No windows looked onto the street. Outside, was a board stating the building's purpose: *SILVER STREET GIRLS REFORMATORY AND RAGGED SCHOOL.* Underneath were the visiting hours. Visitors were permitted on Friday afternoons only. Seeing the reality of the place did two things: it made me tremble at the thought of entering; secondly it told me I mustn't delay, because the idea of Hilda being in there, whatever her need for punishment, was terrible.

At half past one o'clock on the Friday I took my little girls round to the same neighbour, with instructions for Ann to collect them when she returned from school, and then I resolutely set off for East Sunderland. A sweet shop in the high street would be my first stop. With a bag of toffees in my pocket I would feel more confident of a positive reception, supposing sweets were permitted, and assuming I was even allowed inside the prison. The day was warm and sultry with little breeze, which meant the stench from the river became overpowering close to the docks. I wondered if the smell would creep into the reformatory too, or if the heavy walls would keep it out.

Standing outside the grim Silver Street building, a deep breath was required to steady my nerves. With a strict word or two to myself, I gathered my skirts to climb the stone steps, ignoring the stares of passers-by. The strong dark doors seemed even more imposing knowing I might soon be behind them. I rang the bell and stood to attention, my senses heightened to what could happen. After a while, there was a great clanging. The heavy doors creaked open, leaving me facing a fierce looking warden clutching a huge set of keys. She was silent while she heard my mission, but indicated to follow her along a dimly lit corridor, which had gates across it at intervals, each needing to be unlocked. The woman proceeded with much huffing and puffing; she was a large person, more or less filling the narrow space between the walls. I was glad there was not a second person of her size behind me. We passed several closed doors, each with its own nameplate, although it was too shadowy to make out the letters due to the jailor's bulk blocking out most of the already scarce light. At last, the warden selected a door, inserted a key and we passed into a brighter space with several windows, barred and high up. Another window was set at a lower level overlooking a yard. Outside, girls were walking round in some sort of exercise routine, although with no enthusiasm.

A little girl of about ten years old, just two years older than Ann, was talking softly with someone who might have been her mother, or perhaps an older sister. They occupied two of six hard chairs, placed opposite each other in pairs in the centre of the room. I was sad then that Hilda would not get a visit from her mother, that she would only have me, whom she barely knew. I needn't have worried. When the girl arrived she was clearly glad to see me, almost grabbing the sweets I'd brought for her. She was never one to miss an opportunity I remembered, such as when Ann saw her stealing coal at the dock. Probably something like that had happened again, but this time had been her downfall. As we perched on our chairs, I tried to ignore the large warden who remained by the door on a tall, slightly too narrow stool. Hilda was content chewing the toffees, with little to say. I didn't press her to tell me why she was in the reformatory, only asking if she was well, explaining how her mother had asked me to visit. The mention of family brought tears to the girl's eyes. Mine filled up too, but I consoled myself with the fact she at least seemed clean and well presented. She was wearing new boots too, although seemed uncomfortable in this footwear, repeatedly bending forward to slacken the leather around her shins. When she'd put the last toffee in her mouth, I took her hand for a moment.

'I'll try to return next Friday, dear,' I explained with a smile, hoping it wouldn't prove to be an empty promise. 'Is there anything you'd like me to bring? Your favourite sweets perhaps?'

She sat silently, chewing.

'You just have a think about it then,' I suggested.

Stepping out into the hazy sunshine, I breathed in the fumes of Sunderland with mixed feelings. I'd achieved what I set out to do. The thought of entering that building again made me feel nauseous, yet I knew I would go back.

I settled at the kitchen table to write to Jeanette Stott. It needn't be a long letter, just a note to reassure her. Once I'd signed it off, I went out to post it to the wife of the ticket clerk, trusting she hadn't had second thoughts about helping me. Then I put the matter to the back of my mind, as there were chores to be done.

The short reply came the following Thursday, just in time for me to tell Hilda on the Friday. The note was signed 'J'. Otherwise it was in the hand of the railway wife. Jeanette thanked me for visiting and sent her daughter all her love. I was startled to find how relieved I felt, both that the ticket clerk's wife hadn't let me down, but also that Jeanette wasn't too shy to let a strange woman draft a response.

'Who's the letter from?' Will asked. I'd popped it behind the tin on the shelf above the fire without thinking.

'Oh, it's just the ticket clerk's wife, filling me in with the gossip.' I slipped the envelope in my apron pocket out of harm's way, making a mental note to tell him about Hilda, when the time was right. Now my husband could read, it complicated matters and I didn't like the deception.

The next afternoon when I set out for Silver Street, it was with more of a spring in my step. The weather was still warm but there was a pleasant breeze, so the walk was almost enjoyable. I expected the same routine as the previous week; that I would climb the steps as before, sticking out like a sore thumb to those passing by, and ring for attention. Instead, I was surprised to find a small crowd, mostly women and children, but a couple of fathers or brothers too, gathered at the bottom of the steps. They were talking amongst themselves, some appearing cross, others anxious. When I made to go up, several of them called me back.

'There's no visiting today,' was what I heard, although it didn't seep into my consciousness immediately. That couldn't be right, surely?

'They can't stop us visiting,' I said aloud, stepping back.

'But they can, and they do.' It was the same woman who had been visiting the little girl the previous Friday. Then, on the hard chairs under the watchful gaze of the warden, she'd spoken softly. Waiting outside, she was frantic.

'What could be the reason?' I asked. One of the fathers laughed. The reformatory didn't need a *reason*. Sometime it was just an incident, but more often that not it was just to teach everyone a lesson, they reckoned.

'Well, I'm going to ring the bell,' I told them, moving up onto the second step. Several of my audience tutted, but a couple said, 'Good for you missus.'

No-one answered for a while, then the same huge warden I'd seen before, filled the door frame. She made the sort of gesture I might make to shoo my children outside into the yard. 'Go home, the lot o' you. Come back next week—if you have the stamina.' The doors closed again behind her with a heavy clang.

I was shaking; just as furious or concerned as the next person. I could only imagine how it would be if my own girls were incarcerated there. All the way home back to Bishopwearmouth the thought of those poor disappointed children dogged me. Hardly noticing where I was walking, I ended up quite lost in a different part of Sunderland. Youngsters were emerging from a church school, happy and eager to go home. Hilda couldn't do that. She was stuck in her prison, completely at the whim of those running it. I needed to talk to someone about the reformatory, to find out more, but I had no idea where to start.

There was something niggling in the back of my mind. Something Will had said when we were catching up with each other's lives before our wedding. He'd visited the rectory where I'd worked for the Rev and Mrs Beard. When he'd rung the old bell, he was told gruffly that I'd left the place two years before. He'd spoken to the cook, but it hadn't been Martha Cherry who answered. The large cook would have recognised Will even if he did resemble a vagrant. Did the new cook tell Will where the Beards had gone? Did she say Martha had moved with them? I had a feeling Will had said so but I wasn't sure. I'd heard no news myself from the rectory since being summarily dismissed by Reverend Beard, four months pregnant with Ann. If Sunderland *was* mentioned, it would have meant nothing to me at that time, I'd hardly heard of the place. I frowned. I doubted my husband would remember the details now.

Still feeling irritable when we were eating supper, after my disappointing afternoon at the reformatory, I had a grumble about the shortage of folk to relate to in our new neighbourhood. It seemed to be a symptom of the larger town. In the countryside, folk would have been knocking on our door the first evening, out of curiosity.

Will read my mind, as he so often did.

'Didn't that large woman, your friend the cook, move here…to Sunderland with the Reverend and his wife?'

'Martha Cherry?' I said, a trickle of delight flowing up my body into my shoulders, loosening them. 'What makes you say that?' If it was true, and Mrs Cherry the cook had really moved to Sunderland, then it was the first glimmer of hope, that I might find a like-minded person to help me investigate the goings on in Silver Street.

24. Suffer the Little Children

Frances

Over the next weeks while searching for the Beards, I combed Sunderland for places of worship. There were plenty. As well as the obvious larger churches, chapels were hidden amongst small communities, missions were found in wooden shacks or simple brick built buildings that mimicked the shape of churches. There were church schools, and church halls. I strained every nerve in my brain trying to work out which of those, the Reverend Theodore Beard might have chosen to relocate to. I pushed open well-oiled doors, struggled with creaky doors, and knocked on locked doors. I read notices, and asked anyone who looked vaguely like a man of the cloth if they knew the Beards, with various responses. Only one younger clergyman asked if I needed help, others told to me to return when it was more convenient for them, or ignored me. I declined the invitation of a dubious character with a leering smile, to go with him into his dark building. I was almost giving up hope that I would find the Beards in Sunderland, when I happened to enter the parish church for the third time.

'Does the wife of this red-bearded reverend you're seeking, run a church school?' The question came from a young verger who I'd not seen previously. I could have kicked myself. I'd seen the very place he meant that Friday, the day I was prevented from visiting Hilda, when totally lost in the maze of shabby streets. I'd watched those children disperse from a church school. It was so out of the way, it was no wonder I'd not come across it again. I would try to find it again at the earliest opportunity.

Meanwhile, I'd had some success at the reformatory. The third Friday was more akin to my first visit, except that this time several visitors sat on the chairs in the centre of the room. It meant additional chatter, which seemed better for Hilda. The extra noise meant she was more inclined to talk with me, probably because the fierce guard sitting on the stool might not hear us so easily. Of course I was more familiar to her by now as well. I began with an apology.

'I'm so sorry I couldn't see you last week, love. I was outside on the steps, but they wouldn't let us in.'

She shrugged. 'It's just normal.'

It was concerning, seeing the girl so resigned. In between sucking her boiled sweets, she opened up about how their days were spent. They were woken by a bell, forced to wash their faces in cold water then make their beds. After queuing for some thin porridge, they sat to eat it at long tables where they remained all morning, sewing clothes or sacks. Sometimes she had to collect the breakfast dishes and hand out the needlework, sometimes it was the turn of another girl. She preferred it when it was her turn, but if she didn't produce the right amount of sacks, she got a whack over the fingers and lost the chance. At midday there was more porridge of the same consistency, followed by lessons which were taken along with the Ragged School. Except on Fridays, when the reformatory girls were pushed out into the yard earlier for their exercise. As Hilda had been sent to Sunderland at Easter time, she couldn't tell me if the same routines existed in the snow. However, wet weather made little difference, unless it was raining cats and dogs. All this information was delivered in a monotone, with none of the sparkle I wanted to hear from an eleven year old child. Why, even the eight year old English boy in the story, found some enjoyment around him. But then, he had Charley, his green monkey, to keep him company, although as I didn't read to the end of the book, I had no idea if Charley survived the cooking pot of the tribesmen who found them.

I asked if Hilda had any particular friends in the reformatory, or if she'd thought what I might bring her next week. At first she appeared to have forgotten, shaking her head to both questions. Then she came out with it. Not something, but someone.

'I want you to bring your Ann, if you please.'

Trying to remember the verger's instructions, I found the place again almost by accident. The chapel and school weren't in the most squalid part of Sunderland, but the area certainly wasn't inhabited by better-off folk either. Could it actually be Mrs Beard's school after all? Still, I thought back to the time we were teaching the Sunday school children together. She hadn't been averse to my concern that the poorest mill-side families had failed to turn up; even if it wasn't her own idea, she had embraced it. Maybe she'd changed since I knew her? Maybe she'd seen the 'light' so that teaching such ragged children was now her priority. Or maybe the verger at the parish church had led me up a blind alley.

Outside the school, all was quiet. I stood in the yard, watching the entrance for a while, resting. Soon children started to emerge from the school skipping or running. Previously, I'd not taken much note of the boys' and girls' appearance, but as expected they were dressed in tidy but hand-me-down clothes. All were wearing shoes or boots. They ranged in age from about seven years up to thirteen. Some were clearly siblings; the older child taking the younger's hand. One girl and boy pair looked like twins. Only a couple of them carried school bags or books. I waited until I thought the last child had left the building before putting my head around the door cautiously, almost afraid what I would find.

A young woman school teacher, her hair in a bun, was tidying the room wearily with her back to me. If as at Ann's school, it was the final day before the summer holidays, it was no wonder if the poor woman was exhausted. The school room had a high roof with enough windows to give a good light. I guessed a door in the rear wall opened into the chapel. There were three benches, a few low tables and a desk at the front, which, as it had no chair set behind it, the teacher would probably sit on, to give herself some height. A shelf on one wall held a pile of slates with a few books beside them. On a board in the front corner an alphabet had been neatly painted. A blackboard graced the other corner. The teacher had yet to rub away the simple sums chalked on it. I wondered if these children studied the phases of the moon. Probably not, as the smoke of the docklands doubtless concealed both moon and stars. It certainly created a haze over the sun. I considered what sort of teacher the young woman might be; searching for any sign of a cane or stick in the room, but could see none. So it might be a gentle class room, unless she hid her punishment rod behind the door.

'Hello,' I said softly.

Even so, she jumped. 'Oh, can I help you missus?'

Rather than immediately state my mission, instead I told her about my little village class at Long Newton. I said how I missed it, feeling the school teacher was the sort of woman who would listen to your story. She listened attentively and nodded.

'I know what you mean. I would miss this lot too, even though it's right hard work when they have their moments,' she admitted. Then she suddenly seemed to worry I was one of the children's mothers. 'Ooh sorry, they're lovely children too.'

When I reassured her, she pretended to mop her brow. 'Well you can come and help me anytime it suits,' she said with a wink.

Looking to see if she was serious, I decided she was. Then I moved on to explain my reason for popping in. Did she perhaps know a Mrs Beard, who was a reverend's wife?

'Mrs Beard?' said the young school teacher. 'Oh yes miss, Mrs Beard oversees this church school.'

A notice board outside the chapel had revealed the Reverend Theodore Beard preached from the platform each Sunday at ten o'clock. At home on the Saturday evening, I announced that I'd be going to church in the morning. 'So you girls need to be good for your father,' I told them with a wag of my finger. They wanted to come with me, of course, but I wasn't having that. The last thing I needed was the attention that three or even just two children would certainly attract. My plan was to be as quiet as a mouse, to creep in unnoticed to the back of the chapel then leave in a similar manner. I tried to pacify them. 'Mebbe next time you can come. I just need to find a friend first.'

While the young school teacher tidied up that previous afternoon, she explained the chapel was too small to have a rectory attached to it. It meant the Beards lived fairly close by, in their own home. The teacher had never been to Mrs Beard's house, and couldn't give me any more information because her employer only ever discussed school business in the classroom.

I would have to be stealthy in the first instance, while I discovered where the Reverend and Mrs Beard lived. Once I'd achieved that, I hoped I would be closer to finding Martha Cherry, if she still worked for them.

'Do you think I look different to when you first met me?' I asked Will. I needed to know if he thought the Reverend would recognise me. Will was no help at all. 'You're quite as pretty as you were in the rectory kitchen, so I'd have no problem recognising you anywhere. You'll just have to pray the chapel is poorly lit.'

I reached Reverend Beard's chapel in good time, approaching it by its main entrance rather than from the smaller road by the school room. I hung back to wait, my bonnet pulled as far down on my face as possible. Worshippers, who'd clearly made an effort with their appearance, arrived in ones and twos. Old men and middle-aged women traipsed in; mothers with daughters, arm in arm. A flustered woman hustled her family through the open door like a hen with her brood.

231

The room would be filling up, so I wanted to make my move soon. The ideal opportunity to slip in quietly came when a cluster of people arrived together.

No-one seemed to notice me, or if they did, they didn't reveal it. Reverend Beard wasn't as yet on his small pulpit. I entered a simple space, high ceilinged like the schoolroom. A gangway ran down the centre, with pews on either side. One side was well lit from a high window, the other side in shadow. I chose the latter, perching uncomfortably in the corner at the back of the chapel. There was hardly time to look around before a young man entered behind me, closed the door after him, removed his hat then sat on my pew at the aisle end. It seemed to be a cue for activity to begin at the front of the room, although how this was achieved was difficult to guess—unless the Beards' time keeping had improved. A small group emerged through another door, which I guessed led from the schoolroom. Apparently they'd been holding a meeting of their own. Two grey haired men and Mrs Beard took their places at the front, and finally the Reverend Theodore Beard entered to take his place at the lectern. He loomed larger than life in the small chapel, although he did tone down his voice to match the size of his audience. His red beard was also muted by streaks of grey.

Whilst the Reverend made the announcements I scrutinized his congregation. Apart from some of those families and individuals I'd observed entering the chapel it was hard to decide who was who, from the backs of their heads or bonnets. One thing seemed certain though, while also filling me with surprise and joy. Mrs Beard's tiny form on the front row was now seated beside a large woman, whom I was in no doubt was Martha Cherry. This would never have occurred at St Thomas', where the cook and I were always relegated to the servants' pews, or those of lesser individuals. Here the pair looked to be friends, or even perhaps equals.

I took mental note of the sermon: *SUFFER THE LITTLE CHILDREN TO COME UNTO ME.* Words of Jesus, I knew. It wasn't a subject he'd lectured on before in my presence, but it seemed appropriate in view of the church school his wife oversaw. I thought no more about it, especially as I was so pleased to have found Martha Cherry. The choice of lesson certainly didn't give me cause for alarm, on that summer's morning.

25. A Completely Different Child

Frances

The Reverend Theodore Beard moved quickly to the church doors to shake hands with his flock. People weren't inclined to stay long after the service so I had a difficult decision to make. I could wait in the shadows in the rear corner of the chapel, with the risk of being seen there and looking suspicious or I could leave with the rest of the throng, and try to slip past him. I decided on the latter, which I thought would give me the best chance of catching Martha Cherry alone.

Fortunately it was easy to avoid his handshake. Most people seemed keen to thank him for his sermon, which meant he was kept busy enjoying their appreciations. I waited outside, standing back from the chapel doors, but neither the cook nor Mrs Beard emerged. Disappointed, I wandered round the block of terraced houses to the schoolroom exit. There they were. The two women were walking away from me side-by-side, one tiny, the other towering above. It was strange in so many ways. Although it was Martha I wanted, for the first time I considered catching up with both of them, wondering if the women were now inseparable. I remained a good distance behind while I gave the idea some thought, and while I watched to see where they would lead me. Soon enough they opened a gate to a tiny garden, forcing me to keep back even more. Mrs Beard approached the front door of a modest house, whilst I was just in time to see Martha Cherry open a small door at the side, before ducking to enter. At last I'd found my friend. Doubtless, the Reverend Theodore wouldn't be far behind though. It was time to leave for home, but I would be back.

As we stood at the top of the stone steps I could feel Ann trembling lightly. No longer quite so shocked myself by the imposing doors and high windowless walls of the girls' reformatory, I could imagine my daughter was.

'Are you still sure you want to go in?' I asked. Her 'yes' was more of a squeak, so I squeezed her hand. The reformatory warden was no less brusque for me having a child clutching my hand, but then why should she be with her occupation?

For all that, I was glad I'd found the courage to bring my eldest daughter, and that she'd been brave enough to agree. Although she was a few years younger than Hilda, they had always got on well, and with someone nearer her own age present, Hilda gave out more details than before. Some of it I'd guessed already. Jeanette Stott's boyfriend had work as a labourer when he could get it, but they rarely saw any of his wages. He would go into the Crown Inn on the corner of Anson Street on the days he was paid, and stay there until all the pennies were gone. Hilda would watch for him to begin his unsteady walk home, because his mood would be sour and his fists flying by the time he got there, so she had to make herself scarce. Jeanette took in laundry and sewing, but times were tough which meant they were often hungry. Hilda had been caught red handed, pilfering in the market. That had been bad enough, the constable said, but it wasn't the full reason for her being in the Silver Street reformatory. In a sober moment, Jeanette's boyfriend had declared he wanted to provide for his family as he should, especially with a bairn on the way, which he assumed he'd fathered himself. The next night he'd shaken Hilda gently on the shoulder then

236

urged her out of bed with his finger to his lips. They'd crept through the streets to the new properties of West Hartlepool, where they'd stopped outside an end-of-terrace home. It was the sort of place a comfortably off family might live. Hilda's part in the crime was to be lifted up and to enter a small window, before opening the front door for her step-father.

'There was no-one at home,' she assured us, 'he told me that.'

Ann and I had both gasped when she'd reached the end of the tale.

'Did you believe her story?' Ann asked when we'd escaped into the street. It felt like an escape each time I left through those hefty doors.

'Aye I did lass,' I sighed, 'enough of it, anyways.' Apparently, there was no shortage of men prepared to drink their families into poverty, then wanting to make it up to their missus in a better moment. But to involve Hilda in a burglary!

'I s'pose we have to be glad they didn't send her overseas to Africa or somewhere.' Seeing Ann's face pale, I could see I'd said too much.

I'd promised to take the children to Long Newton to visit our family, so it was two weeks before I could take

Ann back to see Hilda. When the Friday afternoon arrived we found a completely different child. Hilda wouldn't talk to either of us for the whole of the visit. She just grabbed the toffees and chewed. We'd warned her we were going to visit our family and wouldn't come for a while, so I hoped it wasn't disappointment about that. I looked at the girl carefully. Her head was down, her eyes red. We asked what was wrong, we tried to make her laugh, and we told her what her ma had written. Nothing helped. I glanced up at the warden on her stool, but her gaze was as noncommittal as ever. The stout woman clearly wasn't prepared to intervene, or tell us what might be going on. In the end Ann and I just had to leave, giving as many assurances to Hilda as we could, that the problem would improve soon.

'I'll be back next week, love,' I told her.

With the worry of Hilda fresh in my mind, I was even more determined to visit Martha Cherry. She'd always been so full of good advice. I decided to make the effort the next afternoon, especially as I recalled Mrs Beard would often go out visiting after lunch on a Saturday. The girls came with me. I wasn't happy leaving the younger ones with Ann because she was still distraught after visiting Hilda. When we got close to the Beards' house, I stopped outside the schoolroom thinking the girls could wait in there, but the door was locked. It wasn't surprising. Next we tried the chapel. That was open. It was taking a chance but I wanted to be sure they were somewhere safe. I pushed them inside with instructions for Ann to sit on a pew and tell the others a story, preferably a Bible one and that there should be absolutely no singing. Once the children had got the message, I retraced my steps until I was outside the Beards' house. I guessed the entrance Mrs Cherry had used that Sunday after chapel, would either lead to the kitchen, or her own quarters. I hovered outside summoning the courage to knock. A small window was set in the same wall, but it was hard to see much through it. All of a sudden the door was thrust open.

'Frances Ferguson. Can that really be you?' The cook ducked her head, and stood outside still wearing her apron, shaking her head in disbelief.

'Mrs Cherry, you won't believe how glad I am to see you.'

Once she'd recovered, she took my arm pulling me into what was obviously her private room, complete with two easy chairs, a small table with wash basin and jug, a narrow bed under some shelves. It was simple, but cosy enough, with crocheted blankets on the bed, a picture of her late hubby gracing a shelf over the bed and a newspaper which lay open on a stool next to her chair.

'So you see I'm well able to entertain guests now,' the cook said, seeing me look around the room. 'I have a door to the kitchen in case I'm bored.' She pointed to an exit at the rear of her room, chuckling. 'Now, sit down lass, and I'll get you some tea.'

Martha insisted I start calling her just that, since I was a grown woman and no longer her kitchen maid. She explained she'd left St Thomas', along with the Beards, shortly after I had myself. The Reverend Theodore Beard junior had returned from Africa from doing mission work at the Cape.

My ears pricked up at that, especially as I had no idea they had a son. I said as much.

'Anyway,' Martha continued, 'the Reverend wanted Theodore Junior to take over from him, while he in turn would find a less demanding role elsewhere. On the other hand, Mrs Beard wasn't so sure. She wanted to enjoy her son's company after missing him those three years. She also preferred not to let the children of her Sunday school mission down.'

'Flipping heck Martha,' I said. 'What happened next?'

'Theodore junior didn't care to be under the shadow of his father, so he persuaded his mother he would continue her Sunday school work. He also assured her a place like Sunderland would offer even more opportunity for teaching good moral sense to children.'

In the end, Martha explained, the menfolk won, as they usually did in her opinion. But it *had* turned out well for Mrs Beard, because along with this chapel, there was a church school to oversee. It meant the Reverend's wife was in her element and quite a changed person too.

I smiled to hear it, pleased for my old employer.

'And the Reverend Beard?' I asked. 'Is he also changed?' My children were waiting in his chapel. I hoped they were behaving and that the clergyman hadn't had business to attend to in his church.

Martha didn't seem to know how to answer. Instead, she changed the subject. 'Now you must tell me all about yourself. What brings you to Sunderland, and how on earth did you find me?'

I filled her in quickly about Will, the girls, and the places we'd lived. While I wanted to get to the subject of Hilda, there was a lot of news to catch up on first, and I was edgy, thinking of my children in the chapel. Martha noticed.

'You'll need to get going, I can see.' she said. 'Now wasn't there something you wanted my *expert* advice on?'

'Might you be free next Friday after two o'clock?' I asked tentatively.

It was settled. We would meet outside the reformatory on Silver Street at visiting time, all being well. Martha grasped me in her large arms. 'It's been a fine surprise Frances, seeing you after all these years.'

After our goodbyes, I walked briskly to the chapel, worrying what might have happened to the girls, such as they'd been locked inside, or Reverend Beard had found them misbehaving and thrown them out. Neither of those things seemed to have occurred, although the three of them were happy to see me.

'Did a large man with a red beard bother you?' was my first question.

'No Ma. We just saw a little old woman,' said Peggy.

Mrs Beard probably—she would have seemed old to my youngsters.

I might have gasped slightly because Ann said, 'she wasn't cross.'

'She asked our names,' Peggy told me.

'And you told her?'

'That's all we said, just our names and that we were waiting for you,' Ann said. 'She said she would come back later in case we'd been 'bandoned. What does 'bandoned mean?' Picking up the baby from Ann's arms, I led the way out of the chapel.

'Let's go girls, before the woman returns.' I explained the meaning but assured them there was no chance at all I would abandon my children. For that matter, I had no intention of abandoning Hilda or the other children at Silver Street, but I kept that thought to myself.

Ruth

She wasn't at all surprised to see the girls occupied at the back of the chapel. The three were well behaved, appeared clean and seemed well-fed. The older girl was bouncing the baby on her knee as if she were its mother. At the same time she was telling them a story, almost certainly it was a Bible story, but with a difference. Children had been abandoned there before, but those had been shabbier. It was also a common haunt for vagrants to spend the night, especially after they'd had a drink. Theodore didn't much like the door left unlocked, but Ruth had won that particular argument, years ago. Still, with the gossip going round Sunderland that summer, it did concern her; particularly that these were little girls. She'd finished her visit to a dying member of the congregation and was making her way back to the chapel, when she saw a woman escort her children out. They seemed a happy family, so no need to worry. The reverend's wife wasn't close enough to be certain, but the girl's mother looked familiar. She decided she must wrack her brains to remember where or when they'd met before.

26. Three Heads Together

Frances

Hilda was reluctant to leave the exercise yard, yet the warden was having none of it. The altercation was visible through the visiting room window. She *would* go inside to see her visitors, or else. I wasn't sure what concerned me more, her reluctance, or that the girl was given no choice. Once she'd sat down heavily opposite me, I introduced Martha Cherry as a friendly cook who'd baked a honey cake especially for her. Hilda showed no interest at all. I broke off a piece of the delicious looking loaf, passing it to her. She pretended to ignore it, but the temptation was too great. Once she'd got the taste, she wolfed it down, taking more from me when offered. I was thankful because she'd obviously lost weight and looked haggard. There were dark shadows under her eyes as if she was getting little or no sleep. In which case, it was no wonder she was so morose. I tried to see Hilda through Martha's eyes. The girl was quite tall for her age, with her height emphasised by her skinniness. Having two of us visit together made it easier to keep a conversation going, but Hilda took no part in it, simply staring at her boots. We didn't make her endure the ordeal any longer than the last piece of cake.

Outside, Martha and I shared worried glances.

'And this was a child who was chatty a few weeks ago?' the large cook asked with a frown. I walked with my friend to her rooms, thinking to go home straightway after, but Martha suggested we sit in her kitchen for a while. I followed her inside, knowing my girls were safe with a neighbour. The room reminded me of the rectory kitchen, so it brought a feeling of nostalgia sitting at her big table. It seemed only yesterday I was chopping vegetables for Martha's stew, sweeping the floor or waiting for Will to visit. This kitchen was also tidy and well stocked, as I would expect from Martha Cherry. Several jars of pickles, sacks of flour and other dried grains were visible in an open cupboard in the corner. The Beards were lucky to have her.

I described my previous visits to Silver Street again, telling Martha more of Hilda's story. In the retelling, I realised the girl had seemed almost proud at one point, especially narrating her part in the burglary. The difference now was unmistakable. Something had happened, and I guessed that whatever it was, it was still going on.

After thinking for a while, Martha looked down at me apologetically. Unfortunately she didn't believe she could be much help to me with Hilda. I tried to contain my disappointment, but Martha could always see right through me. She touched my hand—but she was acquainted with someone who *might* help. One of her neighbours regularly went behind the walls to collect or return laundry, so she would probably know any gossip that went on in there.

'I can mention it to her if you like?'

With a big smile on my face, I said that it would be very helpful, thanking my new accomplice warmly.

'Bring your hubby and girls to see me soon,' she called as she waved goodbye at the door.

I decided to tell Will about my visit to Silver Street with Martha Cherry. The effect was instant. His face dropped like a ton of coal, so at that moment I knew not to mention the previous times I'd been to the reformatory, either alone or with Ann.

'This is about those folk behind 'docks in Hartlepool again, isn't it?' he shouted. The broad Yorkshire brogue meant a raw spot had been touched, deep inside him, but I wasn't about to be cowed into subjection. 'Aye, it's about Hilda, Ann's friend from school and she's in trouble.'

'No doubt she was stealing again. You just can't help folks like that.'

'It's more than that, Will,' I said quietly, cutting him off in full flow.

It was the worst argument we'd ever had. The New Testament says not to let the sun go down on your wrath, but we did that night; even when the moon was out, we were still fuming.

Although it shook me up, I tried not to give our disagreement too much attention; there were more important things to occupy my mind. Within a week, Martha Cherry had new information. As promised she'd spoken to the laundry woman who had come straight out with it: children, both male and female at Silver Street were wetting their beds more than usual, although the woman was unable to say which individuals in particular. I raised my eyebrows. This I was not expecting.

'There's anxiety then, for sure,' I said eventually.

'Aye, yet my friend said there's no talk of the punishment room being used much.'

I had a thought. 'Did your friend say there were any new wardens of late?'

She shook her head. 'If anything she said there was less gossip than usual, that everyone was very tight lipped and cagey.'

'It's puzzling for certain,' I said scratching my chin.

If I wasn't so concerned for Hilda, I might have enjoyed the detective work, sensing that Martha might do too.

'What will you do next?' she asked, a glint in her eye.

I confessed I had no idea yet.

'We need to know which outstanding pillars of the community are trustees of Silver Street,' I announced a few days later, with a hint of sarcasm. I'd come up with the idea from an advert in the Newcastle Courant, where a church school was seeking a new trustee. Martha kept a pile of old newspapers for cleaning the windows or lighting the cooking stove so we'd decided to scour the back issues for clues. Perhaps there would be notice of a Silver Street meeting, or some other public information about the reformatory or Ragged School. I'd taken my girls to visit that day and we were seated around Martha's kitchen table. Ann helped too, once she knew what we were looking for. As we finished with each page, we passed them to Peggy. Martha showed the little girl how to tear the paper up into a bowl of warm water to make a pulp. 'We'll add some flour soon, so you can make a ball,' she told her to Peggy's delight. My middle daughter was soon soaking wet up to her elbows, covered in ink.

'It's hopeless,' I declared after a while, sitting back and sighing. We'd looked through perhaps a dozen papers but found nothing of any help.

'Then its time we sought Mrs Beard's assistance,' said Martha firmly. 'She'll know how to find the information.'

Ruth

Ruth Beard had been wracking her brain, but it wasn't until she stopped thinking about the woman she'd seen leaving the chapel with the little girls, that the answer came to her. It seemed so obvious now. After all they'd spent many hours in each other's company teaching the Sunday school mission. Seeing her in a new context, a mother with three children, had completely thrown her. Fanny—or was it Frances? It had been a perfect ending for the girl to throw that missile at them after Theodore had sent her packing. Ruth tried to remember if she'd been upset by Frances' words. She might have been, but then she'd been somewhat of a different person in those days. She'd missed the girl, who she recalled was extremely good with the Sunday school children and intelligent with it—a natural teacher in fact. Perhaps she should have shown more appreciation towards the girl. Ruth suddenly remembered something else. It had been Frances' observation about the poor mill-side children being absent. Could that have been the beginning of an awakening for the reverend's wife? She recalled having to fight Theodore for permission to provide refreshments. It didn't bear thinking about now. Most of the children currently at the church school were from poor families, which she was proud of.

Ruth was aware there were visitors in Mrs Cherry's kitchen. She'd heard the giggles. It was time to make an entrance. She opened the door quietly. There they were, those same children, the two older girls busy at the table with their hands in a bowl, the baby on a rug well away from the stove. The two women were clearing up a pile of newspapers, their backs to her. Despite the difference in age, the pair looked completely comfortable in each other's company. She cleared her throat.

'Ahh, I *was* right. A very good afternoon to you, my dears.'

'Hello Mrs Beard,' Frances said, turning round with a blush on her cheeks. Ruth wasn't sure if Frances was going to curtsy, as the woman seemed at a loss for a moment. Close up, Ruth could see the visitor looked tired, as if she had the world upon her shoulders, but when Frances spoke it was with the same spark that she remembered.

'We were just thinking about you Mrs Beard, me and Martha. Actually you're exactly the person we need to help us, if you've a mind to.'

Ruth Beard listened carefully. It was quite a tale although not in the least surprising. 'Let me see what I can find out for you,' she agreed.

For one thing, her husband, the Reverend Theodore Beard was one of the reformatory trustees, but she said nothing of that to Mrs Cherry and Frances Bell. It looked as if the visitors were preparing to leave so she said goodbye, quickly retreating upstairs to her lounge. First of all she would question Theodore. He was out that afternoon so she had time to think how to approach the matter.

Finally, when they were relaxing in their easy chairs after an excellent beef stew cooked by Mrs Cherry, she broached the subject.

'How do you find the children at Silver Street these days, Theodore?' she asked without looking up from her sewing.

'What a strange question, Ruth.' His voice was even, with no hint of emotion. 'Why I'm sure they're quite fine.'

'Except I heard some of the girls were more anxious than usual. Would you know of any reason? Is there a new warden or anything similar?'

'I wouldn't worry your head about that place, my dear. I would have heard if there were any concerns to attend to.' Her husband's tone made it quite clear the conversation was over. But his words had the completely opposite effect on his wife. She felt the sharp prick of the sewing needle before she saw the drop of blood. What was the matter with her? She couldn't remember the last time her needle slipped like that. Her concentration must be completely awry.

By coincidence, the following day was the first Thursday in the month, the day the Reformatory and Ragged School trustees met. A little while after Reverend Beard

253

had left the house, Ruth Beard entered her husband's study. It was a smaller room than at St Thomas' rectory, so it looked even more cluttered with the same large desk in its centre, full of papers. Her husband wasn't a tidy man. She would have her work cut out finding the information the three women wanted, but she could be methodical. Starting with the desk drawers, she worked her way upwards. The bottom drawer contained old sermons with crossings out and markings all over them. The next was full of letters, their seals lying open as she flicked through them. She wouldn't have to time to digest everything she read, some of which would have been fascinating in itself, but instead concentrated her searching for words such as *SILVER STREET, RAGGED SCHOOL or REFORMATORY.* The two upper drawers yielded no better results. She turned to the desktop. The task was taking even longer than expected, with so many papers in such disorder. Ruth glanced at the clock in the corner of the room. The trustees' meetings had been going on for longer recently, but even so, her husband would be home before long. Standing at the window for a moment to check for his return, she was dismayed to see his top hat and frock coat approaching, his red beard glinting in the sunshine.

Ruth Beard wasn't one to curse; instead a flush crept up into her cheeks. She did a rapid calculation of the time it would take for him to reach the house, open the front door, hang up his hat then make his way upstairs. She did an even more rapid search of the remainder of the desk. Actually, the final pile was at the front so perhaps those were the papers he had most recently been viewing. There it was: a list of five trustees for the Silver Street reformatory. There was no time to copy the names down, which was a shame because she'd brought pen and paper for that purpose. Similarly it was too dangerous to borrow the paper if it was amongst those he was currently perusing. All she could do that day was to take a careful look and try to memorise the names of the two men that were new to her, before beating a hasty retreat. She slipped the list back under a few other papers, peered around the door and crept out, listening for her husband's heavy tread on the stairs.

27. The Detective Work Continues

THE railway engineer stood at his library shelves in Kirkdunham House searching for a suitable book to read to his son. There it was: *The English Boy at The Cape, An Anglo-African Story.* It was the same book that Frances Bell had borrowed when she worked as a maid for his wife. Of course she would have had a different name in those days. The book was in good condition, with the pages un-creased. Bell's wife had clearly loved that book and he was always interested to know why. He'd not read the story as a boy, because it hadn't been written at that time. He'd bought the book on a whim years later, when he heard the protagonist's name was the same as his own, and would therefore be that of any firstborn son his wife bore him.

He'd spotted William and Frances Bell from his desk at the ticket office on the day the railway verdict was made public. As he watched them with their brood of children he'd been surprised at the feeling of envy which crept up on him. He'd known with regret it could never be quite the same for his own family, yet surely he *could* put more effort into getting to know his son. He could even show some interest in his newborn daughter. As a start, now his boy was old enough, he would read the book with him.

Kirkdunham House still felt claustrophobic, so he took the boy into a summer house which faced a pond in the wildest part of the garden. Not quite Africa, but it would have to do. Once they were settled side-by-side on the cushioned hammock, he began to read, '…..Charles could not but *like* every individual at the government house…..yet he formed no attachment there save to the little green monkey named Charley like himself…..'

Perhaps he should consider buying a monkey for his own boy? But he had a better idea. Just a week later, the railway engineer sighed with satisfaction as he squeezed past customers entering the new Sunderland toy shop. His purchase would do very well. He'd ordered a clockwork train-set to be posted to Kirkdunham House for Charles. They would enjoy it together. He also had in mind to bring the boy to Sunderland on his first real train journey, then they could browse the books in the high street. But shopping wasn't his foremost concern that first Thursday of the month. He had a meeting to attend, and not a railway one on that occasion.

It had all begun on a day a few months back when he was equally busy, at a time when the railway accident involving William Bell had yet to be resolved. On the day in question it had been entirely railway business which took the engineer north of Stockton. He needed to deal with another safety concern, which was handled easily. Those days, while awaiting the accident report, the engineer had awarded matters of safety the fullest attention. Monkwearmouth railway station was on the north bank of the Wear, almost opposite to the malodorous docklands of Sunderland which did little to enhance the south bank. It was a dreary day, with winter still in its throes at the time, but visiting the station was not in the least bit dull. It was a fascinating building, while the railway engineer did enjoy unusual buildings. This particular edifice was built like a classical Greek temple, so he had difficulty tearing himself away. By contrast, he recalled, the geology had been a commonplace mix of sand, gravel and till.

The journey home wouldn't be as straightforward as he would like. There was an annoying gap in the railway network, which was the fault of the river Wear. Monkwearmouth station was separated from Fawcett

Street in Sunderland, by the river. He predicted that a rail bridge would eventually link the two, perhaps even built by the famous Robert Stevenson as the road bridge had been. At that time though, the station on the north bank served South Shields and Newcastle, while Fawcett Street was the gateway to Hartlepool and other stations south, such as Stockton-On-Tees, which was closest to Kirkdunham House. The inconvenient break in the line meant the railway engineer had to take the ferry back to Sunderland, with a cold drizzle penetrating his coat as he stood waiting for the vessel to turn round. The water was packed with sailing ships trying to negotiate their journeys in a brisk wind from the North East.

'Not the best weather for waiting about is it?' observed a man who looked about thirty years, standing beside him.

The engineer agreed wholeheartedly with the other man's opinion. He was also happy enough to engage in conversation to take his mind off his discomfort.

'Henry Coulson,' the younger man said in a friendly manner, extending a cold, wet hand. 'Most folk call me Harry.'

'Nice to meet you,' the railway engineer said. Bowing slightly he revealed his own name. 'Charles,' he said, 'although my friends used to call me "Woolly".'

Cordiality thus quickly established, Henry Coulson pointed towards one of the larger vessels out on the Wear. 'My ship,' he said proudly. 'I've another out on the ocean.' The engineer remarked that in that case, the young ship owner had done well for himself. 'Aye,' Coulson continued, 'and I've more plans, too.' He shifted about a little. 'I hope to be a politician before I'm thirty five.'

The engineer looked suitably impressed then explained his own profession. They both agreed that the railway would be the future for land travel.

'So, Woolly, if I can call you that? What is it that *you're* passionate about, besides railways that is, if you don't mind my asking?' Coulson said.

The ten minutes before the ferry arrived had passed affably, with the engineer describing his passion for literacy amongst his workers, while Coulson admitted he sought to clothe and feed those folk that were struggling. Born near the banks of the river Tyne in Newcastle, he'd seen what poverty could do to a person. As they boarded, Lamb remarked that between them they might even save the world.

Now, several months later, as the railway engineer climbed the stone steps to be admitted to the monthly meeting of trustees, he thought back to that winter's day. The two men had disembarked from the ferry, but rather than go their separate ways, by unspoken consent they'd continued walking together. The walls of the Ragged School had loomed dreary in the grey afternoon as they passed by. When he felt the engineer shudder beside him, Coulson had surprised him by saying he'd recently become a trustee for the place. Soon, over a welcome drink in the Dog and Pheasant, Coulson had persuaded the engineer to put his own name forward.

The trustees' meeting that Thursday was the engineer's fourth and it was a typical one, even down to the final point on the agenda which was 'any other business'. Harry Coulson asked his usual question about the diet the children were being fed, to which another trustee who neither of them liked, but who was also the children's doctor replied, also as usual, that the porridge was nutritious enough. The railway engineer then asked his usual question about the children's literacy. Reassurances were given by another trustee who was a clergyman and whose 'good wife' oversaw his church school. After that the two friends had to rush off. Coulson had work to attend to, while the engineer had a train to catch. The other three men remained seated, with their heads together. Outside, the engineer exchanged a knowing look with Coulson. As yet they were both novices with little influence around the trustees' table, but both were privately determined that situation would change.

Ruth

She was ready for a rest after the afternoon rummaging through her husband's desk, not to mention the tense moment when he arrived on the landing. But instead of putting her feet up, Ruth went straight downstairs to the kitchen, to find Martha Cherry. The cook was preparing vegetables for their supper and the reverend's wife stood helping her for a while. She didn't exactly say how she'd come by her information, but disclosed she now had names for five trustees of the Silver Street reformatory.

'Oh, that's grand Mrs Beard. You found out so promptly as well.' Mrs Cherry said with delight, looking down at the tiny woman beside her. Ruth chopped a turnip up a little too vigorously, before admitting she was concerned about the whole affair. She went on to explain she was acquainted with some of the trustees. One was a doctor, and another a magistrate. She would personally talk to the doctor to ask if he had any concerns for the reformatory children, but it would be less straightforward speaking with the magistrate, who would probably be too busy. Ruth waved the kitchen knife around a few times and frowned: then there were two trustees completely unknown to her, whose names were H. Coulson and C. Lamb.

'I've not heard of them either Mrs Beard, but I can pass their names on to Frances. Perhaps she can ask around,' said Martha Cherry, gently taking the knife from her employer.

Next morning, Ruth sat in her doctor's waiting room, listening to the muted cries of pain coming from his surgery. The noises put her teeth on edge, but only briefly did she reconsider her mission. Once the corpulent physician had bid goodbye to his patient, a man who seemed all too keen to leave, he ushered the reverend's wife into his musty office.

'This is a pleasant surprise Mrs Beard. How may I help you today?'

Once he'd closed the door behind them, she explained she'd had a cough for quite a time and would appreciate some advice.

'I hope you're not suffering from damp as I am,' he joked, pointing to his mildewy walls. Puffing a fair bit, which made Ruth wonder if he *did* need a physician himself, he bent down to put his ear to her chest, on one side then the other, lingering for a little too long each time. Then he straightened again with equal difficulty, announcing, 'well all seems well in that department. Now open wide my dear.' She gave a cough to encourage him. He completed his tests in a jolly manner, informing her she would live, and that her symptoms were certain to disappear very soon without intervention, which she knew already. Finally she came out with the real reason for her visit.

'Theodore said he saw you at the Ragged School yesterday.' It was only a small untruth. 'I assume as their physician you'd be aware if any of the girls in the reformatory were unduly anxious?'

'Yes, yes,' he said quickly, slightly flustered, his cheeks reddening. 'I mean no, no, the girls are doing splendidly.' He looked down at her chest absent mindedly. Then he bent again, but this time to whisper something confidentially. 'In fact I visited some of them yesterday evening after the trustees' meeting. You need have no concerns there my dear.' His words were almost identical to her husband's two days before, although the doctor delivered his with more condescension. Ruth felt her stomach churn. As she passed through the waiting area on the way out, she could tell her discomfort was obvious to the youth who was next in line for the doctor's attentions. She felt sorry for worrying him. She considered how the visit might have increased her own anxiety too, but that her cough had miraculously stopped. Even the deep breath she took when she stepped onto the street failed to set it off.

Ruth passed by the magistrate's court on her way home, but there were no obvious signs of that individual being in residence. She wasn't even sure the man would receive her readily if he was present. If he met her, he would have to be civil, as a gentleman must, but he would give her short shrift without Theodore being there. Those were excuses, she knew, but even she had limits to her bravery. Frances would probably have faced the magistrate head on.

For the three of them to find out anything of further use about events at the reformatory, particularly to help young Hilda, it seemed they would need to seek out the two as-yet-unknown trustees. As she walked, head down, barely aware of the traffic passing her, she reviewed the evidence the three accomplices had gathered between them to date: Hilda—a girl she'd not personally met—had become deeply unhappy and silent, despite being fine and talkative previously; girls or boys, or perhaps both were wetting their beds, which had not happened before in such high numbers; finally the assurances of two of the trustees, including that of her husband were suspicious. She felt her face drain of colour. God forbid that Theodore was up to his neck in something sinister alongside the doctor. Surely the magistrate couldn't be involved too? Well she had no choice. She would have to approach him. She lifted her head up, turned round and headed back towards the magistrate's court.

28. The Threat

Frances

We called at the sweet shop to buy two bags of mints, one for Hilda, the other for Ann and Peggy to suck while I was inside. Even with my daughters slowing me down, we arrived at Silver Street early. That day, a motley group of people had gathered outside the reformatory. A few looked struck down with poverty, their clothes threadbare, any colours washed out years ago. Most of the visitor's eyes rested on an elderly man with a pocket watch. Once he declared it was time, they would ring the bell. I'd begun to recognise some of the folk over the weeks as we shared grimaces about what we would find inside. For me though, there was a glimmer of hope since Mrs Beard agreed to help us. It was two days since the reverend's wife entered her kitchen to find me visiting Martha with the girls. She might already have some new information for the other two detectives.

A collective sigh sounded when the burly warden let us in. Being prevented from visiting for no good reason was still fresh in our minds. I told Ann and Peggy to stay close together outside and not wander away. With the state Hilda was in lately, it wasn't right taking Ann in with me, let alone Peggy, yet on this occasion I had nowhere else to leave them for any length of time. The baby would be none the wiser at her age, strapped across my chest. We allowed ourselves to be led deep into the prison, our chatter ceasing for a while. It was always an experience to enter along with other visitors, wondering what they were thinking and feeling. The small group was ushered into the same visiting room, which meant we soon filled most of the chairs. It felt less daunting than the days I'd been alone in there, especially as I hoped the extra hubbub might bring Hilda out of her shell. If not, then perhaps seeing the baby might cheer her up.

One by one, girls arrived to take their places at the centre of the room opposite their visiting mothers and sisters. I kept one eye on the emptying exercise yard, the other on the door leading from it. Occasionally I turned, trying to read the face of our hefty guard who sat uncomfortably on her stool as usual. Eventually one of the other visitors noticed my girl hadn't arrived. She pointed the empty chair out to her daughter, who was an older girl of perhaps thirteen.

'Hilda was chosen again,' the girl said simply, her face falling.

'*Chosen*?' My voice shook—'*Again?*' I didn't know exactly what she meant but a feeling of intense anger rose up through me. Looking around, most people were pretending they hadn't heard, although one couple nodded their heads knowingly.

Picked up the baby in my arms I strode over to the guard.

'Will Hilda Stott be coming today?' I asked, my voice cracking by then.

She held my eye and spoke roughly. 'Obviously not miss. I'll ring for them to let you out.' By that time the whole room was silent. Approaching the girl who volunteered the information, I begged her to take the toffees to Hilda. 'Have one yourself too,' I added, pushing the paper bag into her hands. I was seething as a second warden escorted me along the passage. Outside the building, I had to sit on a wall to recover my balance. Ann rushed across the road dragging her sister behind her, barely escaping a passing carriage as they cut across its path.

'Ma, what's wrong?'

I couldn't answer, just pulled them close to me. What had the girl meant by '*chosen*'? By her tone of voice and demeanour it couldn't be a good thing.

It took a few minutes for my dizziness to ease then we wandered to the end of Silver Street to sit down again by the river. There, slowly, watching the toing and froing of ferries, my tension began to soften. One thing was certain, I wasn't wrong to question the goings on at the reformatory.

It made sense to share the new development with Martha Cherry as soon as possible, so we took that route home despite it being out of our way. It was a wasted journey, like everything else that day. There was no reply after knocking loudly at her downstairs entrance. We couldn't keep waiting; neither would it be wise to ring the bell at the main entrance, in case the Reverend came to the door. All in all it was a disappointing afternoon. We were tired, with the girls getting more irritable by the minute. Jeanette Stott kept coming to my mind. How I would explain if something really bad had befallen her daughter? I would have to pull myself together to be any use to them or my own family. After a quick stop at the chapel informed me Mrs Beard and Martha weren't to be found inside, we started for home. It was then that Peggy began wailing in earnest, 'I've lost little Peggy.' I last remembered seeing her clutching her peg doll when we were by the river. With one glance at her face, both Ann and I knew we'd have to go back.

Will

'Mrs Cherry,' he said, recognising the cook immediately from her big frame and smile. The engine driver had just returned home from work exhausted, late on the Friday afternoon, with no idea where his wife and children were.

'It's no concern that I've missed her,' his visitor said cheerfully once she was inside the Bell's small kitchen in Bishopwearmouth. 'I'm glad to see you instead, William. It's been too long. I'll get you to pass a message on to your wife, if you're willing?'

Martha chatted away as women often did in his experience. It made his head spin. She'd never been to that side of Sunderland before, she said, but had found the place easily, following Frances's description, noting how much wider and cleaner the streets were. Also, despite being a warm summer's day there were none of the smells they got in East Sunderland.

'Aye, we're happy enough here Mrs Cherry,' Will assured her when she'd paused for a breath. 'No doubt it'll be about the reformatory. Your message, I mean,' he added quickly, in a tone which should have told Martha he was less than happy. 'She's been there again hasn't she?' He was worried.

'Aye, she'll have been there earlier this afternoon for visiting,' Martha admitted too easily. 'I thought she might have called to see me on her way home, but maybe she did when I was in the yard getting coal. Or we might have just missed each other.' She frowned for a moment. 'I hope she's home soon.'

She told Will the message she'd come to deliver, carefully pronouncing the names of the two reformatory trustees the women needed to trace.

He hesitated. 'H. Coulson and C. Lamb? I've not heard o' them—but I suppose I could ask around at work.'

'I reckon Frances would appreciate that.'

Will wondered how much Mrs Cherry knew of the enormous row he and Frances had engaged in. It bothered him that Frances might have spoken of it to her friend, but then the duo had been thick as thieves back at the old rectory, making him feel a stranger at times. This latest tension between husband and wife had lasted several days until they'd arrived at a truce. Now, as little as possible was said on any subject that might prove inflammatory.

Will remembered something. 'Did you know it were me who found out you moved here along with the Reverend and his wife? Otherwise Frances would never have found you, Mrs Cherry.' It was time he got a pat on the back for something.

'Aye, Frances said as much,' said Martha with a sigh. 'You're a good man, William Bell.' As she stood up to leave she wagged her finger at him. 'When I saw the two o' you in my kitchen at the rectory all those years back, I knew you were made for each other. Just make sure you don't lose her again.'

Frances

The river path was busy with late afternoon traffic as we arrived back there to search for Little Peggy. Waggons and carts rattled past, additional stall holders had set up and were flogging their wares to folk who were making their way home. I knew then it would be unlikely we'd find the doll. Still, we carefully retraced our steps. Ann and I tried to recall where Peggy had skipped off to previously and might have dropped her toy, as my second daughter was seldom still. We searched diligently in the dried mud at the edges of the path, but of Little Peggy there was no sign. Ann tried to comfort her sister by saying another child must have picked up the doll and would be looking after her; we would make another the next day. Nothing went down well, but I'd had enough. I was exhausted from lugging the baby around as well as trying to make sense of what had gone on earlier.

'That's enough girls. Let's go home now. Your daddy will be worried.'

Ann wasn't keen to go back along Silver Street. 'Its just bad that place,' she moaned, not wrongly. Instead, I led them along a street which lay behind the reformatories. Ann and Peggy were too small to look over the wall up at the grim buildings beyond, but I could if I held my head high. I could just see the grilled rear windows and imagine the luckless boys and girls inside.

Unexpectedly, we came to an opening in the street wall filled by a high barred gate. Behind it, a path led to stone steps at the back of the buildings, similar to those on Silver Street. A door at the top of the steps opened at that same moment, and I stood captivated while three gentlemen emerged in their frock coats and top hats. The first was silver haired with an upright stance and important look, the second was extremely plump, and the third was—well he was the Reverend Theodore Beard. The shockwaves coursed through me. If the Reverend Beard was somehow involved at the reformatory, then why wasn't he aware of Hilda's treatment and acting to stop it? It could only mean one thing—he must be a guilty party himself.

The group was rapidly approaching the street gate, so I urged the children to stand behind me out of sight, while I stood as close to the wall as possible, trying to blend into its ivy covered brickwork. We heard the Reverend bidding his companions a 'good evening,' then the sound of a key in the lock. It wasn't clear if he noticed us as he turned round to shut the gate. I suspected he didn't register our little group. As a woman with three children, we were probably of no significance. Added to that, I was dressed plainly and greying. If Will was to be believed, my searching eyes were the part of me that drew you in, but I kept them averted until the clergyman was well gone. If he did see us, he made nothing of it, but set off briskly towards his home.

'Who was that?' Ann whispered seeing my expression. I put a finger to my mouth. 'Shhh.' The two remaining men were in conversation on the other side of the wall so I wanted to hear every word. The pair wasn't visible, but it was easy to guess which voice was which. The person with a haughty air was almost certainly the silver haired individual.

'Beard's ridiculous little wife confronted me earlier today,' he sniffed. 'Wanted to report there's anxiety in the reformatory. She mentioned the Stott girl.'

I gasped but quickly held myself in check. Mrs Beard had confronted him!

'Unbelievable.' The second voice was squeaky. 'The silly woman came to my surgery too; clearly there was nothing wrong with her, she was just after information. I told her there was absolutely no need to be concerned about our girls.'

'You said nothing else?'

'Do you take me for a fool?'

'Yes Doctor, I'm afraid I do.'

There was silence for a moment so I braced myself for them to emerge through the gate, but *Silver Hair* had more to say. 'The Stott girl was chosen again yesterday. I believe she's popular?'

'Yes, but it shouldn't have been a problem, with her mother living miles away in Hartlepool,' squeaky voice said. 'Someone else must be visiting the child.'

'You can leave that matter with me,' the other said grimly.

I urged my girls to move back further. They shouldn't hear this.

'Who have you got coming in tonight?' *Silver Hair* asked the fat man, but he spoke a name so quietly it was hard to make it out, especially since I was literally shaking by then. After that, the gate began to creak open, making me step back even further into the shadow.

'Those children would be more grateful, if they understood how we afford their new boots and three good meals a day. Schooling too….' The voices trailed off as the men disappeared down the road.

We must have trudged home to Bishopwearmouth through the usual streets that evening. We would have skirted Mowbray Park. The park was normally our highlight. We loved to watch the progress from quarry to public space. It was the landmark that on other days told us we were nearly home, but I remembered none of it that Friday. Only two things were vivid in my mind afterwards: the first was the conversation I'd overheard, the second was meeting Will. My husband had left the house to search for us. When he caught sight of our dejected figures in the distance, he started running. He gently took Mary from me, and with his free hand he took hold of mine; Ann, I noticed then, was already gripping Peggy's. We remained that way until Will briefly released me to open our front door. With tears in my eyes, I realised my husband was back. I had no idea what had happened to change him. All I knew was we were on the same side again, and I'd never been more grateful to have him.

29. New Rules

Will

Next morning, as Will drove his engine past the docks on the early shift, he caught a glimpse of the reformatory looming in the distance. Perhaps his wife was right to be so concerned for the children there. He couldn't bear the thought of his own girls being incarcerated in that building, let alone being abused in some way. Frances had shakily mentioned the conversation she'd overheard and he attempted to make sense of it. He suspected she'd not told him everything, but what was going on with that Hilda girl certainly sounded sinister. He was worried for Frances' safety.

Midmorning when he sat down with some of the other drivers and their firemen to drink his tea, he put the question to them, 'have any o' you heard of a "Mister Coulson" or another called "Lamb" round these parts?' He added that the two individuals would likely be gentlemen or businessmen, not just common folk like most of them. 'That's with the exception of you, obviously.' The last comment was aimed at one of the freight managers in the room with them. They all laughed because the freight manager was a popular fellow. One of the firemen reckoned he'd heard the name Coulson when he worked in the ship yards. Will checked exactly which ship yard it was. He would go and investigate at midday before the afternoon shift began.

The river bank was one solid mass of activity. Men and boys hammered at their blacksmith stalls, ships were in various stages of production. North Sands on the far bank looked similar. In between, the water was packed with vessels vying for position. He hardly knew where to start. He took a chance. Several men were pulling a raft across the muddy beach onto the harder surface. They seemed glad to pause while he asked for their help.

'Do you lads happen to know where to find a Mister Coulson?'

'Harry Coulson? If ye're after a job you'll need to see the foreman, not the owner.' The ship worker indicated a sturdy hut a few yards away. 'But it looks like ye already have work?' He pointed at Will's engine driver's cap. Will nodded his thanks. *'The owner'*, well that sounded about right. He smiled to himself having got some new information to tell Frances.

He'd already picked up his bag ready to go home at the end of the day when the friendly freight manager called him over. 'I've got something as might interest you, Will.' Will followed him intrigued, into one of the yard offices where a clutter of papers was stacked on a table in the middle. The edges of the office contained an incongruous mixture of ledgers, engine parts, clothing and tools. 'This notice came yesterday,' the man said. Will took the paper the man held out for him. It was an invitation for any North Eastern Railway Company worker to improve their literacy. Classes would be held on Tuesday evenings. The notice gave the address and details for taking part.

Will fumbled with the sheet in his hands. 'Thanks mister, but I don't reckon I need much help now. I went to the same class in Hartlepool when we lived there.' He felt his heart sink a little. Perhaps the company was dissatisfied with the way he wrote his weekly reports. He held out the paper to return it to the other's hand.

'Aye lad, you're a good writer. I meant for you to see the name at the end.'

Will did as the freight manager bid him, scanning down to the bottom. Under his sprawling signature the sender had neatly printed: Charles Lamb, Head Engineer, North Eastern Railway Company, Stockton-On-Tees, County Durham.

Ruth

Ruth Beard called a meeting on the Monday afternoon. It was a time when she was free of chapel duties and she knew Martha Cherry could also be present. That just left Frances Bell. After chapel the day before, Ruth sent one of the Sunday school children to Bishopwearmouth with the message. So the three women detectives were all present, around the kitchen table in Martha's domain; three Bell children safely occupied in Martha's sitting room.

Of the women, Martha Cherry seemed the least distressed to Ruth, but then her cook had least to report, only sharing that the bed wetting reported by her friend the laundry woman, had continued.

Ruth went next, reporting her abortive and suspicious conversations with two of the trustees, a doctor and a magistrate. She was careful not to reveal her husband's role, while at the same time hoping the others wouldn't notice her anxiety. The situation could prove embarrassing. Instead, she suggested quickly they should hear what Frances Bell had to say.

Frances was also clearly struggling. In fact she appeared downright uncomfortable when Ruth asked her for the second time to fill them in with any other developments.

'Tell us what you know my dear. Have no fear.'

'Yes, Frances, please tell us everything,' agreed Martha.

In the end with some further encouragement, Frances began to speak, although she told her story piecemeal and in such a faltering manner they both had to continually urge her on. She stuttered when she had to explain seeing the Reverend Beard emerge from building with the others, but she had particular difficulty narrating how the two gentlemen trustees had referred to Ruth. But that part didn't concern the reverend's wife nearly as much Frances seemed to imagine it would. Ruth had already guessed the magistrate's low opinion of her, even if her overweight doctor's words did come as a shock. Instead, there was a much more pressing question to ask.

'Let me get this straight Frances,' Ruth said. 'Theodore was not part of the conversation you overhead between the doctor and magistrate?'

Frances confirmed that was the case, the Reverend Beard had already taken his leave by the time she overheard the threatening conversation at the rear gate of the reformatory. Ruth took the information in, fidgeting in her chair for a moment. Then she took a deep breath.

'In that case I will tell you something which I've kept from you.' She turned to them both, and admitted, 'Theodore is the fifth trustee at the reformatory.' She looked back and forth between the women detectives. They'd done well, she thought, to conceal their gasps.

'I reckon it's as good a time as any for one of my fresh currant buns,' Martha declared decisively, leaving the table to fetch them. 'We need a break.' She busied herself pouring each of them some tea and handing the cakes out.

'Now,' said Martha when Ruth was feeling calmer. 'What shall we do next?'

Frances had apparently pulled herself together too. She told them about Henry Coulson, who her husband had discovered was a ship owner, then about the railway engineer, explaining how Will had discovered the latter's name.

Martha remarked that Will had been busy since she'd seen him three days ago. 'He's turned into quite the detective, just like us,' she said, lightening the mood in the kitchen, making Frances blush. Frances explained how she'd had plenty to do with Charles Lamb in the past and now she realised she *had* known his name when she worked for him at Kirkdunham House, just forgotten it. She told them she preferred not to remember her time at that place, before she went to the rectory.

'Anyway….' Frances went on, she felt certain that the railway engineer would know what to do. He'd helped her before, twice. Her task would be to write to him without delay. The other women agreed it sounded a good plan, but Martha said she felt they should also be watching the rear door to the reformatory, despite being aware it wasn't a helpful suggestion, being impossible to keep up. Ruth, for her part, felt herself blush as she vowed to keep a close eye on her husband's comings and goings that week. Neither Ruth, nor Martha it seemed, wanted to remind Frances of the threat to her safety if she dared to visit Hilda again. They knew nothing would stop her.

Frances

'A penny for your thoughts,' I said wearily, pulling myself up against the iron bedstead. It was Thursday night, the day before I would return to the reformatory. We were both restless.

'I worry about you, and I keep thinking what if our girls were in that awful building instead of Hilda.' Will sat up next to me gripping my clammy palm in his.

I agreed that didn't bear thinking about, but neither did Hilda and the other inmates deserve the treatment they were getting, assuming our suspicions were right. My voice sounded shaky. 'That's why I have to help Hilda. It's a terrible thing to have no one on your side. The girl needs a friend, with her mother being so far away.' I knew that from bitter experience, when I was so lonely in that first housemaid job I'd made a friend of the English Boy in Africa, a fictional friend.

I was scared though; afraid something might happen so Hilda would have no-one again. I was worried for our own children's safety too. I think Will could tell.

'Look. Tomorrow you'll leave the girls with Martha Cherry while you visit this Hilda, won't you?'

'Aye, that's what we women decided.'

'Good. After visiting, you must go straight back to Mrs Cherry and the children, but don't leave again to come home. It's not safe for you to walk home alone. Wait for me instead. I'll call for you at six o'clock when I've finished my shift and we can all come home together.' He waited for my response, but I didn't speak again. Gradually, I felt my breathing become more even.

'Get some sleep now, you'll need it for tomorrow,' he said more gently.

The steps felt steeper than usual as I climbed them with one of the mothers. It was the same woman whose daughter had told them Hilda was 'chosen'.

'It worries me what we'll find today,' I murmured as the great doors creaked open.

Her glance told me she felt the same.

We didn't have long to find out. Instead of the heavy-set warden perching absurdly on her stool, a skinny warden was seated at a small table inside the door of the visiting room. In front of her was a note book and pen.

'Full name of inmate to be visited?' she barked without looking up.

The unexpected change of routine threw my companion for a moment. She faltered, so I spoke up from behind her. 'We've not had to give those details here before.' We'd already given our children's names to the warden who let us in at the main door, so they could to be brought from the exercise yard.

'New rules,' said the thin faced woman, unsmiling.

'Visitor's name and relationship to inmate?' she barked again.

We chose seats as far from the doorkeeper as possible, sitting down nervously on the hard chairs, to wait for our children to be brought in. My companion had turned pale. What was going through her mind, I could only guess.

Our thin faced guard reminded me of someone. I racked my brain to think who it was. Finally it came to me. It was the housemaid who'd taken such a dislike to me when I was nineteen. It was the same sour look. I considered if it might actually be her but this version was too old. This woman looked as if she'd spent a whole lifetime practicing being fierce.

Thin face continued to scratch in her notebook. It grated on my ears like chalk on a blackboard. To take my mind off the waiting, I tried to remember something pleasant. I thought of Will wrapping his strong arms around me before he set off for the freight yard that morning, with the promise he would see me later. I thought how we would walk home together that evening. The girls would race on ahead, their elongated shadows dancing with them. Normally nature would spring to mind too. Perhaps the buff tailed bumble bees busy on a patch of wild comfrey at the edge of the quarry. I was glad the park developers had missed that remnant of the past. But on the way past Mowbray Park that Friday I'd paid no heed to the bees, my mind fully occupied on Hilda and what I must tell her. I had another thought while I waited for the girl to be brought in, perhaps Will would bring news from Charles Lamb later that evening, to say he had also noticed the sinister happenings and would act soon.

Nothing was working. No pleasant memories or images were sufficient to quash the feeling of doom those grey walls and dirty windows provoked. *Thin face* had stopped scratching so it was quiet. That was something. I imagined how it must be to work in such a place, or even be imprisoned there. I shuddered. What or who were they turning the children into?

When eventually the heavy-set warden ushered Hilda into the visiting room, I saw the change. For the first time I saw a look of defiance, even a flash of anger in the girl's face. It was directed first at her large escort, then at the skinny warden at her table. It was hard to tell whom she hated most.

By contrast, the girl took her toffees from me with a quick smile. I pulled myself together abruptly. I had a mission to attend to, a message to give her.

'I hope you're well dear, I missed you last week,' I said in a loud enough voice for the doorkeeper to hear. Then I spoke softly. 'I know what's happening Hilda. I know what they're doing to you.' She glanced at me sideways. 'And I'm going to get it stopped.' I made sure she had eye contact with me, so she would know I was serious. After that I reverted to the normal line of conversation, at a normal volume, telling the girl what was happening in the outside world or asking what she'd been doing, even knowing she wouldn't tell me.

When the skinny warden rang the bell early, I'd long since run out of subjects to talk about, so was partly relieved. My eyes widened when her large colleague came in to collect the two girls. The woman took hold of Hilda, but the child was having none of it, snatching her arm away. My heart beat a little faster, but the warden made no sign she would slap Hilda or punish her. It seemed almost as if the girl had some sort of power over her, although I couldn't think how that might happen.

Her new behaviour occupied me all the way along the passageway, down the stone steps and out onto Silver

Lane. I barely noticed the shady looking character waiting nearby.

30. Pursued

Frances

I saw him again out of the corner of my eye as I turned at the end of Silver Street. The same man had been hovering outside the reformatory as I emerged with my head in a cloud. It was his peculiar manner that alerted me. Hands in pockets; a kind of slouching; an attempt to blend into the wall. Even after weaving in and out of the usual backstreets to reach the Beards', he was still there behind, not near, but he had me in his view. If I picked up speed he did too. Rather than take a dark alley as normal, I took a longer route, moving as swiftly as I could without breaking into a run, my heart beating loudly in my breast. Should I hide somewhere? Or divert into the chapel? It may be locked though, and what protection would it give me if he followed me inside? No, I would just get to Martha's as quickly as my legs would take me. I could see the house ahead—I just had to reach it to be out of danger. Without stopping to shut the garden gate behind me, I rapped loudly on Martha's door and said a quick prayer. Thankfully she came out swiftly, worry written all over when she saw my red face. Feeling safe at last, I spun round boldly to check. The man had continued slouching past. I stared at his back. There was no doubt in my mind he'd noted the Beards' house, along with Martha's side entrance.

'Would you know him again?' Martha asked biting her lip.

'I'd know him by his walk.'

The street door firmly closed, Martha led me into the kitchen. 'The children are happy enough playing in the back yard, so just get your breath back.' She put a welcome mug of coffee in front of me. 'Now let's think it through sensibly.'

'He pursued me from the reformatory,' I groaned. 'What about my children? They could be in danger.'

'He saw you come here, Frances. He doesn't know where you *live*. Anyway Will's picking you all up, he'll protect you.'

I doubted even a combination of Will's wiry frame and determination would be a match for my pursuer's solid weight. Still, it was comforting to hear Martha's reassurance, so I let her persuade me.

Will

He was feeling positive as he strolled away from the freight yard. He was used to driving an engine in all weathers, but had to admit it was an advantage to finish a shift as dry as when he began it; it was better for his knees especially. For once, Will wasn't even particularly bothered by the heightened odours coming off the river or from the town's privies, due to the summery weather.

Frances had explained how to find the Beards' modest home. She'd told him to knock firmly on the side door so Martha Cherry would hear him from the kitchen. He chuckled to himself, thinking it would be just like old times at the rear of the rectory of St Thomas', except of course that door had a bell. The other thing putting him in a good mood was that he and Frances were together again after the row. He was even looking forward to the walk home across town with Frances and the girls, which was such an ordinary thing.

He found the place with no trouble. Ann answered the door, with Peggy hard on her heels, 'Daddy, I'm right glad you're here.' But it wasn't the normal excitement from his eldest daughter he'd come to expect when arriving home, this was something different. Something was wrong. He followed them through a small sitting room, into the larger kitchen. It looked as if Mrs Cherry had served the girls with supper, which he'd interrupted.

'Ma's disappeared,' Ann cried.

Ruth

Ruth Beard was also engaged in the act of following someone that Friday. She was trailing Theodore. Earlier on the Friday afternoon he'd been at the reformatory, doing his rounds, checking on the boys' spiritual wellbeing. He'd told his wife as much when he returned at sometime after four o'clock. It was at a quarter past five, when he told her he must go out again that she grew suspicious and followed him. The good thing about trailing Theodore was he was easy to distinguish in the distance with his red hair and tall frame. She on the other hand was tiny, and therefore almost invisible. The difficulty was the relative length of their legs. Ruth had to hurry in a most unladylike way to match his pace.

She'd followed Theodore the previous afternoon too so she was getting quite proficient. On that occasion, the Reverend had been to visit the Methodist minister. Still out of breath from her exertions, she'd watched him enter the large house adjacent to the Methodist chapel. The whole thing was noteworthy because the two men had never agreed on anything, to her knowledge, yet this meeting had appeared civil as they exchanged greetings at the door. She'd noticed that much before slipping away.

On her latest pursuit, at a quarter to six on the Friday, they were clearly approaching Silver Street, but instead of continuing on that route, Theodore, with his wife not far behind, diverted behind the reformatories. He must be heading for the rear entrance where Frances had overheard the trustees' disturbing conversation last week. The route seemed busy at that time of day with rich and poor alike. Gentlemen were heading home in their Broughams; other folk were off in their gigs to wherever they would spend the evening; while a donkey cart was being driven too fast. Ruth found a moment to cross safely, keeping to the far edge of the pavement, almost parallel with her husband on the other side. He paused when he reached a tall gate. It was obviously the rear entrance, but he didn't proceed through it. Instead, he paced up and down, or stood, moving from one foot to the other, waiting. Man and wife remained in their positions for perhaps half an hour, although it felt a lot longer to Ruth. She longed to take the weight off her legs. Instead, she stood quite still in the entrance to a blacksmith's premises a few yards down the lane. She prayed Theodore wouldn't look across the lane too carefully. Eventually when she was wondering whether to call it a day, a carriage pulled up almost opposite her, from which a short built gentleman alighted with some difficulty. Ruth recognised him as one of the town councillors. The little man nodded to Theodore, who was standing still at that point rather than pacing, opened the gate and was let in promptly at the heavy door at the top of the steps. It must have been what her husband was waiting for, because after that he turned and strode home furiously.

Frances

I'd only stepped out to fetch water for Martha Cherry. It was the least I could do. She was busy preparing supper for the girls knowing it would be their bed time by the time we'd walked back to Bishopwearmouth. I'd not previously noticed the narrow passage behind the pump, a low brick wall separating it from the back yard.

Two hands grabbed my arms roughly from behind.

'If ye know what's good for the children, ye'll follow me now,' hissed a man's voice. He held me in such a grip it was impossible to see his face, but I was in no doubt it was the same individual who'd pursued me earlier. I didn't argue. Looking up at the house, I could see no-one at the windows. Putting the pail down carefully I slid over the wall after him.

Not for one moment did I believe it an idle threat. My children would be in danger if I disobeyed him. Why, the girls had only just left the yard and gone inside to play. He could have kidnapped any one of them. My mouth was dry. With everything in me screaming that it was a bad idea, I followed him into a quiet backstreet. He turned then, coming close enough to feel his sour breath. I waited for the pain, but instead he grabbed me by the arm again pushing me ahead of him.

'Walk.' He slouched behind me as he had earlier that afternoon, but closer now, seemingly making no attempt to hide our situation from the few people we passed. They would think him my controlling husband, with no reason for them to intervene. At each turning he gave a hissed instruction. I didn't recognise the streets, or the people, who looked of my captor's ilk—far from virtuous. Even so, I felt a strange calmness.

'You won't get away with this,' I said at one point. 'My husband will find us.'

Trying to keep my wits about me, I looked for landmarks that might help me find the way back. We wove rapidly in and out of shadowy passageways shaded from the last of the afternoon sun, past filthy dwellings and equally dirty children. Sweat was trickling down between my breasts. I tripped on something baked into the mud so he swore behind me.

'Keep going.'

The docks weren't far away. I could sense the repellent smell, but still gasped with surprise when we emerged from an alley into Silver Street. So he was taking me back to the reformatory. At least he wasn't dumping me in the water. Not yet anyway.

The building loomed large as we skirted the front of it. I searched frantically for anyone that might see us ascend the stone steps together and disappear within, but the pavement was empty save for one shoeless beggar boy.

The huge warden, complete with the usual bunch of keys, let us in quickly. She must have been expecting us. I stood in the dark while the two of them conferred quietly out of earshot, before the warden pushed me roughly in the direction of the visiting room. But we'd soon taken too many turns to be going there. We climbed a short flight of stairs then descended again. It was such a maze of corridors, the idea of finding my way back to the main door struck me as impossible. I'd already left my sense of calm outside that enormous wooden entrance. Instead there was the dread that enveloped me each time I entered the high stone walls, but a thousand times worse. The small room we eventually entered, had no window at low level looking onto a yard, just a small door leading to somewhere unknown. Yet this was clearly a visiting room of sorts, with pairs of chairs in the middle. I imagined the same thin warden as earlier, seated at the table by the door, the notebook and pen before her. Surely they wouldn't be bringing Hilda in again?

'Sit.' The heavy woman pushed me towards the chairs. Then she left, surprisingly nimbly, locking the door securely after her. It took just seconds to understand I'd been imprisoned in the reformatory.

The hot sweat from my rapid walk under duress was replaced by a cold one. I shivered under my damp blouse. The room was cool, probably due to the building's thick walls. The stink of the town's waste hadn't penetrated either, but the space had an odour of its own. I tried to identify it. It was the smell of fear.

31. The Sneeze

Frances

Martha would tell me to consider my situation calmly. My husband would say the same. The thought of Will warmed me for a moment. He would come to find me soon, but would it be in time? Still, I must be ready for whatever they had in store for me. I moved to the door, checking it. It was locked as expected. I flopped down at the warden's table, seeing the visiting room from a gatekeeper's perspective. The wall facing me had barred windows high up near the ceiling. That must be the side of the reformatory visible from the back street, where I'd eavesdropped on the threatening conversation. So this was what the silver haired magistrate had meant when he said, 'leave it to me.' He meant 'leave *her* to me.' No doubt once he knew I'd been captured he would decide my fate. It was strange the wardens hadn't simply prevented me from leaving earlier that afternoon.

I picked up one of the chairs to feel its weight, practicing to see if I could use it to protect myself. Then I waited, my weapon at the ready, fully expecting the magistrate to arrive to deal with me, now he had me at his mercy. After a while when nobody came, I turned my attention to the room again. The windows weren't an option for escape, being too high. I had no means to climb up, nor the will to drop down to ground level outside. I considered the second, narrower door which probably led to a cupboard, but maybe not? I leapt up and rushed over to it, grasping the handle. The hinges groaned with disapproval, until I was peering down a corridor. Why hadn't I thought to check it before? No-one had bothered to lock it!

The passageway was wider than its narrow exit from the visiting room, otherwise I could imagine someone like the huge warden struggling to pass along it. The route was well lit from windows on one side, making it far lighter than the corridor leading from the main Silver Street entrance. I found myself tiptoeing gently downhill, before emerging into a room of a similar size to the visiting room. It was a study, much like Reverend Beard's office at the rectory, except for a lack of book shelves. A clock in one corner read five minutes to six o'clock. No-one seemed to be around at that hour in the late afternoon, so I kept going, deeper into new territory, peering through each door carefully before proceeding.

Naturally, in such a place, it would only be so long before I encountered a locked door, but this part of the building seemed dedicated to staff rather than inmates. After passing through another room, furnished with several easy chairs, I spotted the large warden ahead of me in a kitchen area, helping herself to the sort of food I doubted Hilda would ever see. I was hungry myself, having had no appetite that morning with all the anxiety about visiting Hilda. Little did I know then, how real the danger would turn out to be. By the warden's unbothered attitude, I guessed no-one had yet reported me missing. Part of me was intrigued by my unofficial tour of the building, but it could only be so long before they discovered me. Still, for the time being, luck was on my side and with the warden so engrossed in her illicit meal, I was able to creep past the kitchen into another passageway, this time unlit. Beyond that through a door, was a square chamber, with a large bed against one wall to my right, a small table holding an unlit candlestick, and one hard chair. A screen stood folded in the far corner.

Having got used to my free run, it was almost startling to find a firmly locked door on the wall ahead. I must have reached another part of the reformatory. I thought about retracing my steps to the kitchen to try another exit, but the heavy warden would probably notice. With nowhere else to go, I sat on the bed to consider what I'd learned. A grilled window in the locked door had revealed a hallway beyond with several exits off of it, including a strong outside door, which apparently lead to freedom. It was probably the entrance the trustees used the previous Friday. The window in the locked door was the only means of natural light in the bed chamber but I could still see my legs trembling.

Just then there were urgent voices, followed by sounds of a key being inserted into a lock. Fortunately there was a decent gap under the bed, so giving no thought to tearing my skirt or getting splinters from the boards, I dived under it. It was the magistrate with the skinny warden in his wake. The silver haired man was shouting. He couldn't believe how it was possible to lose this ridiculous Bell woman, when she should have been securely locked in, pending his decision. The man appeared to think all women ridiculous if they had a mind of their own. I was happy to be put in the same category as Mrs Beard, whom he also thought ridiculous. I held my breath and prayed they wouldn't search under the bed. The skinny woman whined that she couldn't help it if the other warden was such a fool not to lock both doors. I should have been concentrating on my survival, but that didn't prevent me reflecting how nasty people were so quick to pass the blame.

They didn't check under the bed. Instead, their voices disappeared in the direction of the kitchen. Perhaps I should have felt sorry for the large warden eating her supper, but I couldn't find it in me.

'Did you fail to lock this door, too?' Skinny barked at her colleague when they'd returned to my range of hearing.

'I did not,' the large woman told her.

'Then where's the Bell woman, you fool?'

The magistrate was no longer with them, presumably he'd stayed in the kitchen or gone to his study, but he'd clearly given orders for the wardens to continue their search. What worried me more was I was just yards away from the silver haired trustee, with no means of escaping from the hard floor beneath me.

I'd found a better position, on my back, staring up at the bed springs. Although not in the least bit comfortable, lying there with nothing to do made me sleepy, especially since Will and I had slept badly the previous night. Perhaps I dropped off, because suddenly the bed springs were a lot closer to my face. Someone was on the mattress above me. I twisted my head slightly to be confronted by a pair of hanging legs, not quite reaching the floor. They were trousered legs with expensive boots. New voices sounded, not those of the magistrate or wardens. One was the squeaky sound of the doctor, who must have just entered the room; the other words came from the man on the bed, whose voice I didn't recognise.

'I do apologise for the long wait,' the squeaky voice was saying. 'May I suggest we rearrange your visit for tomorrow, the same time, at half past six o'clock?'

The other asked what the problem was, as he may not be free on the Saturday. He didn't sound at all happy.

I felt sick to the stomach, taking every ounce of willpower to keep quiet.

'Once again, I do apologise,' the doctor squeaked. 'Of course in that case we'll refund your donation, but unfortunately we've have an incident. We have a lunatic loose in the building.'

The idea that I might have saved one of the reformatory girls from this awful man's unwanted attention that evening caused me to exhale with pleasure. It could have been the upwards flow of air which dislodged some dust. Alternatively it could have been the man redistributing his weight above me, to send a fragment of straw down from the mattress. Whichever it was, I sneezed.

Will

The child's words didn't intrude into her father's cheerful mood immediately, not until Martha Cherry suggested the girls go back to their supper, so she could talk to him. As she turned to face him, Will saw the old cook was only keeping the situation calm for his children—underneath, she was frightened.

'I'm so sorry Will, I didn't notice Frances was gone immediately, being busy at the stove.' Martha was wringing her hands.

'How could she just vanish?' he muttered.

Will listened to Martha's story standing in the centre of her sitting room. She perched on her sofa, but he couldn't bring himself to sit. Frances had been pursued from the reformatory. Then, after stepping into the yard to fetch water from the pump, she had completely disappeared.

'I told her to wait here to keep her safe,' he groaned, the first signs of panic in his eyes. He turned towards the front door. 'I'll have to look for her. Can the girls stay here?'

'Will. Wait,' said Martha putting her hand on his arm. 'Let's think this through. We don't want the girls to misplace their father too.'

It was then he understood the danger they might all be in. He agreed Martha should call the reverend's wife downstairs first, but when the large cook returned far too slowly for Will, she was more flustered than he'd ever seen her.

'Mrs Beard's disappeared too—and there's no sign of the Reverend Beard. It's so unusual for…'

He put his hands up to stop her. 'Look, I'm going to search the streets. Frances may have had an accident. You say she disappeared from the back yard? I'll be back as soon as I can.'

He scoured the streets at the rear of the Beards' house first, fanning out further and further as systematically as he could. It meant he had to keep retracing his steps but it would be worth the effort if he found her. With his heart in his mouth, he examined every side alley in case she'd been accosted and thrown there. There was absolutely no sign of his wife. The street's inhabitants were rough looking, poor. Most people he asked simply scowled at him or laughed. He would normally avoid such places with every bone of his body. He enquired at a market stall which was being dismantled in one of the wider streets. There was no point describing the grey dress his wife was wearing when he left home that morning. Most women would be in the same washed out colours. Even so, they might have noticed a woman being coerced? But no, not one person admitted seeing a smallish woman of about thirty years of age with mousy hair, with or without a dubious looking companion. He would have to return to the Beards' house without her. Unless,—unless his wife had been taken back to the reformatory. It wasn't a comforting thought.

32. The Punishment Room

Frances

My sneeze produced a reaction. The short legged man jumped off the bed and ran to the door yelling to be let out. All previous bravado and power had disappeared, with the guilty man revealing his pathetic self underneath. The doctor couldn't help himself either; he cursed the silly man, thus ensuring he lost his custom from then onwards. Despite my predicament, I smiled, realising that was a good thing. Then I felt the bed springs descend towards me again, with a good deal of puffing above me from the doctor. His hand appeared, vainly exploring the space under the bed trying to grab hold of me, but I wriggled to the far side.

'Come out you foolish woman,' he told me when he realised his quest was fruitless. Doubtless, his protruding belly prevented him from bending down, so he had no means to make me obey. But the magistrate did. When he and the two wardens arrived, summoned by their customer's hammering on the door to be released, I was dragged out, and then pushed unceremoniously onto the bed. I found myself resisting, just as Hilda had done earlier that afternoon with the large warden. My teeth found the magistrate's thumb.

'OW! You bitch.' He struck me across the mouth. 'Now stay there woman. Calm down before I do something a lot worse.' A look of pure contempt spread across his reddening face. 'What did the Stott girl tell you, you interfering bitch? And what were you doing at the Reverend Beard's House? Did you expect him to help? Were you going to pass on what the girl told you?' He spat out the words like venom. 'Well you've made a big mistake.'

I gasped. So that was why I'd been brought back to Silver Street. This was about the red headed clergyman. The magistrate was concerned I would inform on them. So *was* the Reverend Beard involved in any sinister goings on, or wasn't he?

'Hilda said nothing,' I cried, 'despite what you're subjecting her to. Who was destined for that revolting creature tonight? Was it Hilda again?' I looked across the room at the cowering little man, whom nobody had yet let out. 'You won't get away with it,' I screamed.

'Oh be quiet woman, nobody else knows anything about it, except you, and perhaps Mrs Beard. What have you been telling her? You'll vanish completely soon so your secret will remain with you.'

'Where shall we put her, sir?' asked the large warden.

'The punishment room will do very well for now.' He sucked his injured thumb crossly.

The three of us proceeded with difficulty, with me resisting using every trick you can imagine. On balance though, the determination of the two wardens plus their years of experience handling wriggling inmates, proved too much for me. They half dragged, half pushed me back via the visiting room where I'd first been held, through a locked door, which I noted the large warden forgot to lock again, then almost immediately down a wide flight of stairs to a lower floor. Making a pretense of continuing to struggle I used the opportunity to look around. We were passing through a boys' section. Classrooms were visible on the right hand side of a long walkway, with several male inmates in similar uniform to Hilda's, sweeping floors or scrubbing desks. Perhaps it was punishment. Crying could be heard through doors on our left. The nameplates meant nothing to me, while the shrill voices from inside might have belonged to girls or boys.

'But those are just children,' I shouted.

My captors laughed. 'How else will they learn to behave?'

My own turn came later when they opened an unmarked door. The two women captors gave a cruel shove, making me cascade down a flight of wooden steps into the dark. There was the grating of a bolt being slid across above me. Lying bruised and shaken at the bottom, I latched onto to the slim hope that when Will came to rescue me, he wouldn't need a key—he would only have to release the bolt. I'd memorized the route we'd taken to the punishment block, and I would be ready for him.

All resolution disappeared once my eyes adjusted to the gloom. It was just possible to appreciate the awful confines of my prison. The meagre half-light leaked through a small grate high up in the stone work, presumably at ground level outside, through a crisscross of webs and other debris. The room was so small I could have crossed the floor in two strides if I had the inclination, but it was foul. From years of soiling, I guessed. No pot was provided. It wouldn't be long before I would have to add to the mix. There was no water, no food. Not that I would trust any of it. I imagined the children locked in that prison even for an hour or two. It must scar them for life.

Moving stiffly back to the top step, away from the cellar's filth, I found a draft under the door diluted the pungent smell slightly. With my mouth still aching from the magistrate's blow, I leaned wearily against the brickwork, my ear to the wood of the door frame, to listen for my husband's voice.

Will

He arrived breathlessly at the imposing building, stood at the bottom of the stone steps and wondered again why on earth his wife would go through the heavy oak door willingly each week. He took the steps two at a time, rang the bell and waited. With no windows at the front of the reformatory, he could only guess what was going on inside. No-one came, and when he'd decided that no-one would, he retraced his steps onto Silver Lane. Spotting a fair haired youth unloading a waggon on the opposite side, Will ran over to talk to him. Perhaps he'd seen something earlier? Had a woman been forced up the steps an hour ago, or even gone of her own accord? The youth shook his head. He'd been elsewhere an hour ago.

A young mother with infants in tow was passing by, so Will tried asking her too, desperate by then. His voice was hoarse. 'Might you have seen a woman climbing those steps about an hour ago?' She hadn't. His heart sank. He was up against a brick wall, literally. Crossing back to look up at the grim facade he knew he was running out of options.

'Are you in there Frances?' He must have uttered the words out loud.

'The woman you're seeking went up the steps with a man. The pair o' them was let in by a fierce warden quick as you please.'

Will spun round to see who was speaking. It was a child's high pitch, from low down on the pavement. A beggar boy looked up at him. The ragged creature looked to be around Ann's age, dressed in torn breeches and half a shirt. His bare feet were brown with grime from the road. Streaks of coal dust told Will he must spend time by the docks too, wherever the most profit was, he supposed.

'When was this, son?'

'Just before that waggon came.' The child pointed to the fair haired youth's pony and cart across the road. 'I'll have a penny now if you don't mind?' His eyes held Will's, testing him.

'You can have two if you're right. How do I know you're telling the truth?' Will crouched next to him to put them at the same level. He didn't trust urchin boys as a rule, but this was no normal day.

'The woman was shorter than you, but curvy here.' He gestured to his chest. 'He was pushing her and she looked red in the face—but she still smiled at me with her eyes. She was kind.'

It had to be Frances. Who else would show such humanity? Will reached into his pockets to drop some pennies in the upturned cap. This boy was wasted on the street. He should have been a detective with those powers of observation.

'What about this man? Do you remember him?'

'He has the look of a toad. I've seen him lots before. He was here earlier by the steps, before he followed the same woman you're after.'

'You're a good boy.' Those were the words every child wanted to hear weren't they? He had certainly craved them.

'Thanks mister.' He indicated towards the great wooden door. 'They don't let you in there, but if thcy do let you in, they don't let you out,' he said sagely. 'An' if they don't like you, they put you in the punishment room, down the bottom.' The boy shuddered.

'You've been in there yourself then?'

'Nay, but me brother has. What will you do now?'

'Reckon I'll try to get in round the back.'

'Aye mister, there's a drain pipe. That's how me brother Jack 'scaped last year.'

Will regarded the animated face. A simple smile from Frances had loosened this street boy's tongue. In return, the ragged child had been more help than anyone else he'd spoken to; had even proved a friend. He worried about him. Shouldn't the boy be heading home to his family? For the first time Will wished he was in a position to do more. He nodded his thanks. Because of the child's help he could be pretty certain his wife was imprisoned within those walls. Gaining entry himself was of course another matter entirely.

33. Dutch Courage

Ruth

Ruth Beard slipped into her house from the rear yard. Theodore would ask awkward questions if she arrived at the front door shortly after he did. She was still trying to work out her husband's part in the unfolding drama. What had he hoped to achieve by his vigil behind the reformatory? Deep in thought, she wasn't expecting to find Frances' girls still in the kitchen, especially with the eldest in tears being comforted by Martha Cherry. After listening to their story she knew it was time to confront her husband.

She found Theodore in his study still wearing his hat and coat, rummaging through the papers on his desk.

'Ruth my dear, is something wrong?'

She wasted no time coming to the point.

'Theodore, when you go to the Ragged School or reformatory in your capacity as chaplain, do you give spiritual comfort to a girl named Hilda Stott? She would be about eleven years of age. I gather she's much distressed.'

The Reverend removed his hat and sagged into his chair. A broad blush crept into his cheeks until they took on the same colour as his beard. He admitted the girl's name was familiar.

'And you have concerns?' Ruth persisted.

He sighed. 'Yes I do worry about her welfare, about other girls too.'

Ruth Beard also gave a sigh, but hers was one of relief.

The churchman explained how the Methodist minister was equally uneasy about the running of the reformatory. He'd met with his previous antagonist only yesterday to discuss it. They'd reached the same conclusion: the best way to acquire evidence was to wait outside the reformatory walls, at six o'clock the following day.

Ruth frowned.

'So that's where you've been this afternoon? ' The slight deception slid easily from her lips. This wasn't the time to feel guilty for lesser sins. He nodded, reddening still further while telling her he believed a member of the town council had visited to satisfy his base desires. Theodore described the extra visits he'd made himself, but his were out of concern for the children. 'You have to believe me, Ruth.' She listened carefully, and then told her husband they needed to discuss another matter too, one which may turn out to be just as serious. She seated herself opposite him at his desk before asking him if he remembered Fanny, their maid from the rectory. As soon as she'd jogged his memory, the answer was a reluctant 'yes'.

'She's known as Frances now, Frances Bell, and she's in danger.'

Ruth explained everything to the Reverend Beard. The more she told him, the more she was confident he wasn't personally involved in anything untoward. She outlined the three women's detective work, omitting to say she'd searched through his desk. She believed her husband was telling the truth when he said he had no knowledge of Frances recently. In fact, not since she left their employ in Northallerton years back. He certainly had no idea she was living in Sunderland with her family, despite her attending one of his sermons at the chapel, and in particular, hadn't heard she'd been visiting Hilda Stott.

'And now she's disappeared. Someone's taken her from the rear yard of our house, of all places. We have to find her, Theodore, and urgently.'

The clergyman stood up stiffly, moving across his study to stand at the street window, beckoning for his wife to join him. She took his arm as he pointed to a piece of fenced-off ground some fifty yards away. 'That's where I saw him this afternoon,' he said frowning,—'the magistrate's henchman.'

'Woolly'

At six o'clock that same Friday evening, Charles Lamb and Henry Coulson were in the Dog and Pheasant, chewing over the letter which Lamb had received from Frances Bell.

'And you trust this woman's judgement, Woolly?' Harry Coulson asked.

Lamb said he did.

They agreed that what she suspected was unsurprising but a matter of extreme concern.

'We have limited powers,' Coulson said unnecessarily, digging a fork into his portion of steak pie. 'Can we assume the Reverend is in on this caper?' They both hoped not. They would need Beard's compliance to put pressure on the magistrate and doctor, but even with a vote of three trustees it would be unpredictable. After all who would believe the word of a ship owner or railway engineer over two esteemed pillars of the community? Of course it would be far worse with the clergyman involved as well.

'When I'm a member of parliament it will be a different matter,' said Coulson, which Lamb could only concur with. As an MP, his friend would be able to demand more respect. The two men were also in agreement about the urgency of any intervention. It wouldn't be morally right to delay. They decided on one more drink to give themselves Dutch courage.

Will

Now he could be certain his wife was being held inside, Will began skirting the building, looking for possible entry points. Frances had heard those trustees in conversation at the rear gate, so that's where he would try next. He peered over the street wall as he went. It was one advantage of being tall. There were windows on that side of the grim building but he guessed they would be too high even for him to reach without a ladder, while he didn't think he was supple enough to go up the drainpipe. Maybe after dark he could attempt it? The sun was losing its heat but it would still be a while before dusk. A moment of panic seized him. What if he wasn't in time? He was desperate to hold Frances in his arms and tell her she was safe.

The tall barred gate in the perimeter wall was surprisingly unlocked, perhaps for an expected out of hours visitor? Well, he would be visiting himself soon— authorized or not. He pulled himself up to his full height of five feet nine inches, pushed open the gate then marched purposely up the short slope. He noted the door had no keyhole outside, was about to pull the bell cord, not really expecting it to be answered, when the door opened abruptly. A small gentleman brushed past him, rushing down the steps as fast as his stumpy legs would carry him, down the slope towards the street gate. When Will turned back to the building, an individual with a huge midriff stood scrutinizing him in the doorway.

'Who the hell are you?' the man squeaked.

'William Bell, I'm looking for me wife. I believe she's in there.' He waved at the place in front of him.

'We don't have wives here,' said the other dismissively. He looked about to shut the door, so Will thrust himself forward, pushing past the man's belly into a substantial hallway with several closed doors leading from it.

'Just let me see me wife, Frances Bell,' he insisted looking as menacing as he could.

323

'You'll regret this,' the stout man whined.

'Well we'll see about that, Doctor,' a third voice said firmly. 'For your sake, I hope the man's wrong and that you are not guilty of holding Frances Bell against her will. I can personally vouch for William Bell, and his wife.'

Will stared open mouthed at the pair of newcomers poised on the threshold. He knew the voice. It was the railway engineer Charles Lamb. The other must be the ship owner Henry Coulson, who was surprisingly young and was lurching slightly. Following Will's example, the younger man pushed his way through the open door, knocking the doctor aside once more, with the engineer hard on his heels.

Ruth

Ruth dashed downstairs to explain Theodore's plan to Martha Cherry. The worry on the cook's face was palpable. This whole affair seemed to be ageing her friend. Ruth patted the floury hand to reassure her, despite the heavy weight of doubt she could feel in her own chest. Then the Beards left their house together.

Out on the street, it was just as impossible to keep up with the Reverend's pace. He didn't slow for her, so every few steps she had to run to catch up, but it meant they covered the ground rapidly. Before she knew it they were behind the reformatory. The gate was swinging open which Theodore said was unusual. Clearly someone had been in a hurry going through it, but whether in or out, was unknown.

The entrance door was thrust open when they rang the bell. It was the magistrate.

'Ah. Beard. Perhaps *you* can bring some sense of decorum to the situation.'

The hallway was full of humanity. That must be Frances' husband who was pacing up and down, demanding to know where his wife was—his eldest daughter Ann was the image of him, with her dark curls and lanky frame. The doctor was nursing a bloody nose and to her shame Ruth found it a pleasing sight. A young man in gentleman's attire with a damaged fist, which she deduced had been in contact with the doctor's face, was being restrained by another—a rugged older gentleman of approaching fifty years old. Both smelled strongly of alcohol. The magistrate seemed to be distancing himself from the general clamour, as if none of it was down to him; as if the hubbub was upsetting his sensibilities. It reminded her of a playground brawl, with the magistrate playing the virtuous onlooker. There had been one or two scuffles like that at her chapel school, before she managed to instil good behaviour into the boys. Now in the rear entrance hall of the reformatory, she almost had to put her hands over her ears to protect them from a similar noise.

But where was Frances? Neither the doctor nor the magistrate was admitting the poor woman was in the building.

'Can't you *do* something, Theodore,' she asked him silently, as the commotion showed no sign of abating. But it was the rugged gentleman Charles Lamb, who had the presence of mind to take charge of the situation.

'Gentlemen, hear me out please.' He stepped into the centre of the hallway with his arms raised. 'Yesterday I received a letter from one Frances Bell, a trustworthy woman previously known to me, advising she had concerns about goings on in this building.' He had everyone's reluctant attention. 'Now as respected trustees of this Reformatory and Ragged School, it must be our duty to investigate.'

Charles Lamb was astute, Ruth could tell. He'd appealed to their egos while getting straight to the point. Whilst he continued, his fellow trustees grudgingly kept their eyes on him, so no-one really noticed the warden

326

pass across the hallway, her huge bunch of keys jangling. For her part, the heavyset woman appeared flummoxed at the sight of her employers in such disorder. Her mind wasn't quite on the task as she turned the key to lock an internal door with a grilled window in it, after rushing through it. It was fortunate that Ruth stood nearby and William Bell next to her. Seizing the opportunity, the clergyman's wife held her foot against the wood to prevent it closing completely, which meant the lock didn't quite engage. None of the Trustees heard her whisper to Will, nor did they see him casually slip through.

Will

He crept along the passage, passing several rooms which included a bed chamber and a large kitchen, but disappointingly after a steady rise, the route came to a blind end at what appeared to be a cupboard door. He'd have to attempt one of the other kitchen exits instead, but curiosity made him check the narrow door first.

He exhaled slowly. It was a small opening, not a cupboard at all. Dipping his head, he found himself in a largish room, empty save for a few hard chairs occupying the centre and another chair on its side near the main door. There were fresh scuff marks across the floorboards. Frances had been in there, he could feel her.

Miraculously the sturdy door opened easily onto a main corridor. But which way should he try next? Rejecting the direction which would probably take him back to the kitchen, he stood, forcing his brain to think. What was it that urchin boy said? If they don't like you they put you in the punishment room, *at the bottom*. Well Frances was about as popular with the magistrate and doctor as a house full of bedbugs. He needed to find the punishment room, which was probably in one of the cellars. He set off warily, keeping to the sides of the passage ready to dive into the shadow.

The clinking of a key in a lock made him freeze for a moment until he could work out where the sound originated. It came from behind him. Someone was approaching. He just had time to lean into the wall to make himself as slender and invisible as possible. It worked. Obviously the warden wasn't expecting to find an intruder loose in the passage on her watch. She was intent on her own business, with her hard angular face firmly set. Will held his breath until she'd gone, keys clanking at her waist, then set off again even more cautiously after his narrow escape. He could probably have overpowered the woman but he didn't want to resort to that. It would make him no better than they.

He needed a back staircase to take him down into the bowels of the huge building. With his heart in his mouth he tried each unnamed door, most of them locked, but at the third attempt, he found what he wanted, a steep, winding flight of steps disappearing downwards. With scarcely any light and no candle he had to tread carefully on the worn stairs, but at the bottom the passage was lit well enough. There were further signs of a struggle; scrape marks on a dusty stone floor. He couldn't imagine his wife would go quietly with her captors. She was nearby, he knew it.

He paused outside each door, bending to whisper her name, increasing to a soft shout as he became more desperate, gingerly testing to discover if any would open. None did and without a key he had no chance. The heavily bolted door threw him for a moment. If he opened it, what might he find? Well if he didn't take the chance, he would never know.

'Is anyone in here?' he called, knocking gently. He almost fell back with shock to hear her voice, muffled by the thick wood.

'It's me Will, let me out.'

Her lip was torn, her arms bruised under the torn blouse, but she was alive and safe now. He pulled her close, breathing in the familiar scent of her, waiting for her to cease trembling. It was she who pulled away first.

'The wardens—we need to leave quickly.'

She took his hand urgently while glancing both ways along the passageway, eyes roaming for signs of the women's return.

34. The Urchin Boy

Frances

We saw only shadows as we hurried from the cellars. There were no sounds of footsteps or keys clinking to put us further on our guard; we heard nothing besides the creaking of floor boards under our feet. As far as we knew, nobody saw us. The sun must have dropped in the sky because it was gloomier than I remembered as we crept past the kitchen, then past the notorious bed chamber, coming to a halt before the grilled hallway door. The raised voices beyond it told us the trustees were still in dispute.

'They've hardly changed position since I slipped out,' whispered Will, peering through the grid with difficulty. The door was still ajar from his stealthy exit. He opened it a shade more so we could hear them better.

'Do you still deny keeping Frances Bell against her will in this building?' the railway engineer Charles Lamb was demanding.

'That's right,' the doctor said shortly, 'as I've repeated several times. Why on God's earth would we do that? How dare you accuse us of it?'

There was a familiar roar. It was the Reverend Beard's thundering voice, just as I remembered it from his pulpit back at St Thomas' church, so I could well imagine the expressions of the trustees in that confined hallway. 'Then tell me this, Doctor—explain why I observed that toad of a henchman loitering outside my house, shortly before Fanny disappeared, while she was visiting our cook.'

Silence reigned for a moment.

'What are you suggesting Beard?' the magistrate enunciated quietly.

'He's suggesting you conspired to have Frances Bell thrown into the river and dispatched, or some other such foul play—if you continue to insist she is not here in this building.' It was Charles Lamb again, his voice steady. I shuddered, laying my head against Will's chest. Lamb clearly thought they might go that far!

The magistrate was clearly having second thoughts after hearing what the Reverend had witnessed, the consequence of which was put so plainly by the engineer. He cleared his throat. 'Doctor, are you absolutely sure the woman's not here with us?'

Taking a deep breath, I grasped Will's hand firmly and pulled him into their midst. I would never forget the shock on the faces of the doctor and magistrate, or the pleasure on those of the others. In particular, the doctor's face took on an unhealthy hue of sloe berries, which clashed with his red nose.

Trying to keep my voice steady I announced, 'as you can see gentlemen I'm very much here after being held captive in the building, bruised but thankfully alive. However if it wasn't for my brave husband and friends, things might have ended very differently. Now where is that poor girl, Hilda Stott? I demand to see her, even just for a moment, to see if she's well.'

Once someone had sent for a brandy for Will and me, and a third reluctant warden had taken me to see Hilda, Henry Coulson arranged for his carriage to drive us to the Beards' house. I needed to kiss our girls goodnight. Ruth Beard had offered to give the children a bed for the night so we could go home to recover. Neither of us was in a position to argue. Likewise, we were too tired to appreciate the plush interior of Mr Coulson's

Brougham carriage while we advanced smoothly towards Bishopwearmouth. It was too dark to see our neighbours twitch their curtains as they watched us alight.

Home felt strangely cold and empty without the children, despite Will assuring me it was a warm night. Curling up on the rug with a blanket wrapped around me, I watched him coax the stove into life, thinking at that moment I never wanted to let him out of my sight. He lay down beside me, holding me tight and we stayed that way until the moon had risen over the horizon, when stiffness drove us to stumble upstairs to our mattress.

Five days later, Hilda sat opposite me in Second Class, her fair hair pulled back neatly in a plait, exposing a pale face. There were creases on her forehead which shouldn't be present in a child. Hopefully the scars from her experience, and those of the other girls, wouldn't run too deep.

'You'll tell your ma everything won't you?' I suggested cautiously. 'She'll want to know.' She shrugged and looked away. The magistrate had reprieved them, albeit to save his own skin, but it was still a welcome outcome. Further, the self-important silver haired man remained adamant he had only meant to frighten me into keeping quiet, not to dispatch me. He was '*a magistrate for goodness sake.*' Despite his fine words, having seen the hatred in his face and felt his hand on my mouth, I would never be sure.

Every girl who'd formed part of the magistrate's and doctor's scheme—which they insisted was only to increase donations to the reformatory—had also been reprieved. That was one of the conditions laid down by Theodore Beard and Charles Lamb. The other proviso was that Mrs Beard would have regular access to the place to check on the welfare of its inmates. Ruth Beard assured me she would indeed be keeping a keen eye on everyone at the Ragged School, including visitors. She would also be talking with Martha Cherry's friend who collected the laundry to make sure the bed wetting ceased.

In the days following my spell in the punishment room, Reverend Beard organised an independent opinion on the health of the children. When I described conditions in the cellars, he no longer trusted his fellow doctor trustee. As fate would have it though, a week later, probably partly from strain, partly from his already poor physique, the doctor collapsed due to apoplexy, thus ensuring his control of the children's fortunes ceased for ever. None of us mourned his passing.

For his part, Henry Coulson arranged for a better supper for each child, instead of the ubiquitous porridge, and set out his ideas for the trustees to increase sponsorship from businessmen like him, without resorting to child abuse. He also asked Charles Lamb to make an inspection of school lessons taught in the reformatory. Finally, he offered to visit Hilda behind the docks of Hartlepool whenever he had business there, to ensure both she and her mother had enough to eat.

I didn't want thanks from Jeanette and Hilda Stott. I'd come to understand that simply doing the right thing was sufficient. Jeanette had no idea of the depths to which the reformatory had sunk, or the part I'd played in Hilda's release. Perhaps Hilda would tell her, when the time was right. I pushed open Jeanette's front door, with its peeling paint and rusty hinges, watched as she clutched her daughter to her bosom, then I took my leave. I would go back to Bishopwearmouth to do the same with my own.

We were all changed after the Silver Street affair but none more so than my husband. It was the urchin boy that was the trouble. Will just couldn't get the child out of his mind. Each evening after his railway duties he scoured the area for him, starting with the spot outside the grim reformatory walls, but quickly extending his hunt to the docks.

'From the coal streaks on his legs, he will have been at the docks, I'm certain,' he told me, arriving home yet again with a long face after another fruitless hour of searching. Apparently the street boy was nowhere to be found.

'You're sure you'd recognise him?'

I was sorry I couldn't add anything to Will's image of the boy. I had no recollection of smiling at a street child as the magistrate's henchman hastened me along Silver Street, then pushed me up the steps.

'He remembered *you* Frances, that's the point. You made a difference to him and that's what I intend to do. I want to help him, just like you did with Hilda.' He looked down at his feet for a moment while running grimy fingers through his hair. A few more greys were stealing their way in between the wayward dark curls.

After all the fuss he'd made about the docks of Hartlepool, the image of Will looking for a boy at the Sunderland docks almost made me smile. Yet there it was: one short conversation with an urchin and my husband appeared transformed. It was mysterious. A nagging thought wouldn't leave me alone: *No street boy actually existed.* Will was in such a panic he imagined the whole encounter.

On the Saturday afternoon a week after my incarceration, shortly after I'd taken Hilda home, Will and I went together in search of the urchin boy. We dropped our girls at Martha Cherry's place then set off hand in hand, as if on a first date.

'You're certain you don't mind going this way again?'

I knew what he meant. The narrow back streets brought back memories of the magistrate's henchman hard on my heels, his hot breath on my neck. Will explained how he'd wound through the same passageways, at every turn expecting to find me slumped lifeless in an alley.

He let go of my hand, slipping his arm around my waist instead.

'I never want to lose you like that again,' he said softly.

'So tell me where you've already searched for this street boy that helped find me.'

When we did find the boy, cap in hand at the side of the river Wear, it was he who spoke first. 'Ye found her then Mister.'

'Aye I did, thanks to you.' I watched in awe as Will dropped down onto the dried mud beside the boy, both man and child immediately at ease. The earnest face came back to me then through the layers of dirt. Maybe I did smile at him that afternoon.

Later, walking back to collect our own children Will was excited.

'I found him, Frances.'

Beckoning him to bend closer, I brushed a now dusky curl away from his ear. 'Aye, but you know the best thing?'

He shook his head.

'The best thing is we did it together.'

'What do you propose to do with yourself, now the matter with Hilda and the other children is settled?' Ruth Beard asked me one Sunday at the end of summer when chapel was over. We were standing in front of the building, chatting with other members of the congregation. I looked down at my girls waiting patiently on each side of me, and at the growing baby, heavy in my arms. Obviously my family took up much of my time and energy.

'Have you considered using your not inconsiderable teaching skills again?' Ruth went on mysteriously. She explained that the chapel school mistress had gone home to care for her mother who'd suddenly fallen ill. It was a great worry, as Mrs Beard didn't imagine she would find a teacher in time for the new school year. The children were due back in one week.

'Ooh flipping heck Mrs Beard, do you really think I'm up to it?'

'You're more than capable my dear, and in any case it would be a short-term arrangement until I can find a permanent teacher, unless you take to it, of course. We wouldn't be able to pay a great deal for your work, but there would be *some* remuneration.'

I was concerned about my own children, but she'd considered that too. Ann and Peggy would both be welcome to attend the chapel school, while she could ask Martha to care for baby Mary.

I only just managed to hold back my grin that evening as I described Mrs Beard's proposition to Will. He listened carefully, stroking his chin. 'And would this keep you out of mischief? I mean would it stop you gallivanting into dangerous places to save children in trouble?'

'You know I can't promise that.'

Was he teasing me?

His face crinkled into his cheekiest grin.

'You blighter.' Brandishing a rolling pin, I chased him round the kitchen table.

When they heard the commotion, Ann and Peggy came rushing in from the yard. Then soon we were all laughing, holding our sides with the pain of it.

'You'll have to watch out, girls,' Will told them. 'With Ma teaching you about the moon and all.'

I looked up in admiration. He'd remembered about the school lessons on my brothers' farm.

'I'll have to practice my arithmetic,' I laughed, 'and check this week's moon phase.'

Beckoning the older girls to me, I held them close for a moment. Will came over too, wrapping his arms around the three of us. At that moment it felt as if all the best parts of our lives, past, present and future, were rolled into one.

35. Ten Years Later

Frances

There was something I needed to do before winter set in. I had to go to Northallerton to visit Martha Cherry. The aged woman was living with her nieces, not far from the rectory where we once worked for the Beards. I explained as much to Ruth Beard as we sat on the front pew, waiting for the chapel to fill up behind us.

'I wish I could come with you, dear,' she sighed. 'I think I'm past it now, but I feel you should take Mrs Cherry something from me. Let me have a think.'

She clearly did her thinking during the new incumbent's sermon rather than listening to his words, which were nothing to do with gifts, or photography for that matter. At the end she whispered her idea. There was a photographer in the High Street and she wanted us to have our image captured together. 'Bring Mr Bell too,' she directed.

We met in the shop almost a week later on the Saturday afternoon, when Will had finished his shift. The photographer had Ruth Beard and me sit together on hard chairs in the foreground, with Will standing behind.

'Do stand still, sir,' the man said to my husband as Will eased from foot to foot. No doubt the man at the camera was tired of taking people's photos, while Will's creaky knees were probably aching from standing all morning. It meant my husband's expression was more of a scowl than his usual youthful grin. The grey curls were much in evidence too. It was easier for Mrs Beard and me, as we were seated comfortably. My own expression was neutral, but she did manage to maintain a slightly proprietorial smile, while we endured the thirty or so seconds until the job was done.

I could see Mrs Beard was rather pleased with the result as she showed me the photograph, before she tucked it back in its envelope with the photographer's details printed on the back. The photo hadn't particularly captured my newly swelling belly. The tiny woman handed it over reluctantly, but it was quite safe in my bag as I travelled to Northallerton in Third Class.

Earlier, with his customary wink, Will said he was happy enough to give me the fare, so long as I said hello to Appleton Wiske as I passed nearby on the train. The two large pies I'd stashed in the larder for his suppers might have swayed him too.

Martha Cherry's nieces lived near the station in Northallerton so it wasn't a difficult journey. The worst part was the bumpiness of the ride, which made the little one kick inside my belly. Sometimes as we rocked along I noticed flora or fauna to make my heart soar and take my mind off the discomfort, smiling to see a row of lofty elm trees, or gasping as a sparrow-hawk swooped for the kill with a flash of striped orange under-belly. Mostly though, the countryside I remembered was becoming littered with mining waste and other paraphernalia.

My friend loomed large in her rocking chair beside the stove, not relinquishing that position whilst I was there. Martha apparently felt the cold those days. I estimated she was seventy years old at least, but she'd not lost her memory or any of her wisdom. She remembered the day I arrived at the rectory, nineteen, lonely, after being shunned by the servants at Kirkdunham House for being able to read; still reeling from being sacked by the mistress before I could finish the book I'd borrowed; bewildered by the master's kind actions.

'You were such a young thing, but I could see you were strong-minded.'

Martha Cherry peered interestedly at the photograph while we reminisced. 'Who'd have believed Ruth Beard would want to be in the same photo as you two,' she cackled toothlessly. When she'd calmed down and stopped laughing, she became serious. 'Now Frances, you must write your address on the back of that photograph. That way when I'm gone, my nieces can return it to you. It's something precious that needs keeping in your family. It should go to your Ann and she can pass it to her children. They'll need to learn the story too. You know—about the Ragged School detectives.'

She was right as usual; the photo should be passed down the generations, so I obliged her with our address in Bishopwearmouth. Just in case, on the envelope I also scrawled Ann and Peggy's addresses, both were in service in Sunderland. It was a shame not to have a photo of the three women: Martha, Mrs Beard and I, but that image would have to remain in people's imaginations.

36. The Ending

Will

For some time, Will had been interested in a sign hanging in another of the shop fronts along the High Street. It read: 'FOR SALE: SECOND HAND BOOKS'. At last, on one rainy day shortly after Frances' trip to Northallerton, which sparked his memory, he summoned the courage to enter. Closing the door carefully behind him, he looked around. It was a low, dark interior filled with the heavy, musty smell of old glue and leather. A man of slight build sat on a stool in the corner with a book in front of him. His spectacles were perched at the end of a large nose and he had the complexion of someone used to being in the sun, although clearly he hadn't been. The face was intelligent, and he spoke with an unfamiliar accent.

'How may I help you, sir?' he asked.

Just for a moment, Will wondered who the man was speaking to. He couldn't recall being called sir before, yet he could see there were no other customers in the shop.

'I'm looking for a book for me wife,' he said hesitantly, starting to scrutinise the rows of mainly brown leather spines, vaguely hoping for any writing he might recognise. The shopkeeper didn't interfere, leaving him to his gazing, but it made Will's eyes hurt focusing on such close details, so eventually he gave in and turned away from the shelves.

The shopkeeper looked at him kindly over his lenses. 'I expect you need spectacles yourself,' he commented quite reasonably.

The thought hadn't occurred to Will, as he barely read anything those days. 'It's a children's book about Africa and an English boy, that I'm looking for,' he ventured, shyly. 'Perhaps you know of it?'

'Let me see,' the shopkeeper said, scanning the bookshelves from his seat. 'Try the second row from the top. Then try the ninth book along from the left, with the green spine.'

Will followed the man's instructions and eased the book from its place, then holding it at arm's length to bring it into focus, read aloud: 'THE ENGLISH BOY AT THE CAPE: AN ANGLO-AFRICAN STORY.'

Immediately his body tingled all over. It was the sort of feeling you get when you find something you want that you know is precious.

'That's the one.'

The book seller was very considerate, letting him reserve the story book until the end of the week when it would be payday.

That Friday morning Frances knew something was going on. 'What's so good that you can't keep the grin off your face?' she asked as she cooked his bacon.

'Nothing,' he grinned. That whole day he felt like one of his children at Christmas, carrying out his routines with far more enthusiasm than was required, until finally it was time to leave work at the end of the afternoon. Despite his grating knees he broke into a run in case the shop closed before he got there, but thankfully the 'OPEN' sign was still swinging encouragingly on its cord.

'Well now, I see you're back for your book,' the shopkeeper said when Will eased open the door again, breathing heavily. The man looked as pleased as he was. He produced the slim volume from a drawer at the back of the shop then began to wrap it deftly in brown paper.

He tied the string and handed it to Will before counting the coins carefully. 'Your wife will like this?' he asked in his heavy accent.

Will laughed. 'Aye, I hope so,' he said, tucking the book into his pocket. 'She's been waiting twenty years or more to read the ending!'

37. Under A Moonlit Sky

Frances

We stood arm in arm at the edge of Mowbray Park, the air crisp for early October that night I held the story book in my hands again. The reclaimed quarry was the nearest we could get to nature in Sunderland, which was the proper way to celebrate. I no longer needed a fictional friend, as I had when I'd taken the book from Charles Lamb's shelves, but I would read *The English boy at the Cape* from cover to cover, absorbed in the tale again. I would treasure the slim volume because Will had loved me enough to buy it. When our son was old enough—I knew it was a boy inside me because the pregnancy was so different—I would read the story to him, telling him about trees and flamingos, flora and fauna, so he would cherish it just as I did.

A low grunting filled the sky, a tribe of geese overhead in majestic formation. We tilted our heads to marvel at the migrating birds, magically silhouetted in moonlight, the hunter's moon as bright as ever in the night heavens. The English boy in Africa, had he been real, would have gazed up at the same side of that great circle in the sky when he was lost in the bush.

As we stood watching the geese on their autumn journey, Will reached down for my hand until I felt the familiar spark of connection between us. Feeling him close under that moonlit sky, I suddenly understood. Even when we were chasing different dreams we were never really lost.

'Our moon, Frances,' he said.

I grasped his hand tighter, 'aye, our moon.'

Acknowledgements

Particular thanks to my friend Joy Perryman for your painstaking work with my first manuscript, and for helping me believe in myself. Thanks also to Louise Walters for your wise comments at an early stage. Grateful thanks too, to Marilyn Rodwell (author of The Wedding Drums) for your timely and generous support, and for introducing me to the Romantic Novelist's Association (RNA). Thanks to the undisclosed reviewer from the RNA's New Writer's Scheme (NWS) for your invaluable suggestions—I've tried to follow your guidance. Many thanks to Jacqueline Abromeit for the beautifully designed front cover which turned a vision into something real. Thanks to the many other friends and family who read the various versions and helped me reach this point. You know who you are: Mum, Beryl, Rose, Glen and Janey, Christina Jones. I couldn't have done it without you.

About the Author

Coral Perfitt likes to see justice done, which is probably why Frances Bell in the story feels the same. Another obsession is her love of the environment, so she's happy Will warms to the wonders of nature under Frances' influence. What about the railways which excite Will so much? Well, the author travelled by rail to the North East of England from her home in rural Oxfordshire, to research the places in the book. She cycled round the villages of Appleton Wiske and Long Newton imagining how it would be to live there nearly two hundred years ago. William and Frances Bell were her 3rd-great-grandparents. This is her first novel, which draws on her rich and varied experiences—more about those another time! Now she will knuckle down to write the two sequels and solve more mysteries.

This book is the first of a trilogy.
For further information please check at
silverslatefiction.co.uk